Pickard County Atlas

Pickard

County

Atlas

Chris Harding Thornton

MCD

FARRAR, STRAUS AND GIROUX

NEW YORK

MCD

Farrar, Straus and Giroux

120 Broadway, New York 10271

Copyright © 2021 by Chris Harding Thornton

Printed in the United States of America

First edition, 2021

Library of Congress Cataloging-in-Publication Data
Names: Harding Thornton, Christina, author.
Title: Pickard County atlas / Chris Harding Thornton.
Description: First edition. | New York : MCD / Farrar, Straus and
   Giroux, 2021..
Identifiers: LCCN 2020034898 | ISBN 9780374231255 (hardcover)
Subjects: GSAFD: Noir fiction.
Classification: LCC PS3608.A725386 P53 2021 | DDC 813/.6—dc23
LC record available at https://lccn.loc.gov/2020034898

Designed by Richard Oriolo

Our books may be purchased in bulk for promotional,
educational, or business use. Please contact your local
bookseller or the Macmillan Corporate and Premium Sales
Department at 1-800-221-7945, extension 5442, or by email at
MacmillanSpecialMarkets@macmillan.com.

www.mcdbooks.com • www.fsgbooks.com
Follow us on Twitter, Facebook, and Instagram at @mcdbooks

10 9 8 7 6 5 4 3 2 1

For Paula

Pickard County Atlas

1 DEEP IN THE LATE JULY NIGHT, the headlamps of Harley Jensen's cruiser carved a tunnel of light above Highway 28. They lit the thin tar-and-chip road and the bunchgrass whose shoots ate its crumbling edges. The glare blotted out all else. North-central Nebraska, the spot where sand met loam, rose and fell around him, cast black against the shadow of sky.

Each night on patrol, Harley absently ticked off names of passing tracts like reading a plat map in an old atlas. Convention out here held that pastures and fields were named for the living who owned them. Homes and outbuildings huddled within windbreaks, their yards lit by single lampposts, were named for their builders. The only exception was Harley's folks' place, the abandoned farmhouse he now approached and intended to speed right by. Once the windbreak's trees cut a dark mound against the horizon, he'd pass the barn and glance to see the front door still shut. Then he'd sink the gas with the sole of his roper.

The Jensen place had been built by a Braasch, and a Braasch owned it now. Before Harley was born there forty-seven years back, other families had lived in the silent two-story, but Jensen was the name that took. Which meant there were two systems for naming, Harley supposed. Industry or infamy. Whichever stuck.

A chrome glint flickered in the overgrown yard and tightened his neck. Somebody was parked down by the barn.

He passed the house and let the incline slow him to a coast. He made a left on the gravel of County Road K and stopped. Elbow propped on the window frame, he took a last long drag of the smoke that kept him awake and flicked a shred of tobacco from his tongue. He brushed a knuckle against a sideburn and debated whether or not to keep driving. Pretend he hadn't seen anything.

The legal drinking age was nineteen, old enough that high school kids gathered in broken-down homesteads dotting the hillsides. Granted, they were generally bright enough to pick a place without highway frontage, certainly one without ties to a deputy who patrolled half the night. But then Harley supposed nothing drew drunk, horny kids so much as a little seediness, some grisly bit of trivia they could spin into full-fledged lore. He wondered what they'd come up with. In his day, rumor had it in the thick cottonwoods lining the quarry, a compound of naked cannibal albinos waited for couples to park on moonlit nights. It'd be tough to beat that.

He threw the Fury in reverse, punched the gas to clear the blind intersection quick, and weaved into the house's drive. The tracks were little more than two slight dips in the knee-high grass. Ahead, his low beams caught a snatch of tailgate. Above the wild rye and volunteer ash saplings hovered the dusty bumper of a red F-250.

Paul Reddick.

Harley gripped the handset where it clipped to the radio. He held the button, not pressing but resting. Protocol was to radio in whenever he pulled someone over. Technically, he supposed he wasn't pulling anyone over. He let the handset go.

He grabbed the flashlight from the bench seat and tensed at the pop of the door hinge he kept forgetting to WD-40. He stood in the brush and trained the beam on the pickup's back window. The old twelve-gauge Winchester lay in the rack behind Paul's dirt-colored hair, which hung well past his shoulders. From the open driver's-side window, a tan and veined forearm jutted like it was signaling a right-hand turn. Its fist flipped Harley the bird.

"Reddick," Harley acknowledged.

Paul dropped the middle finger and let his arm dangle from the window. "Jensen," floated back just as how-do-you-do.

That how-do-you-do-ness, that unshakable calm, made Harley's teeth grit. It wasn't composure, and it wasn't reserve. Harley knew a good bit about composure and reserve himself. What Paul had was the hostile indifference of a person who valued nothing. The kind of rarefied spite that came from never having known a single thing he'd mind losing.

It no doubt stemmed from a brother dying eighteen years back, when Paul was surely too young to even remember him. In Paul's case, Harley thought not remembering was probably worse. All Paul would've known was the wake of it.

Dell Junior, the oldest of three Reddick boys, was seven when he was killed by a farmhand named Rollie Asher. Dell Junior caught Rollie off guard while he was shoveling dirt into a collapsed cellar at the old Lucas place. Rollie hadn't been right since Korea. He caved in the boy's skull, called the sheriff to say he'd done it, then blew a load of buckshot through his own. All Rollie neglected to mention was where he put the body. The summer of '60, Harley and the department searched every vacant building, scoured every grain of dirt in the fields and ditches. Never found him. They'd found the spade, matted with hair and skin. They'd found a spot of earth soaked in more blood than Harley knew could course through a seven-year-old boy. Just no body.

Sometimes Harley suspected if the department had found that body, the Reddicks might've fared better. Maybe the mother,

Virginia, wouldn't have become a shut-in. Maybe Dell Senior wouldn't have moved out and left the two young boys as her caretakers. If the department had just found that body, maybe Paul's sense of the size and gravity of things, of knowing how and when to be fazed, would've been halfway normal. As it stood, not a whole hell of a lot qualified.

Harley's boots moved forward, flattening the grass and grinding the dirt till a movement in the cab stopped him. He rubbed the holster's thumb-break. Another head, this one covered in long, crumpled blond curls, surfaced from the seat. A pair of eyes sleepily squinted back at him. A girl, sixteen maybe. Paul had to be bordering twenty-two by now. It was worth a check.

At the open window, Harley trained his light on Paul, who didn't squint. Instead his head tilted back, as if he were studying the glare through a pair of bifocals. The angle made his hard-set jaw look more square than it already was. His silver-gray eyes held steady, unblinking.

"Sightseeing?" Harley asked.

"Getting a little air." The words seemed a touch too loud, an effect of the pitch, not the volume. Paul's voice was clear and low. "While I'm still on the right side of the sod."

It was a quip old men would exchange at a feed store. But then, the only thing young about Paul was the age on his license. The hairline cracks at the edges of his eyes, lines from working in the sun and wind, resembled crow's feet.

"Time being, at least," Harley said.

"Sounds pretty foreboding." Paul glanced away easily, without a trace of readable meaning, toward the house. In profile, his bones were thick, prominent. So much so, they seemed ready to surface and split the skin. The flashlight shadowed the dark hollows below Paul's deep-set eyes, between his cheekbone and jaw.

"Kindly step from the vehicle."

Paul looked down in his lap and busied himself with his hands. Harley nudged his holster break with a snap. The rasp of a zipper's teeth filtered from the cab in reply.

The pickup door opened, and Harley watched for Paul to blink at the dome light stuttering on. Nothing. Paul slipped his hands in the pockets of his too-tight jeans and strolled through the knee-high grass toward the house. His threadbare black T-shirt faded into the night's darkness, a whiff of Brut aftershave lingering on the air behind him.

Harley gripped the wheel and used the running board to hoist himself into the driver's seat. He turned the beam on the girl, although the overhead made her clear enough.

She was wide-eyed, pinching her bottom lip between her thumb and forefinger.

"You here of your own volition?" he asked her.

She sat there, dumb and dazed as a sleepwalker.

"I said, you out here on purpose?"

The girl said nothing.

He shifted the light from pupil to pupil. They worked fine. Harley reached across the cab and pressed the button on the glove box. The compartment fell open with a thud.

"Ain't nothing in there," Paul called out, more or less jovially.

There probably wasn't. Once, there'd been a half bottle of quaaludes prescribed to Paul's mother, but Glenn, the sheriff, flushed them. Glenn told Harley to forget it, that poor woman had enough problems. What exactly those problems were was a matter of small-town speculation, since she never came out of her house.

There was nothing in the glove box besides the registration and some coarse paper napkins. Rifling through Paul Reddick's F-250 always felt about as productive as clipping off the lit end of a fuse. Even if it put the spark out, Harley sensed the fuse getting shorter each time.

Across the way, Paul swung a foot, not kicking but swiping his worn motorcycle boot through the grass, like he was searching halfheartedly between the blades. "Stop by for old times' sake?" he asked.

"Saw your pickup," Harley told him, running his flashlight beam over the dash, the floor, the seat. "Thought I'd make sure nobody lost a foot or got brained on a rock yet."

The silhouette of Paul's head was shrouded in long hair so it looked hooded. It bobbed in agreement. "My burden, apparently. I know it. Always bearing witness."

"Just a bad penny, huh?" Harley said. "You know, you turn up often enough—wrong place, wrong time—you seem less like an omen than a reason."

"Got any evidence to that effect, Deputy?"

Harley didn't. He wished to hell he did. He turned to the girl again. He asked her age.

Seventeen, she said.

She probably was. Her back had shrunk to the corner of the seat and passenger-side door. She looked repentant, like a child, but given the cut of her cheeks and her shape, draped beneath a thin Wilton Panthers T-shirt, she was old enough to know better. Harley asked for her ID.

The girl's forehead shriveled into folds. She stammered she'd snuck out, forgot her purse, that her parents would kill her. Her shoulders racked with a sob that crumpled her toward him across the seat. He flinched and slid away. He grabbed the wheel to keep from falling out the open driver's-side door. His elbow nailed the horn, and the loud, clipped blare rang through the quiet. Harley didn't care for being touched. Not unexpectedly.

If Paul was concerned about the horn, he didn't mention it. "Nah," he said in answer to some question Harley hadn't asked. "Don't guess you stop by the home place much if you can help it."

A deep breath burned in Harley's lungs. He held it there. He told the girl to pull herself together, go wait in the cruiser. When her sniffling bubbled into a panicked stammer again, he told her to calm down, he didn't want to deal with some idiot girl's parents at 4:00 a.m. any more than she did. He'd drop her a block from the house and she could take her chances sneaking back in. She got out of the cab and went to the cruiser to wait.

Paul kept talking, offhandedly. "How'd she do it, again? Gun? Hanging?"

Harley slid down from the seat. He held the burning breath tight in his chest and walked across the yard to Reddick's black outline. "Guess that's why you stopped by. Figured I wouldn't. Knowing I drive right past on patrol."

Paul sighed a breath. "Don't read into it. I misplaced something, is all. Thought it might've drifted out this way. Surely you've done that—lost something, drove yourself half nuts looking for it." He gave a pause, perfunctory, not waiting for a reply. "I been all over this evening. Here's where I happened to land. Where our paths crossed. It's happenstance, Harley. No accounting for fate."

The flashlight bled a long, oblong mist across the grass and toward the house. Toward the kitchen windows. Harley didn't look there. He kept his focus on Paul's dark figure. With the yard's incline, he stood a hair taller than Harley.

"Seem distracted." Paul craned his head to look back.

"Let yourself in, then? Have a look inside? There's a root cellar out back. You check there?"

"Now, that'd be trespassing. You ought to know I learned my lesson about trespassing."

The night of the water tower, he meant. That'd been the charge in the end, trespassing. For an instant, Harley pictured Paul dangling upside down in the tower's floodlights, barrels of the Winchester trained toward Harley and the cruiser below. "You're trespassing just parked here," Harley said. "I'm seeing if we can tack on breaking and entering."

Paul's voice briefly lowered. It took on a tone of discretion. "I suppose you'll need to call Braasch, then. See if he wants to press charges. Loren Braasch owns the place now, don't he?"

The flashlight's glow had crept upward a touch. The waved pane of a kitchen window winked back. Harley pushed the beam down again. "Want to say what you're looking for?"

"I would not," Paul said. "If it's all the same to you. Not that county law enforcement's sleuthing expertise wouldn't be helpful, of course."

Harley wanted to grip him by the Adam's apple and shake the nonchalance right out of him. "Leave," he said instead.

Paul looked skyward. Harley thought he might've squinted a bit before his gaze dropped back to the shadows. "Oh, now. I wasn't insinuating. You always think I'm insinuating. You need to let some shit go, Harley. You don't let that shit go, it'll give you ulcers."

"Leave."

Paul stayed put a beat, then ambled toward the cab. He hopped in and closed the door. Harley followed and trained the flashlight on his face again. Under the low-hung lids, the beam shrank Paul's pupils to little pits. Little pits of irises, drilled in like aluminum funnels. Like they'd been carved out by the light. But Paul didn't flinch. He never flinched. Not when his nighttime game of chicken left the Sawyer kid crawling in a ditch, feeling alongside a flipped Chevelle for his severed foot. Not when the Ferguson girl, on a dare, missed the quarry water and dove head-first into dry granite. Paul was the only kid out there not frantic or vaguely giddy. "Pretty clean," he'd deemed it. "Not near as gourd-like as you'd think." He hadn't flinched that night at the water tower, either. Harley saw then. There wasn't something off about Paul Reddick. There was something too on. He was too lucid for anyone's goddamn good.

"I don't want to see you here again," Harley told him.

"Nope." Paul stared straight into Harley's eyes, though he couldn't have made them out past the glare. "I can't imagine you do."

The key ring jangled and the engine churned to life. Reddick pulled out in a broad curve, no hurry, tires rolling over what was once a yard, nicking the corner of what was once a carefully tended flower bed. The hairs on Harley's arms and the back of his neck rose in needle pricks. Then the Ford passed, and the tail-lights brightened where the drive met the highway. The pickup turned right and passed through the blind intersection. It disappeared over the hill.

When his eyes adjusted to the stars, Harley saw his shadow

was missing, swallowed by the house that loomed at his back. He walked slowly to where the cruiser shone in the moon.

AS HARLEY DROVE east toward the station, morning broke in a still-life fire of receding clouds to light a jagged sand hill the color of honey. Bunchgrass and spires of soapweed yucca rooted most of the thin topsoil in place, but in a bald divot of erosion, a rancher had lined spent tires tread to tread like a dark scab. The rubber kept the blowout from spreading. Within the turn of an odometer's digit, the dune lay in the rearview. A ditch of cattails and reeds gave way to a plain of wine-stain bluestem.

Pickard County's dirt was erratic as the weather. The place was a cusp, and it'd once drawn people accustomed to life on cusps. Farm kids, immigrants, children of freed slaves. They'd come a century before, for cheap railroad land or cheaper homestead tracts. Hordes left with the droughts and dust and then again when the combines rolled in, when crop rows snaked longer and longer to make the same ends meet.

The cruiser coasted toward the county seat huddled in a green wedge of trees. Alongside the highway, the abandoned railbed's shaggy embankment blurred by. The pink ballast and creosote-coated ties were why the town of Madson came to be, a spot to fuel up trains in the days of steam.

Harley checked his speed as he crossed the wood-planked bridge spanning a loop in the Wakonda, and he slowed-and-goed through the town's sole four-way stop. He passed the business district, the K–12 with its sprawling addition Madson would be lucky to ever pay off, then the courthouse, where boxes of county assessor paperwork had squeezed out the sheriff's office two years before.

He made the right on the gravel and headed toward the dusty white portable they'd been consigned to since then, the Fury's leaf springs groaning across the train tracks and past the footings of the old railroad water tank. The concrete footings rose from the grass like a plot of graveyard obelisks. Wilton, thirteen miles down the tracks, had a matching set.

He parked and headed up the steps. Inside, across the wood-paneled room lit yellow by fluorescents, the sheriff sat at his desk filling out paperwork, bald head propped on a fist. "Harley," he said in tired greeting without looking up.

"Glenn." Harley made a beeline for the cafeteria tray by the coffee maker. On a mug emblazoned I'D RATHER BE FISHING, a red-cheeked, pudgy man cast a makeshift pole. Glenn's wife donated the cups, probably because they didn't match her china. She could be particular. "You're early. Where's the cruiser?" The lot had been empty.

Glenn Cox was a doughy man who waxed to a pink, high-gloss sheen when frustrated. He was clearly frustrated. At the shop, he said. Engine had a hiccup. His luck, it'd be the carburetor. He asked how Harley's night went.

"Mostly quiet." Harley's thumb ran up the edge of the thin phone book on his desk. The pages whispered like worn playing cards. He briefed Glenn on the night's calls: a brush fire in Oakview Precinct, out by the time he got there; a complaint about an unmowed lawn; a stolen gas can down on the south edge of town. Probably misplaced.

"Had a run-in with Paul Reddick," he finally said.

Glenn made a soft suck noise, tongue against teeth. "Tread

light there." He reached into his desk drawer for the Mylanta. "Guess they had a service out at Red Cedar. Would've been good to know—wasn't even in the paper. Had to hear about it from Kirschner."

Bill Kirschner was caretaker at Red Cedar Cemetery. He had a sideline carving monuments. He likely did better business than anyone else in town, given nearly every young person left Madson the day after graduating. They had to. A town Madson's size had about three dozen jobs, give or take, and if one opened, you could bet Kirschner was carving a headstone. Your best options were to be born lucky, inherit a cow-calf operation as the only child of parents not prone to longevity, or walk beans and detassel corn with junior high kids for two bucks a day while you waited for the school janitor to keel over. "Who died?"

Glenn stilled in his seat to stare and look grave. "They filed the certificate. On Dell Junior. It was in the notices, you know—thing ran thirty days. Paperwork went through Friday."

Harley remembered Paul's little dig about the department's sleuthing expertise. The same needles that pricked the back of his neck hours before tingled again, but he didn't let on to Glenn. "Last I read the notices, I saw I was getting sued for divorce. It's a whole page of nobody's damn business."

"Public servants ought to read the public notices, Harley."

"I'm hourly."

Glenn shook the antacid bottle and apparently didn't care for the sound of it. He chucked it in the wastebasket with a thunk, then pulled out a fresh one. "Funeral with no body. Can you imagine?"

"Not sure it's much odder than a death certificate eighteen years late." Harley knew it was a mistake from the beginning, letting the family go without filing a death in absentia. But it'd been Glenn's dad's call. He'd been sheriff back then. And he'd said it didn't feel right, forcing the Reddicks to sign off on the boy's death when the department couldn't find the body, much less serve any kind of justice for the killing. Whatever the hell that would've been. Rollie went above and beyond with the load of buckshot.

"Where'd you pull him over, anyway? Reddick."

"I didn't. He was parked with some girl from Wilton. Over at my folks' place. Said he'd lost something, was there looking for it."

Glenn went silent. He was picking and choosing what to say next. "Hell of a spot for you to run into each other." He took a sip of antacid. "Were you checking the place out?"

"No, Glenn, I was driving by."

"Wouldn't blame you. Kids always up to no good in those empty houses."

"They're bored. No harm in it." Harley almost asked if Glenn hadn't done the same thing when he was younger, then didn't. Even if his dad hadn't been sheriff before him, his mother was a notorious battle-axe, and then, well, then he had Miriam.

Glenn was quiet again. Picking and choosing. "You can't keep letting that kid get under your skin."

Harley slid open his desk drawer, flipped folder tabs, tried to let Glenn know he wasn't the least bit concerned. But Paul being parked in the last place Harley cared to be wasn't chance. Not when it came just days after the Reddicks held a funeral for a body the department never found. Whatever it was, it wasn't chance, and it didn't bode well. He pulled out a blank patrol activity report.

Glenn was sweating, shining like a bulb. "Look. This thing between you two. Especially since the water—"

"Don't start."

"You tried to get him goddamn committed. Jesus H., Harley. Every town's got some dumb, drunk kid who climbs the water tower, pulls a jackass stunt—"

"That dumb, drunk kid's on his way to prison or dead." Harley checked his watch. He filled in the date on the form. The phone rang. Harley felt a flash of gratitude for the ring, then braced himself for the blunt bark of Otto Ziske. Nine out of ten, it was Otto Ziske.

He picked up. It was Ziske. Today the old man called about his weekly *Pickard Post-Gazette* not showing. Gene, the *Gazette*'s owner, delivered it every Tuesday before dawn. Ziske railed on, voice like a mallet pounding a barrel, ringing in Harley's ear. To make it stop, Harley interrupted to ask why he hadn't just called Gene and asked for another. Why bother calling the sheriff's office?

"I did. I did call him. Know what that son of a bitch says?" Ziske stopped and waited.

Harley shut his eyes. "Nope."

"Says, 'I didn't know better, I'd think you're trying to get a second copy out of me for free.'" He waited again, apparently to let this sink in. "Now, what the hell is that?"

"Well, Otto, my guess is a joke."

Across the room, Glenn managed to lighten a bit. He gave a bounce and titter at the mention of Otto's name.

"I don't need no goddamn Jack Benny," Ziske went on. "I need my paper. And if he's gonna cast aspersions, I'm gonna press charges. He don't have no trouble cashing the check."

"You know, we got a paper right here I can—"

"I bet you do. I bet you do got one right there. You're the law. Even Gene's not stupid enough to steal from the law."

Harley rubbed his eyelashes with a thumb and forefinger, cleaned them of the sleep he wouldn't get for another hour or two. He suggested they see what happened with the Thursday supplement. If the supplement didn't show, somebody'd run the station's copy out to him and they'd go from there.

The old man huffed. Through his nose, it sounded like, a little flute note behind it. But he reluctantly agreed and hung up with a short, popping pair of clicks.

"Otto want an APB put out?"

"Says he wants charges pressed against Gene."

Glenn chuckled. "Hate to say it, but I'd expect an uptick in Ziske calls, now that he don't have Christiansen to antagonize."

"End of an era," Harley said.

The two old men—Otto Ziske and Jack Christiansen—had parked at the counter of the Range every weekday seemingly since time began, a stool between them, cups of quarter coffee untouched. Folks called them Pershing and the Kaiser. Jack wore his WWI American Legion lapel pin on a freebie seed company hat, and Otto was half German. They were there four days ago when Jack dropped dead. "How'd you like that," Ziske supposedly said. "Man survives a shot through the drumstick at Château-Thierry only to die of bad ham." The hospital said it was a coronary.

"Know what time Christiansen's service is today?" Glenn asked.

Harley shrugged and tossed him the paper. Glenn was quiet then. He flipped pages, stopped to read. Harley deciphered the night's notes and jotted down a two-sentence account of the brush fire. He soaked in the quiet, which was too brief.

"Think they filed so they'd feel right laying a headstone?" Glenn was still stuck on the Reddicks. "Wouldn't think they had insurance on him."

"No, wouldn't guess they did."

Glenn sucked his tongue against his teeth again and winced out, "That poor woman."

The wince made Harley bristle. Glenn had a good heart, but there was only so much of it a person could take in one sitting.

Glenn went silent a bit before saying, "I know you think we had a hand in it, how Paul Reddick turned out. But you—and Dad—hell. We all did all we could there. To find that boy."

"I know it," Harley said.

"Not like we could've done a damn thing different."

"I know it, Glenn." Harley did know it. That was no doubt the worst of it.

2 THE DRY TOWELS PILED on the bed radiated heat. Pam worked the tips of her nails and tried to loosen a knot of frayed terry cloth that bound a dish towel to a bath towel. The box fan in the trailer window moved the morning air but didn't cool it. Pam was being cooked. She was being cooked like those hobos her mother once told her had roasted in a freight car. Pam didn't know what the difference was, when it came right down to it, between a trailer and a freight car. Wood paneling, maybe. Carpet. Freight cars were probably better built.

The knot wouldn't give, and a bead of sweat tickled the back of her knee. She clawed at it, then slapped the spot so hard it stung. She yanked the fabric. It hissed with a rip. She chucked the tangled mound at the fan, which slammed cockeyed into the screen, blades rattling. She yelled to Anna. Told her to put on her shoes. They were buying some new goddamn towels.

Pam felt the hollow beneath each step down the hallway, the give under the burnt-orange shag and the avocado lino-leum that never stayed clean, not because of the three-year-old who should've made a mess every ten minutes, but because of a twenty-four-year-old man going on two. From the cabinet closest to the fridge, she pulled down the green Tupperware container for flour and lifted out the bag. The bills lay scattered in the bottom. She counted them. Six tens, two fives, three ones. Lot rent was due in two weeks, and that was fifty. They'd need groceries and gas. Utilities came due the week after.

She eyed the smaller, matching sugar bin at the back of the

cabinet. She didn't touch it, and she wouldn't open it. She didn't need to count what was in there.

Right now, it was only ninety dollars, but if Rick's scotch-swilling, snake-oil salesman of a dad, Dell Senior, came through on the double-wide he'd found, their share of the sale would go straight into that sugar bin. It'd go straight toward a down payment on a place with no axles. A place not parked up on cinder blocks like some beater car nobody ever bothered to fix. That money would go toward a house with the kind of sturdy foundation she never once thought about before living in a trailer.

The familiar clatter of sheet metal drifted through the window screen. Rick's work van rumbled up the road.

Anna waited in the room's entryway, quiet and wide-eyed with concern. That stare. Maybe it was nothing more than expectation, attentiveness whenever Pam yelled something snippy. But Pam swore she'd seen Anna stare like that at only one other thing: a wall cloud that'd once rolled in outside the kitchen window and colored the sky deep green, right before the tornado sirens wailed. Anna could stare at Pam with just enough alarm to make Pam alarmed. Not knowing what Anna saw or expected to see. Maybe for Pam to turn into a whirling torrent of baseball-sized hail.

Aside from the stare, she was a three-year-old miniature of Rick. Same dark hair, same complexion that tanned beneath a light bulb, same short, soft nose, rounded at the tip.

None of it was Pam. Dishwater-blond Pam turned pink in the shade and had a nose shaped like the rest of her, long and fairly sharp. Some said Anna had Pam's eyes, since Rick's were blue. But Pam's were hazel. Anna's eyes were the same deep brown as her grandpa Dell's. Anna's eyes were all Reddick.

"Never mind," Pam said.

Outside, the van's engine shuddered and choked into silence. Pam dropped the flour back in the bin, burped the lid, and shoved the canister onto the shelf. Tar-caked work boots clomped up the stairs, and the screen door whacked the jamb. The spring was broke. Or the chain. Something Rick said he'd replace or fix a year ago.

"How's my girls?" he said. Anna rushed excitedly to his side. He propped her on his hip.

When he leaned in for a kiss, Pam tried not to breathe the roof sealant. All his work jeans were ruined with silver swaths of it. She asked why he was back already. "You need a shave," she said.

"Do I?" He nuzzled Anna. She squealed with a giggle. Paul hadn't shown at their dad's, Rick said. "Kid needs to get his shit together." The two brothers always met at Dell Senior's before work. Today, apparently, Paul called and said he'd be there about noon. Rick had coated some old lady's roof north of Wilton by himself and had driven home for a bite to eat while it dried. He'd swing by and get Paul, go back to Wilton, and they'd finish it after he ate. "One more coat should do it. Tomorrow we start some single Dad picked up in Arnold."

A single in Arnold. Another bead of sweat tingled at the back of Pam's knee, but she didn't scratch it. The next job was supposed to be by Newman Grove. The double-wide. The next job was supposed to be the trailer that'd be a quick sell, with a decent profit this time. "Arnold," she repeated.

"West of Broken Bow about thirty miles. On 92."

She knew where goddamn Arnold was. She breathed, and the sealant stung her eyes. "What about the double-wide?"

Rick gave Anna another nuzzle. She didn't squeal. She burrowed her head into his collarbone. He squatted to set her down.

"Tea ready?" He asked it so brightly not even a three-year-old would buy it. Anna was going through a tea party phase. Pam didn't know where she'd picked it up. TV? They'd never had any tea around. Pam didn't even know anyone who drank tea. Tea seemed like a drink for prim old ladies in white gloves and pillbox hats.

Anna shook her head and bit her lip. When Rick squatted down to her height, the two of them were a pair of bookends. He was just darker from the sun and dirtier from work.

"I'm pretty thirsty," he said. Anna nodded and smiled at him before she took off down the hall.

Rick rose with a grunt and a crunch of the knees. He grabbed a can of beer from the fridge, pulled the tab, and dropped it on the counter.

Pam snatched up the tab and threw it in the trash below the sink. "Is he fronting you this time? To get to Arnold?"

"Pam—" He said it on a high-pitched sigh that made her teeth itch. "The man gave us a place to live. I think he's good for it."

She stopped and searched his face between the sweaty shags of hair pushed behind his ears. His skin was leathered and creased and pocked with pores. Everything about him was rugged and rough-edged but his eyes. Those were blue as pilot lights. She searched them for some sign, any sign, that he knew better. That he had the tiniest inkling of the shyster everybody else knew Dell Senior to be. All she saw was that Rick was growing a mustache. A Fu Manchu. There was something caught in it. A piece of scrambled egg, it looked like.

"What?" he said at her stare.

"Any word about the double-wide? About the bond, even?" A savings bond started the whole thing. Somebody'd bought it when Rick's older brother, Dell Junior, was born. Dell Senior said it'd be worth enough by now to pay for the gravestone plus the place near Newman Grove.

Rick's mouth went tight. His eyes dropped to the linoleum, and he gave a frustrated, pressed-lipped huff. There was something he wasn't saying.

"What—did it sell? Before he could put in a bid?"

His chin puckered into a pout. He rubbed beneath his nose, and the piece of scrambled egg fell loose to the floor. She didn't know when he would've eaten scrambled eggs. Maybe it was carpet padding. "Face value," he said. "Bank says the bond's worth face value."

"For the love of Christ." She felt the familiar, unwelcome quiver beneath her sternum. The shiver of a ghoulish laugh that broke out during fights and funerals. She swallowed it back. She looked past him, past the glow of the screen door, and eyed the hall to the bedroom where ratty towels waited to be ripped apart and put away.

"Real nice place, that double-wide." He leaned back against the counter and took a drink. "Something else'll come along."

She wiped down the already clean sink. Her hand holding the dishcloth was numb.

"We get by," he said, voice exaggeratedly gruff and singsongy at the same time. Like he was Smokey the goddamn Bear. He reminded her they had more than some people had. Roof over their heads, health, Anna—

"Don't." Pam shut her eyes. The glow of the sun through the screen door lit red behind her lids. Her jaw cramped with that damn smile that came whenever a smile was least warranted. If her mother told her some aunt had dropped dead, there that grin would be. Proof positive that Pam was a horrible person. She tightened her teeth and bit it back. "Do not."

"I'm only saying—"

"You don't have to."

He looked confused. Then he didn't. "I wasn't even talking about that."

"You're never not talking about that." Every time she tried to tell him they were in trouble, every time she tried to say what little they had was one minor inconvenience away from disaster, that they were one blown tire away from living in a cardboard box, he brought up Dell Junior. That she should be glad they didn't have a dead, missing kid like his parents did.

He gulped another drink. "What about your parents?"

"What about my parents?" She searched his face again. Those pilot-light eyes could plead in a way that left her wrung out. They were doing it now. Pam wasn't up for being wrung out.

"If you think we need a cushion. I don't know. A hundred for backup."

"What—ask Babe?"

"She's not that bad." He must've heard how stupid it sounded. "What about your dad?"

She didn't answer. Her hands and feet throbbed, and the trailer air thickened. She squeezed past him and snatched her purse straps from the finial of a kitchen chair. "Jesus Christ," she said.

"Pam—"

"Go have your fucking tea."

The storm door slapped behind her, and the landing vibrated with her steps. Her legs carried her across the dirt and past the trailer's shadow, into the full sun.

She slipped into the bucket seat of the half-Bondo-and-primered Nova SS and twitched at the scalding vinyl beneath her cutoffs. The engine roared to a high idle. She'd asked him a dozen times to check the timing. She punched the gas once, quick, to make it settle before she pulled out.

She drove to her parents' place north of Madson but not for any goddamn money. She drove to drive. She drove because she needed some air.

By the time she was far enough down the gravel to see Dad's pickup wasn't there, it was too late. Her mother always knew when somebody was coming, and if she saw Pam's car turn around, she'd get the smug satisfaction of thinking her youngest daughter was afraid of her. Which Pam was. Babe Reinhardt had the parenting style of one of the meaner breeds of birds. If she thought you were old enough to leave the nest, you did, or she pecked out your eyes. Not to mention she was just dark. Always ready with some anecdote about hobos melting in train cars.

At the back door, Pam's fingers coiled around the pull of the screen. Through the wire mesh and across the kitchen, Babe had her back turned, doing something by the sink. Maybe she didn't know Pam was here after all. Maybe she'd had the water running and didn't hear the tires. Maybe Pam could still leave.

"In or out." Babe's short salt-and-pepper perm bobbed when she spoke. Even her perm was curt.

Pam picked the path of least resistance. She crossed the short length to the harvest table and sat in Dad's chair. On the counter by the sink, Mason jars wafted steam. It rippled in waves as Babe poured stewed tomatoes straight from the pot. She wiped the lips and worked the lids and rings. The sight of steam in the heat put Pam on edge. "Where's Dad?"

"Feed store. To get salt, he said."

"Salt?"

She craned her head around, face flushed from the steam, and eyed Pam to let her know she was a moron. "For the water soft-ener. How long did you live here?"

Too long, she wanted to spit, but she wouldn't have meant it. Not completely. There were things she missed. For one, she could breathe here, beneath the high ceilings. She missed those. She missed walking into this room before dawn to see Dad at the table with his percolator, listening to livestock and grain futures on the AM radio. Always there, like the jars in the pantry.

"Salt, my ass. Those old men are a bunch of hens." Babe took the lid off a simmering pot, filling the air with more wet clouds. "So? Where's Anna and what are you pouting about?"

"I'm not pouting."

"That'd be new."

"With Rick. I needed to run errands. We need towels." She heard how it sounded after it came out. Babe probably thought Pam was after hand-me-downs. Never mind Pam never asked Babe for a goddamn thing.

"Some in the linen closet, top shelf. Pretty raggedy, but if you want new, you're out of luck."

"I'm headed to Gordon's. To see if they have any sales."

"Oh. Well. La-di-da, then." She changed the subject. "How's his mother?"

"Still crazy as a shithouse rat, I'd guess."

"Watch your mouth," Babe said, but her thick torso bounced with a short, silent laugh. "What do you mean, you guess? She didn't go to the funeral? Or the memorial—what do you call something like that, with no body to bury?"

And there she went. There she went throwing dead bodies into a conversation like somebody else would mention chairs or spoons. "I don't know. I didn't go. Anna's too young to understand." In truth, Pam had used Anna as an excuse to avoid the funeral, the memorial, the whatever it was, in case Rick's mother did go. The whole thing was morbid, and Virginia Reddick gave Pam the creeps. The woman had the same pilot-light eyes as Rick, but they didn't plead. They didn't wring you out. They landed on you and lit so you swore you could hear the whoosh of a furnace. Then they stared like they meant to burn a hole straight through you.

"Understand what? A funeral with no corpse? I think I'm probably too young to understand," Babe said.

"How about corpses in general?"

"Well, that'll be a nice rude awakening down the road." Babe dropped her emptied pot in the sink and turned on the tap.

Without being told, Pam got up and grabbed a towel to dry. Above the rush of water, Babe tried making small talk. She asked how Rick was. She asked if Pam was feeding him.

"Feed him, patch the crotches of his jeans, vacuum his dirt—"

"So you're married, then."

"At least yours isn't helpless."

Babe sputtered a breath between her lips and eyed Pam like she was a moron again. "They're all helpless. Only more useful than babies when they can hold down a job." She passed Dad's coffee cup for Pam to dry.

"I'll let him know that's why you keep him around."

"It's what 'married' means. You keep somebody around. Hate to think what the hell you thought it meant." She stopped and held a fork above the foamy basin. "Speak of the devil." She told Pam to put his cup front and center on the cabinet's bottom shelf. Otherwise he'd never see it.

Pam listened for tires on the drive, but there was nothing until the screen door spring creaked. She breathed relief till she turned back and looked. Red stepped in and smeared the dust from his boots on the rag rug. He really was turning into an old man. He looked ganglier in his threadbare gingham and worn denim. His ears looked bigger, poking up higher and more sunburned than they used to.

He called out to no one in particular, "Why's a chicken coop got two doors?"

"Hope you remembered what you went for," Babe said.

"If it had four, it'd be a sedan," he said.

"And Sis here's asking why I keep you around."

"My good looks." He winked at Pam before he gave her a one-armed hug. He strode to Babe and tapped her shoulder. She kept washing but ducked the bill of his Cargill hat for a peck. He gave her back a stroke like it was the neck of a cow.

If he'd been to the feed store, Pam realized, he might actually have some cash. Not a hundred, not enough to make a dent in a down payment, but maybe enough for some gas, some groceries so she didn't have to dig into the savings again.

She went to tug the thin fabric of his sleeve right as he stepped out of reach. He gave a wad of bills to Babe. Pam's hand fell empty and useless. She'd been stupid to even think it. She'd been stupid for a lot of things.

Babe asked him when the gas truck was coming. Thursday, he said. There was plenty of diesel but only enough regular to fill the car and combine. Babe opened the lid of the ceramic beehive cookie jar and dropped in the cash. Then Dad headed off through the dining room and into the hallway.

Pam dried a pot and nested it inside another on the counter.

"Plan on putting those away?"

Pam carried the pots to the cupboard.

"Mother," Dad called from the bathroom. The word echoed, and even in the thick heat, Pam felt a chill.

"Medicine cabinet," Babe yelled. "I moved all his garbage off the sink when I cleaned this morning. God forbid he open a cabinet and look."

He'd called Babe "Mother" tens of thousands of times when they still had kids in the house. And Pam was here now. But suddenly she wondered if he did it when the kids weren't around. Pam suddenly wondered if he ever called Babe anything else. And if he didn't, Pam wondered if that meant Babe was right, that all of them really were a bunch of giant, helpless, goddamn babies.

The thought, or maybe it was the adrenaline from the argument with Rick still wearing off, made her a little light-headed. She wanted to go upstairs to her old room and crawl beneath the quilt and the fresh, bleach-smelling sheets of her twin bed. She wanted to wake the next morning as the Pam Reinhardt she'd been before Pam Reddick ever came to be. She wanted to walk into this same kitchen to the low monotone of cattle futures and the smell of the percolator. But there was no bed up there anymore. Only a bunch of boxes and Babe's sewing machine.

Pam dried the silverware in silence and set the forks and spoons in the drawer. She said she should go. She needed to head home so Rick could get back to work.

Babe dried her hands and followed Pam out. The two parted

ways wordlessly. Babe rounded the back of the house to the garden, and Pam slipped into the Nova's bucket seat. When the vinyl scorched this time, she didn't twitch. She punched the gas to quell the engine's roar and made a three-point turn toward the road.

The car crested the hill where drive and road met. Pam idled and leaned into the wheel automatically, leaned in as she always did when straining to get a clear view past the fuel tanks.

High on a set of spindly steel legs, the rust-red reservoirs jutted from the brush like a pair of headless mechanical heifers.

She eyed the Nova's fuel gauge. A little less than a quarter tank.

There was enough regular gas to fill the car and combine, he'd said.

She checked the rearview. Babe's shadow was a low mound. It rolled darkly across the dirt.

Pam made the turn, headed for home.

3 WHEN PAM GOT HOME, Rick drove to his dad's double-wide across the court. He sat at the kitchen table waiting for Paul, who needed to get his shit together. The kid did decent work when you could get him to, though. Rick admired the full remodel they'd done on the trailer a few years back. They'd lined the raised kitchen with aluminum railing, lightweight but powder-coated to look like cast iron. Two short steps dropped down to the living room, where the walls were done up in bronze velvet flowers. The wallpaper was a bitch, but it looked good. Worth the wasted roll gummed up by paste, even if Dad gave them hell about it. The lower level's floor was a sea of deep white shag that hid the base of an armored knight statue guarding the hall. Little guy wasn't quite full-scale, but then people were likely smaller back then. Either way. Neat little guy.

Rick had to admit, his old man had an eye for what'd look sharp, right down to the retractable lamp pulled low above the table's veneer. Under the glow, Dell Senior's bifocals pored over his spiral job notebook. The sheet was filled with writing sunk so heavy into the pages you could read the back as well as the front. He turned a page that crackled as if it could break.

At least Paul's not being there yet gave Rick a chance to ask about money to get to Arnold tomorrow. He got as far as saying things were tight.

"Can't loan you none. Least not till I get paid on this Wilton job. Shelled out two hundred for a headstone the other day, in case you forgot."

Rick hadn't forgotten. At the cemetery, Dad said he was

lucky he'd worked a discount on the plot, given no hole would ever need digging. For a second Rick had been glad Mom wouldn't come out of her house for the funeral that morning. It sounded bad, talking money when they were there to put Dell Junior to rest. Or at least put the idea of Dell Junior to rest. Eighteen years without a body, Rick couldn't blame Dad for trying. Anyway, Dad wasn't one for tears and speeches. The way his fingers shook when he squatted down, inspected the carving, said enough.

Today the same hand was steady as he turned another page. A few brassy chunks, one with a Mason insignia, ringed his fingers. Most men couldn't pull off rings outside a wedding band, but Dad did.

"I didn't mean a loan. Just, Pam wondered—"

"Cut the shit, son. Whatever you're asking, ask."

"Some cash up front for gas, the motel."

"I don't know. Think you can keep hold of the receipts?"

"I said I was sorry about that."

The white-streaked crest of Dad's pompadour was trained so well it hardly needed any hair grease. The peak pitched forward a bit as he studied the notebook, and the slim, close-trimmed line of his skinny mustache gave a twitch. Like something on the page didn't smell right. "No need to tell me sorry. It's your pay gets docked when you can't keep hold of the receipts."

Dad scratched the little triangle of curls jutting from the V of his collared shirt, not like he had an itch but like he was finger-combing it. His Action Slacks whispered below the table. He leaned back in the chair and reached for his wallet. He pulled out five crisp twenties, fanned them like a hand of cards, and put two back. He dropped sixty on the table and returned to his notebook.

"Should cover two nights' motel, gas there and back, and leave me with change. That's worst-case scenario, three days."

The front door opened as Paul gave his usual pair of knuckle raps. He came in smoothing his bed head. He'd no doubt remembered to slap on the aftershave but couldn't be troubled to run a comb through his hair. Long strands caught the light that shone in behind him. They made him look electrified.

"Get it done in two," Dad said and turned his attention to Paul by way of raising his voice. "Glad to see you could pencil us in."

"Interviewed a new secretary last night. Good help's hard to find these days."

Rick said, "Need to get your shit together is what you need to do."

Dad's thin mustache tucked up on one side in a grin. "Good help's hard to find," he repeated on a low breath. "Was about to call your boyfriend, Jensen. See if you were shacked up down at the courthouse."

"Nah. Won't let him get past second base. You raised me better than that."

Dad gave a snort. Dad thought Paul was a real riot. "Your mother been up to the cemetery yet?"

"What am I, my mother's keeper?"

"Long as you want to live on my dime," Dad told him.

Paul asked if Rick was ready to go and said he'd drive himself. He had some affairs to attend to later in Junco, he said. Rick didn't know what the hell that meant. He knew he probably didn't want to know.

Rick stood and slid the twenties behind the can of dip in his pocket. He wished he had time to swing home, tell Pam he got

Dad to front the money. It'd be one less thing she'd worry about for no reason. Sometimes it was like her brain kicked into high gear and ran hot till it fried the wiring. He didn't know why she got so worked up. They managed. They got by. She should've known by now: Rick did whatever he had to where family was concerned.

RICK AND PAUL drove separate back out to the Wilton job to put a second coat of sealant on the roof. They propped the ladders at each end of the mobile home, climbed up, and met in the middle to mop their way backward.

A few strokes in, Paul belted Black Sabbath's "Electric Funeral." He jeered the wah-wah of guitar between verses.

"Keep it down." Rick was pretty sure the old lady who owned the trailer was inside. No old lady needed to hear about atomic bombs and angels from hell. Likely kill her.

Paul bellowed louder.

Rick had no patience. Not after Paul's no-show this morning. "You hopped up again?"

"'Hopped up,'" Paul repeated. "Spoken like a true hep cat. Nah. Got some in the pickup if you want. Rarely touch the stuff these days. Don't need it. High on life."

"Great thing to keep around, cop pulling you over every other day."

"Jensen? He lacks creativity. Never checks outside the glove box. Meanwhile, I got it hid behind the horn pad. One side popped loose, and I said, *Lemons into lemonade, friend. Lemons into lemonade.*" He tapped his temple. "Resourceful."

"You better hope. Last thing Mom needs is you going to jail."

"First thing she could use is a tranquilizer dart to the neck."

Rick gripped the mop handle tight and reminded himself: all Paul knew was after. After Dell Junior was gone, after Dad moved out, after Mom took to cursing Dad into her short glass of scotch on the recliner arm. All Paul knew was after her tall yellow pile of hair slid to a permanent tilt and the ropes of smoke colored a shadow on the ceiling above her. She spent every night like that, smoking, sipping, till the cursing turned to that little bird trill of hers. It'd trail along with George Jones. Trail along with whoever was on the big console Zenith radio.

Paul had been barely four. He didn't even remember Dell Junior. Rick tried to imagine that sometimes and couldn't muster it. He didn't want to. When he was a kid and still at Mom's, anytime Dell Junior's face faded, Rick studied the picture on the hallway wall. There he was. Dell Junior standing astride the Schwinn in the yard.

"She ain't been up to the cemetery?" Rick asked.

"Could not tell you."

"Why not?"

"We should talk about that, but I'd rather not do it on a roof."

The fumes and glare from the aluminum sealant made Rick's eyes water like somebody'd tugged his nose hairs. "What's going on?"

Paul slapped and mopped on the silver coat, widening the wet line between them. "Mother has quit the premises."

Rick stopped. "The fuck does that mean?" The wood handle of his mop was thick and sticky with old tar and sealant.

Paul squinted up at the sun, white teeth glaring back at the light. He wiped a temple with the shoulder of his T-shirt. "She took off," Paul said. "Don't overreact."

"What?"

"Told you she wouldn't care for the headstone deal. She left the night before last." Paul said she'd taken her old powder-blue Plymouth Savoy. Dad paid her bills, so all she would've had to go on was whatever gas was in the tank. Who knew how much was in there. Probably not much. The car sat in the garage for years. Paul went out once a week and started it, put it in gear so it didn't seize up. "She was pissed as a feral cat," he said with a little laugh, as if it were a hell of a thing. "But vindicated. Ask me, she's been waiting all along for him to pull some shit like this."

"Where is she?" Rick kept tight hold of the mop handle.

"Vicinity of Dell Junior, I suspect."

"She don't know where he is, Paul."

"She'd beg to differ."

"Goddamn it," Rick snapped, then remembered the old lady in the trailer. "If he was wedged in a crawl space or stuffed down the chimney of some old house, they would've found him."

While the cops were still looking, while they dredged the creeks and drained the quarry, she kept saying: *Check the houses. Check the houses. Check the houses.* It made sense. Old empty houses had the most nooks and crannies. But Rick tried to tell her. *They checked the houses first, Mom. That's where they started.* Then, after they quit looking, once in a while she'd say she knew right where he was. Rick thought he heard her wrong the first time. The second time, he asked. *Check the houses*, she said. *They checked the houses first, Mom*, he told her again.

"For chrissake," Rick said. "If she knew where he was, don't you think she would've said by now? She gets hammered and says all kinds of shit."

"All kinds of crazy shit? That what you're insinuating?"

"Paul." Rick wanted to say yes. Yes, she got hammered and said all kinds of crazy shit, and that was why she couldn't be left out wandering around.

"That's Dell Senior talking," Paul said. "I'd take his assessments of our mother's mental fitness with a shaker of salt."

There was no use fighting about it again. All Paul knew was after. After was normal to Paul. "She'll get killed looking." Rick thought of her wandering and muttering. Combing the ditches and fields. Crawling under a house and getting crushed in a chimney collapse. Meanwhile, here was Paul, coating a roof like any other day, any other job. "Bullshit." Rick dropped the mop handle and headed for the ladder.

Paul called out, loud and hard and even, "What's your plan there, buddy? Go tell the old man?"

Rick stopped at the roof's edge and eyed the ladder.

"He wouldn't piss on her if she was on fire."

Rick stared down at the cracked dirt and patches of crabgrass.

"Real idea man, Dell Senior," Paul said. "Planting a headstone that says where he's not."

"He meant well."

Behind him, Paul dunked his mop, then slapped it across the roof. "He might've meant well with that bucket of ash. I won't speculate about that. This time, though, he meant to save face while turning a profit. That and piss her off, decreeing an end to it. Again. Worked great the first time, didn't it."

It wasn't a bucket. "It was a tin," Rick said. "You don't even remember."

The day they called off the search—suspended it, they'd said—Mom changed into some old jeans and a flannel shirt and walked out without a word, without looking at him or Paul in the front room. Paul was stacking blocks so he could kick the bottom out and watch the rest fall.

Near dark, she was still gone and Dad was in the yard. He scooped ashes from the burn barrel into an old hinge-lidded tin for cookies or cakes. Rick didn't know where it came from, the tin. Likely something Dad salvaged from a trailer. He held up a pair of jeans and a T-shirt from the boys' dresser. He lit the shirt, let it flame, then stomped it out. He did the same with the jeans. He threw the charred scraps in the tin.

She was gone two nights. Both nights, Rick watched the moon through the porch screens. It was the boys' room, the back porch.

She came home in daylight, muddied and scraped, flannel shirt torn. Her pile of blond curls was dark from dust and soot and fell so it clung to her shoulders. She passed Rick and Paul again without looking and weaved into the kitchen. She weaved like she was treading air. Like the floor couldn't hold her to it. She stopped at the sink and stared out the window. Her fingers locked on the counter like she could've floated away.

When Dad came in, it was too fast. The speed of him churned in Rick's stomach. He followed her through the kitchen's open entryway.

He's— she breathed.

Dad slammed the tin on the counter with a scrape and a puff of dust. *There*, he said. *There. They found him and here's what was left of him. So get the hell on with it.*

She stared at him. She stared at him stunned, like somebody in a movie who'd been slapped out of some panicked, ranting fit. When she did come to, she stared at Dad harder than Rick had ever seen her stare. Harder than Rick had ever seen anyone stare. She pulled a Salem from her breast pocket and lit it.

No more of this shit, Dad said. *Dell isn't your only anymore*, he told her. *He might've been once, but now he isn't. So you'd best get the hell on with it.*

She looked at the tin, picked up the swatch of burnt collar, and squinted through strands of smoke. She thumbed what was left of the label. She coughed a short, crackling laugh and let it fall to the floor. She grabbed the bottle of scotch and a tumbler from the cabinet, went to the front-room recliner, and clicked on the Zenith.

Nothing else to say, then? Dad said.

Nothing that can't wait, she said. If she ever elaborated, if she ever spoke another word to him, Rick never heard it.

Dad charged back outside.

Rick crept to the kitchen and looked at the label. The shirt was one of his own. A hand-me-down. Dell Junior hadn't been that size for a year. Dad must've not known the difference.

In the front room, Paul was collecting the blocks and stacking them like nothing had happened. Rick had wondered, right then, what Paul would remember—if all Paul would ever know would come after.

"He's a goddamn jackass," Paul said now.

"He lost a kid, too, you know."

"You just focus on keeping shit normal," Paul said. "Copacetic," he added because he was a little prick. "Go doing something out of the ordinary, he finds out Mom's gone, he'll throw her shit in a dumpster, sell the house. Keep claiming her on his taxes like he tried with Dell Junior. Last I checked, you got two people besides yourself you're on the hook for, and they're barely dangling. Dell Senior catches wind of this, you'll be screwing her, too."

"And you." Like Dad said, Paul was living on Dad's dime.

Paul stopped again and pressed the mop head to the roof. One of his eyebrows tucked up, like Dad's mustache had earlier, like Rick had said something funny. "Yeah. I'm living the life of Riley." He dunked the mop and slopped it across the roof. "I suspect I'd figure something else out. Any rate, I'll take care of it. Always do."

"Seems like you're in a big hurry."

"Even a feral cat's got a right to be where it wants to be, brother. It's called personal autonomy. Liberty," he said. "Besides, I already had one run-in with Jensen over it. Best to proceed delicately."

"The cops know she's gone?"

"Sure. I went straight to the cops. Love cops. Use your fucking head. Everybody in town thinks she's nuts. Dell Senior says so to anybody who'll listen. They'd throw her in a padded room. I'd sooner take her out back like Old Yeller." Paul pulled the belly of his T-shirt up to wipe the sweat from his eyes. "Shit, they probably wouldn't even bother looking. Just read me my rights and wait for a body to turn up."

The thought of Old Yeller, the thought of a body—Mom's body—made Rick's own move forward. A boot stepped into the fresh sealant.

Paul casually lifted the mop so it stuck out from his side like a lance. It reminded Rick of the statue at Dad's. Paul was wirier and full-scale. "What'd I say about overreacting?"

Rick stood his ground a breath, then stepped back.

Paul lowered the mop.

He was right about the cops. They had it in for him. They'd trained their sights on Paul since the night Jeannie Ferguson died at the quarry. Or earlier, even, when Vern Sawyer flipped that Chevelle. Like both were Paul's fault, just by his being there.

Christ, that meant they couldn't even go to the cops, for all the good the cops had ever been. A slow panic twitched through Rick's veins. "You're supposed to take care of her, Paul."

"Never haven't." He dunked the mop and dripped thick clouds over the stretch he'd already coated.

The sun pressed into the back of Rick's neck like the tines of a wire brush. They finished the job in silence. When they were done, Rick told him to load the ladders, buckets, and rollers. Rick said he needed to tell the lady who lived there they were done.

Paul didn't question it.

Rick slipped around the front of the van to Paul's pickup. He reached through the driver's-side window and nudged the horn pad. Beneath the plastic strip, Rick felt two wads of cigarette cellophane. He pulled them out. Each was stuffed with off-white, partly crushed tablets and sealed with Scotch tape.

He listened for Paul. An aluminum ladder screeched against the van bed.

It wasn't just for Mom's sake. It was for Paul's own good, too. Sooner or later he'd understand.

Rick hid the crinkling plastic mounds in his fists and rounded the van again. He opened the door and stashed the pills beneath the driver's seat.

IT WAS NEARLY seven by the time Rick got a chance to talk to Pam. She'd cleaned while he'd downed a pair of beers and watched TV without taking any of it in. Anna had drifted off beside him on the couch. Last winter, when he wasn't still pulling hail-dimpled siding off mobile homes out west, the whole of her fit on his chest. She'd had to pull her knees up to fit, but she'd sleep like that. Drawn up like a little egg on his chest while he watched Johnny Carson. He supposed it was good, that she was growing.

It was probably too early, but he carried her to the crib she was getting too big for.

He went to his and Pam's room and sat on the edge of the bed. He pulled off his boots, which didn't breathe for shit. He peeled away the soaked socks that left his skin pale, water-bloated, and split. He scraped the soles of his feet over the ridges of the heat register. Pam would be pissed. He always left ribbons of dead skin to be vacuumed up. But he was tired, and it felt good when the skin sloughed off. Like a deep itch and a scratch at the same time.

She walked in as he was doing it, a stack of folded laundry propped in her arms. She stopped cold by the dresser, looked down at his feet, then turned her back. She yanked and pushed drawers, put clothes away.

"Just don't mess with it," he said. "I'll vacuum tomorrow."

"You'll be in goddamn Arnold tomorrow."

Speaking of which, he told her he got some money from Dad, to get to and from.

Her back expanded and contracted with a breath. "That'll help."

He tried to think of a way to ease into what was going on, but there wasn't one. So he came out and said it. "Mom's missing. She took off."

Pam turned to look at him and squinted like he'd spoken gibberish. He wasn't sure if she hadn't heard or if she'd drifted off in her thoughts or if he'd really said something that made no sense. Then it seemed to register. She looked tired around the eyes. Pale and clammy. It struck him that he was glad Anna got his coloring. His coloring took the sun better. It wasn't so delicate.

Pam sat cockeyed at the end of the bed so her side was to him. She closed her eyes and pinched the bridge of her nose. "Morbid," she said under her breath. "Just goddamn morbid."

"You got a headache?" he asked her.

She didn't answer.

He told her everything Paul had said about Mom leaving, about why he wouldn't go to the cops for help.

She was quiet for a time. She braced her palms on her knees and looked straight ahead at the wall. "He's right, you know." She said it more to the wall than to him, which made him uneasy. It made him think of Mom muttering curses into her scotch. Trilling along to George Jones on the Zenith.

"I suppose. Cops'll either lock her up or not do shit. Go right for Paul, thinking he did something to her."

"No," she said. "About how she's got a right. About letting her go."

He watched her. Pam was thinking. That was rarely good news for either of them. "Can't exactly let her go wandering around and expect her to come back. She ain't all there."

Her eyes focused, aimed at some knot in the wood-grain paneling. She looked like she was putting something together. Figuring something out. Rick watched her think. He pictured popped fuses. Melted wires.

"You're tired," he said. "I shouldn't have laid all this on you tonight."

"Come back to what?" She looked at him then. Her cheeks went reddish. She looked like she was about to smile, though she didn't. "What's her life, Rick?"

He scooted down the mattress edge and put a hand on her back.

It'd all turn out fine, he told her. She was tired. She just needed some sleep, was all.

4   THAT EVENING, HARLEY WOKE and rolled up to sit on the sofa. He polished off what was left in the tumbler, a swallow of mostly melted cubes, caramel-colored by the morning's bourbon. The couch was shot. He'd bought it in '68, shortly after the divorce and his switch to nights. The burgundy upholstery was some kind of polyfiber rougher than wool, the cushions chintzy. But in ten years he'd never grown used to sleeping in a bed through daylight. Dozing off to the black-and-white set on the end table felt more natural.

He lit a cigarette and came to in a haze of tiredness and smoke. Every other hour, a spring had dug into his kidney, and each time he woke, he rehashed the brush with Reddick, wondering how it related to the death declaration.

When Harley reached the station, Miriam Cox's Studebaker was in the gravel lot. He girded himself before opening the door, then breathed relief to see Glenn alone in the portable, no sign of his wife. He was working late, which wasn't unusual. He did more often than not, though Miriam drew the line on weekends. "Still no cruiser?" Harley asked him.

"Carburetor rebuild." Glenn was pink and shining. There was nothing worse to wake up to than Glenn's sheen. "Get some sleep?"

"Not to speak of." Harley sat at his desk and stretched an elbow above his head to work out a kink.

"Don't get comfy, it was a pleasantry. June Christiansen called. Jack's widow. Somebody broke in during the damn funeral."

Harley released a surprised breath, a sound like *shoe*.

"Yeah, it ain't all." Glenn dropped the volume, though no one was there to overhear. "They stole Jack's clothes."

"What?"

"Somebody waited till his just-widowed wife was out burying her husband, broke in, and stole the man's damn clothes."

It was a hell of a violation, all right, burglary during a funeral. And the clothes deal was just weird. But Harley tried to curb Glenn's impulse to jump straight to some worst-case scenario. He had a tendency. "Only the clothes," Harley said.

"Jewelry, TV, hi-fi—all there."

"So maybe somebody was trying to help. I don't know. Get things packed up."

Glenn stood and plucked the flat-brimmed Stetson from his paper tray. He said everybody helping out was at the cemetery. June dug around in Jack's closet before she left, looking for a different tie to bury him in. Everything was there then.

Since his cruiser was at the shop, Glenn needed Harley to drive. The two men made the short trip across town.

The gravel road that reined in Madson's southernmost edge passed Virginia Reddick's house. Paul lived there with his mother. Harley slowed only enough that Glenn wouldn't notice. Between the low-hanging limbs of locust trees, there was no sign of Paul's F-250.

The slim road veered left like it was eager to avoid that shroud of locust trees. Harley pulled to a stop at the third house and cut the cruiser's engine. Past Glenn's window, the narrow alley's edge dropped off in a deep ditch before a field of puny corn swelled to meet the sky.

The Fury's door opened with its loud pop. Glenn flinched.

"Need some WD-40 for that thing." The man nudged and puffed his way across the bench seat, said he'd get out on Harley's side rather than take his chances with the ditch.

The steep slope of the Christiansens' yard made the clapboard one-story look taller than it was. The round porch, topped by a dome and ringed in pillars, resembled a child's playhouse. The houses in Madson's oldest addition were miniatures of the Victorians near Main. Only the years evened things out, put the same wear on roofs and paint.

As the men mounted the stairs, June Christiansen appeared in the doorway, draped in a quilted pink housecoat, hair a thinning mass of white. Her smile was tight-lipped, the eyes behind her horn-rims rheumy. She invited them in.

Glenn asked how she was doing, voice so thick with sympathy it clung to the air like a recent downpour.

"Been better," she said flatly. She had a reedy voice, vowels that came pinched from her throat. With a pained, lopsided gait, she led the men through the living and dining rooms, into a short hallway that ended in a bedroom. Light through the sheers caught motes above the quilt. Harley once heard dust came from a person's skin. He briefly wondered how much of Jack Christiansen was in the motes, here in what was his room just a few days ago.

Glenn stepped to the scene of the crime, the open closet door. Bare hangers lined the wood rail. He asked if she'd noticed anything else missing since she called. She pulled open a dresser drawer. Harley was closest. He peered over to see it empty.

"Underwear and socks," she said.

"The man's underwear and socks." Glenn's forehead wrinkled like an old fruit.

Even the holey stuff, she said. And that damn, ratty DeKalb

hat she'd threatened to throw out a hundred times, because, evidently, he couldn't remember the things were free. Her breaths were heavy as she hobbled across the room. Meanwhile, she said, there was forty bucks sitting right in the nightstand. She snatched open and slammed shut the small compartment like she was insulted to see the cash still there.

Glenn looked crestfallen. "Makes you wonder what the world's coming to."

June squinted at him, suspicious at the borderline emotional outpouring. Harley bit back a smile. She tempered Glenn's dismay with a quick, "No harm done." She said she wouldn't have bothered to call if the whole thing hadn't been so weird.

"Any sign of how they got in?" Glenn asked her.

"Didn't know where the keys were myself till I looked for them today. Unless they wanted a challenge, guess they walked through the door."

Harley jotted notes to look occupied.

"Not worth the paper and ink." June tightened the knobs on the drawer before shutting it.

Glenn said if she didn't mind, he'd take a look around. She shrugged, and Glenn left them standing in the bedroom. Harley's pen scratched the paper. He felt her stare.

He supposed he should say something. "I'm sorry about Jack," he said. He'd known Jack in passing, mainly from the diner.

She gave another thin smile. "Yeah, me too." She brushed her hand across the lip of wood not covered by the dresser top's doily. She checked her fingertips for dust and wiped them on her housecoat. "Jensen," she said, like she was trying to change the subject and place the name.

His jaw set. The muscles there rose beneath his thick sideburns like a pair of stones.

Was he one of Hans Jensen's boys? she wondered aloud. No, he said. No, they were cousins. He concentrated on his pen. He wrote the word *underwear*.

There was a spot of silence while she acted the part, pretended to be piecing things together, drawing limbs on a family tree. Then he felt her hand lightly grip his elbow. His shoulders stiffened.

Behind the lenses of her horn-rims, those rheumy eyes looked like they might've been watching a puppy drown. He took a soundless, steadying breath through his nose and stuck the notepad in his back pocket. He reminded himself it was probably simpler for her today to muse on somebody else's tragedy than deal with her own. He gave her hand a pat. A silent reassurance that this, too, would pass, even if it likely wouldn't. "It's all right," he said. "Long time ago."

Glenn stood at the room's threshold again. "Senseless," he proclaimed the break-in. "Just senseless."

The woman gave Harley's arm another soft squeeze. His nostrils fluttered.

"Well," she said, like she was winding up a phone conversation. "Guess somebody needed some holey underwear."

When the men were in the car, she gave a single wave from the porch, a swat like shooing a fly. She turned and went inside.

Glenn took off his hat. All that was left of his hair was an apron of salt-and-pepper bristles. He daubed the bare skin above with a hankie. "I can't figure why the hell, much less who."

"Could've owed Ziske a cup of coffee," Harley said, trying to lighten his own mood as much as Glenn's.

Glenn gave a one-beat laugh. "Petty crime. Ziske fits the bill on petty."

"Not too stealthy, though." Harley slid the key in the ignition.

"Can you imagine?" Glenn brightened. "Kaiser helmet and all, wheezing up the lawn and back with that walker?" He chuckled. "Glad bags full of Jack's clothes?"

In the rearview, Harley eyed the locust trees, the unpruned elderberry bushes that hid all but the shingled roof and stovepipe chimney of Virginia Reddick's. He was staring there when he turned the key.

Glenn braced a hand on the dashboard and huffed to strain around, see what Harley was looking at. "Don't go jumping straight to the weirdo," he said. "Could've been anybody."

Harley slid the cruiser into drive. "Wasn't," he said.

Glenn settled back in the seat as the Fury pulled away. "Know she got caught burning trash naked?"

"June Christiansen?" For a flash, Harley imagined what might've been beneath the pink housecoat. He tried to think of anything else.

"Virginia Reddick. Dad was still sheriff, right after Neiderbaugh started garbage collection. Folks on the edge of town were still burning their trash. Hell, Liebig was doing it on Fifth and Spruce. You want to see somebody have a conniption—Liebig at that council meeting. Heard cusses I didn't know there were."

"She was naked?" Harley pictured Paul dangling upside down that night at the water tower. He pushed that image from his head, too.

Glenn nodded. "Dell Senior called, few days before he moved out. Dad didn't have the heart to deal with it." When Harley lit a cigarette, Glenn cranked open the wing window on his side.

"Dad never got over that, you know. Never finding the boy. So he sent me down there."

"What'd you do about it?"

"Got her covered with a blanket. Had her in the cruiser—Dell Senior wanted her thrown in the drunk tank till a racket come from the house. Bickering. One of those 'give it here' deals between brothers. Dell said forget it. Leave her. Boys need a mother, even if theirs is a crackpot."

"He's something else."

"Yeah, piece of work. But he'd just lost a boy."

Harley avoided looking at the field past Glenn's window. It spread to the highway bordering the old Lucas place. He'd scoured every inch of that field when they'd searched for the body. "Find out why she was naked?"

Glenn looked at him, baffled. "What good reason would she have, burning trash naked?" He scooted in his seat to hold his head out the window like a traveling dog. "No, just moved the burn barrel. To the far side of the house. You want to keep that thing outside?"

Harley took a drag as they rolled onto the paved road at the alley's end. Though he'd just lit it, he let the cigarette fall to the pavement as a courtesy.

HARLEY USUALLY WAITED till dark for patrol, when the air was a little cooler. But if Paul really had lost something at the home place, it'd be easier to spot with some daylight left. Who knew? Maybe Paul was up to something halfway normal for once, trafficking in stolen property or drugs. Maybe he hadn't been getting a blow job solely to kill time lying in wait. Harley wasn't prone to that brand of optimism, but in this case he'd entertain it.

He sped past the house to turn and park around back, where nobody would see the cruiser. The gravel of County Road K kicked up a cloud of dust between a rise of high yellow grass and the windbreak growing untended. He made a right on the old Schleswig-Holstein road, two worn ruts running along the back property line. Harley saw the road had been newly named "15" by a green reflective tag screwed to a T-bar.

He turned and drove down the backyard slope. When he got out, he waded through the knee-high grass toward the front, passing a pile of rotted, splintered wood that was once a buckboard wagon. It'd been there, piled by the windbreak, as long as he could remember.

In front, he passed the house to check the barn, sliding open one of the double doors Braasch should've secured, though there was nothing in there to steal. There was nothing outside to steal, either, that Harley could see. He threaded his boot through the grass where Reddick had done the same the night before. He saw nothing pitched from a window to avoid arrest.

As long as he was here, he'd make sure Loren Braasch at least had the sense to keep the house locked up. Harley went around back and mounted the two short steps to the entrance they'd used. The front door, his folks had joked, was for visitors and vagabonds.

He gripped the brass knob. The head-level panes were sheathed in a cloudy film, but he didn't care to look in anyway. He turned the knob. The wood pulled inward from the jamb like the door was eager to open itself. He yanked it back, till it latched.

The first thought he had made his face flush. For an instant he'd wondered if this was Paul's whole purpose the night before, bringing Harley back to the last place he wanted to be. To crawl under his skin, like Glenn said. After all, that was what Paul did. Got people to do idiot things like it'd been their idea all along. He'd done it to the Sawyer kid, the Ferguson girl, and likely as not the Wagner boy who stole the snowmobile. He'd tried it with Harley that night at the water tower. But Paul wasn't subtle. He went for lost limbs and crushed heads. Blaming Paul for standing here was letting him get under Harley's skin solely out of fear that he could. Harley wouldn't give Paul that much credit.

Harley turned and descended the steps. If he thought of it, tomorrow morning he'd call and tell Loren Braasch to get the place locked up.

On the way to the cruiser, he spotted his folks' old burn barrel and stopped. He pictured Virginia Reddick naked in the glow of flames and the empty drawer and closet at Jack Christiansen's, just three doors down from her house. Nakedness and clothes, the death declaration for Dell Junior and Paul showing up out here—if all of it was connected, Harley didn't want to guess how.

Beneath the buzz of the cicadas, he took a breath and looked past the burn barrel at the old root cellar's upright door. From the side, a person could see the clay slope that led into the earth. But if you stood straight in front, as he often had as a kid, you could catch it at just the right angle. At just the right angle, it looked like a portal into something else. Something beyond the grass, beyond the hill, beyond the pile of splintered buckboard wagon and the dying windbreak.

5 AT TWO O'CLOCK THAT WEDNESDAY MORNING, Pam sat in the Nova. Her big brass P key chain hung down from the steering column and grazed against her knee every few minutes. She'd slap it, thinking it was a bug. Past the windshield, the lamppost spread white haze and zigzagging moth shadows over the trailer siding.

The bills from the sugar container lay scattered in loose wads at the top of her purse. Some came from the last job she'd worked, at the Snack Shack in Madson, till she'd gone into labor. The rest was from birthdays, Christmases. Fives Dad slipped into cards when Babe wasn't looking. Three months ago, there'd been twenty-five dollars more. Three months before that, there'd been a hundred and forty.

At that rate, even if she could suck it up and stick it out, learn to live with broken screen doors and the hollow beneath the plywood floor and the dead foot skin curled around the heat register, that ninety dollars would be gone well before Anna was old enough to go to preschool. It'd all be gone before Pam could get a job and keep them out of the hole.

And even then, Reddicks would be Reddicks. And she'd still be chained to them and all their morbid problems. Even the most morbid Reddick of them all, Virginia, had the sense to cut ties and disappear.

The gas pedal brushed the ball of her foot. She'd left her shoes on the counter when she'd grabbed the money. If she went back in, she might wake Rick and Anna.

She didn't need the shoes. They were fifty-cent drugstore sandals. She could pick up new ones later that morning.

Pam squeezed her eyes shut, as if that might insulate the sleeping world around her from the choke and rumble of the motor. She turned the key. The engine roared. Still in park, she punched the gas and the idle hummed low. She pulled out. Bare foot on the brake, she watched the trailer windows, made sure a drape didn't slide over and gape with the darkness inside. Nothing. Of course not. Nothing ever woke him up, anyway. Not so long as he had that damn box fan going in the window.

Pam gunned it down Whitmore, past trailers with names like Ambassador and Silvercrest and Prestige. Rick rattled them off like classic cars. "That one there's a '72 Shangri-la," he'd say, and she'd eye the skirting, the corrugated sheet metal that hid the piles of cinder blocks propping the trailer above the dirt. Shangri-la, her ass.

She took the gravel county roads to the north of Madson, where buildings grew sparse and the hills were carved into wide terraces of corn, dried to straw-yellow. When she saw her parents' lamppost, she cut the headlights and pulled alongside the fuel tanks. Babe always bitched about the tanks being at the end of the drive. She'd nagged at Dad to move them closer to the house for years, probably so she could be ready with a shotgun if anyone tried to pull what Pam was about to. But fifteen gallons would get her three, four hours away. In three, four hours it'd be dawn, and the stations would open so she could refill.

Not wanting to take a chance on the high idle again, Pam kept the car running. As she stepped onto the gravel, the sharp granite shards dug into her feet. She closed the door enough to turn the dome light off and walked slowly, carefully to the tank. She snatched up the nozzle, went to the fuel cap, and listened. No creak sounded from the screen door's spring. Babe didn't holler up from the house. When Pam pulled the lever, she listened again, this time for the flow. The tank gurgled, and the hose went silent. She tried it again. Nothing came. She pulled out the nozzle and whipped the tube in case something was stuck in it, in case something inside needed to be jarred loose. Then she listened again, this time for the pump of Babe's twelve-gauge. Pam wondered if her mother would fire a warning shot or just take her out.

She squeezed the nozzle lever once more. Not a sound. The tank was drained.

Pam drooped the slack hose over the gauge, got back in the car, and sank down in the seat. She pulled the door softly till it clicked. After she shifted into drive, she coasted, her toes too numb to press the pedal.

At the far end of the county road, Pam sat, calves shivering below the knees, till the numbness gave way to a surging, useless energy. The drive out here left her with a sixteenth of a tank. At best. She could make it as far as Madson, as far as the gas station, and wait. But Rick was headed to Arnold in the morning. And the first place he went before out-of-town jobs was always that gas station, right when it opened.

There was nowhere to go but back. Back to that sweltering, ramshackle, wood-paneled can. Back to that broken storm door and those shitty towels and Anna's stare of perpetual alarm. Back to Rick and his torn-up jeans and his dead foot skin.

Gripping the wheel and gritting her teeth, she stifled a scream from her gut. It came out long and grainy, an oscillating grunt.

She flipped on the lights and gunned the Nova, fishtailing through the intersection.

She sped down gravel roads, made turns too fast, pounded over a mile-long stretch washboarded from a heavy rain that must've fallen months ago, until she tasted the dust thick on her tongue and her body felt the weight of adrenaline wearing off.

The Nova slowed to a stop at the highway, on the lip of "the Bowl," a low plain rimmed by hills. She made a right and looked for what was left of the Lucas drive. She'd parked there in high school. They all had. They'd come there to smoke cigarettes and drink beers pilfered from parents' fridges. That and scare the shit out of each other with the Dell Junior deal, wondering where his body was in proximity to their own. He'd died not far off, somewhere in the valley between the Lucas place and old man Ziske's, just north.

She needed to breathe. She needed to get out of the car and breathe.

She pulled into the weeds, parked, and walked to the back of the Nova. She sat on its sloped trunk and eyed the darkness across the way. On the other side of the Bowl was the blind intersection and the Jensen house. The place was so overgrown, she might never have known it was there. But of course Babe told her about it. Babe was just dark.

In the Oldsmobile, between snaps of cinnamon Dentyne, between crooning along to Jim Reeves songs, her mother dropped matter-of-fact bits, haphazard bombs about dismemberment by farm implements, grisly murders, child molestations, suicides. Women who dropped dead and blew up because, as Babe pointed out, "A body bloats in the heat."

Pam had been big enough then, her toes brushed the mammoth car's carpet. "See that house over there?" Babe began.

"Jensens lived there—God. When was that? Late thirties? In '38, it happened. He farmed, Pete. Marge kept house." She said they'd gone to the Lutheran church in town, had two kids, a boy and a girl. The girl was a grade or two below Babe, the boy younger.

When she'd finished the preamble, she said, "Close to dinnertime, Pete was out in the field, kids were in the yard doing something or other. Marge finished cooking, set the table, laid out the bowls and plates and silverware. Then she went and blew her head off with Pete's shotgun. Right there in the kitchen."

The cinnamon Dentyne snapped. Pam flinched. And the anecdote, if you could even call it that, settled like an oily dust coating the inside of the Oldsmobile.

Pam finally asked, more to move the air than anything, how come.

"Oh, I don't know," she said in that low, gruff, what-kind-of-a-jackass-asks-that-kind-of-question voice. "Why the hell does anybody go and blow their head off with a shotgun?" Then she'd crooned again between chews of Dentyne, sung along to "I'm Beginning to Forget You." Until the whistle part. "Do the whistle part," she'd told Pam.

Babe ruined her. You start out a kindergarten-age kid on a steady diet of housewives who blow their heads off with shotguns or knock down their husbands with pickup trucks and line the wheels up just right with their necks and run them over—who was that, a Pooley? A Pooley. You rear a kid on that kind of shit, it's no wonder they're skittish when it comes to marriage and having babies. Or folding goddamn towels, for that matter.

Pam flung herself back against the window. She shut her eyes. She listened for the Wakonda at the bottom of the Bowl, thinly bubbling through its slice in the earth.

Instead, a drier sound rose. The static of tires on gravel. Pam lifted her head, looked for any cars across the way. There was nothing. But the grinding continued, breaking up, each rock's pop and clang beneath rubber and wheel well more distinct. A pair of headlights shot down the county road through a cloud of dust. They were aimed toward the blind intersection with the highway.

Pam slid from the trunk and headed for the car door, taking as few steps as possible on the rocky path. She got in, started the engine, and looked back toward the lights. They'd already turned and crossed the rusted bridge. She put the Nova in reverse and backed out as the other car flew across the plain, headlamps a strobe through the corn tassels. She pulled out, and it sped up. Then it put on the cherries. A cop. Pam righted her wheels and pulled onto the shoulder.

The cruiser made a looping U-turn across the empty highway to pull in behind her. She cut the engine and watched her side mirror as a tall, broad-shouldered figure, a black silhouette against the star- and moonlit blue of the highway, unfolded like a jackknife from the car.

When he reached the driver's-side window, his flashlight cast a glow across her legs. A thread from her cutoffs tickled her leg. "You one of Red's girls?" he asked.

She tried to squint past the glare, which was now on her face. He lowered the beam so it fell across the shoulders of her threadbare T-shirt. She blinked hard, trying to see him around the void burned into her retinas. "What?"

"You a Reinhardt?"

Pam nodded, cast her eyes downward, and dug her nails into the itching jean thread. When she looked up again, his image sharpened like he was rising from murky water. Below his dark-eyed squint and cheekbones, dark caverns emerged into a pair of thick sideburns ending at a broad, hard jawline. As he formed and surfaced, the hair at the back of her neck tingled with the sense she knew his face. That she knew it intimately.

"How do I know you?" The question came quieter, breathier than she'd meant it to.

He straightened and turned the beam of his flashlight across the distance. "Don't see how you would."

"No—but I do."

"Everything all right? Car troubles? Not waiting on somebody, are you?"

"No, it's—I'm fine. Did you go to Madson?"

His lip crooked up on one side, deepening a crease between his cheekbone and mouth, and his head dipped a bit. She knew that smile. It was a smile in spite of itself. A half smile that was part sad, part something else. Something that made Pam's face warm. Something that froze her like the sudden sight of a downed wire in her path.

"Sure," he said. "Graduated about the year you were born, probably."

The trophy case. From the hallway right outside the gym. In a black-and-white picture, he'd already had a five o'clock shadow. His hair was a thick Brylcreem wave. He'd looked like a darker, rougher James Dean. "Harley Jensen?"

He nodded. He pulled a cigarette from a soft pack whose foil poked from his shirt pocket. He clanked open a lighter. When he spoke, cigarette lit, he exhaled puffs of blue that rose in the air. He asked if she wanted one. She said she did.

She took the cigarette as the lighter clanked open again. His thumb raked the barrel. He brought the flame to the tip, shielding it with his cupped hand so his palm glowed gold. She puffed, and the flame grew and diminished in small pulses. When it was lit, he still held the flame at the tip, and she caught herself scanning his bare ring finger. Her eyes rose to meet his, and she sensed that downed electric wire again, felt heat in her face.

"Which one of the girls are you?" he asked.

"Pam. The youngest. How'd you know?"

"There's a resemblance."

She pictured Dad, all ligament and bone in worn cowboy plaid and denim. The permanent sunburn of his oversized old man ears jutting from the sides of his Cargill cap.

"The eyes," he said without looking at her. "And the lank." His flashlight's white haze traced across tips of nearby stalks and disappeared short of the distant uphill rise, short of the trees and brush steadily overcoming the abandoned farmhouse. "So what brings you out at two in the morning, Pam Reinhardt?"

She didn't correct him. "Needed some air."

He eyed her without turning his head, gave her a look that was unsure. Like he was reading her. Then he seemed to see whatever it was he was looking for. Or decided whatever he was looking for wasn't there. "You haven't seen anybody else out here, then?"

"No, why?"

His words rose in winding sheets of blue smoke. "No matter." His light was trained on the pavement now, casting a long, thin spotlight there. "Not sure you want to be out here all by your lonesome, though."

She reminded herself she was talking to a cop. "I guess no place is as safe as it used to be."

"Not sure when it used to be."

The night's quiet broke with a squawk that made Pam twitch. His CB. He excused himself and walked back to the cruiser.

Pam waited and looked toward the black rim of hills against the sky. She saw visions of threshers, of necks beneath tractor tires. She felt that strange, wretched smile coming on and tightened her teeth against it. A chill ran down her back despite the temperature.

He came to the window again at a quick clip. His voice was deep, sturdy. "Not sure where you're headed, but you want to get there. There's a fire, half mile from here. All it needs is a little breeze." His eyes were cast downward, into the car. She looked. Her thighs were white against the dark vinyl, a ghostly pale trailing down to her calves, her bare feet. When he made eye contact again, he tapped the car roof. "Next time, be sure to wear some shoes." The half smile crooked. "Catch you again, I'll have to cite you."

Pam hadn't realized she'd been holding her breath till she exhaled. She nodded.

He rapped the roof again, twice, and stood back. He glanced toward the distant abandoned farm before he went to the cruiser.

Her keys rattled with a tremor as she turned them, and the roar of the engine filled her head with a jolt. She revved, and it settled. She waited to see if he'd pull out and head down the highway first. He didn't. The car sat there, no lights inside or out, save the dim cherry of his cigarette. It pulsed once, like an orange lightning bug.

She put the Nova in gear but watched her rearview, even as she dipped down into the Bowl and up again. She made a point not to slow by the windbreak, by the dense cloak of a yard. The yard where one early evening, she knew, he played in the grass till a shot rang out from the kitchen.

6 RICK FELT BURIED ALIVE. He lay on the flat dirt, floor joists two feet above him. It was morning but cellar-dark and dank beneath the mobile home. The batteries in his good flashlight were about to go.

He'd been on edge since he woke and drove to Dad's. Paul strolled in late, and when Rick stared hard at him for some hint, some update on Mom, Paul stared back just as hard. Dead-eyed. Then, when they took off, Paul insisted on driving separate. They never drove separate on jobs more than an hour out. Never. It was stupid, spending that much on gas. Maybe it meant he planned to take off and deal with this Mom thing. Get her back home.

Then again, maybe it had something to do with Rick stealing the drugs.

Whatever it was, was a gray area, and Rick didn't like gray areas a whole lot.

While Paul took his sweet time getting to Arnold, Rick saw the trailer was a mess. The belly was in miserable shape. The pipes froze last winter. Copper pipes, good pipes, but they'd thawed, broke open, and flooded the place. It'd sat empty for months, insulation bloated behind the tarp like fiberglass boils. They'd been tore open, either by rot or some animal. Now the insulation hung down in woolly pink shreds.

While Rick moved the flashlight beam across the joists, Paul's pickup pulled up and parked. "When the Levee Breaks" blasted from the cab. The engine and the harmonica both cut. Then the music blasted again. He must've planned to listen to the full seven goddamn minutes.

Rick worked his box knife at a dangling scrap of tarp, the blade gnawing through the pink batting. He spit dust from where it fell and settled in his mustache, and he made the mistake of thinking, for a split second, what his lungs must look like. Caves of pink fiberglass, sparkling like quartz.

When the song ended, Paul's pickup door squealed open and slammed shut. He yelled, asked where Rick was. Rick called back and heard Paul shimmy under the trailer. Rick asked how it looked down his way.

"Like cotton candy." Paul rustled against the dirt. "Tastes like shit, though."

"Dad wants it done in two days. Three, tops."

"Want it done in fifteen minutes?" Paul said. "You kick over the turpentine, I'll drop the match."

Rick was almost tempted. He knew Paul sure as hell would. All Rick wanted was to turn around and go home. Except when he got there, he wanted it to still be before dawn. And he wanted Pam to still be in bed, asleep, like he'd left her this morning. He'd crawl back under the sheet and bury his face in her hair. It usually smelled like warm soap. This morning he thought it smelled a little like stale smoke. He wondered if she'd been out sneaking cigarettes again. Right about now, she'd be watching *Donahue*, vacuuming during commercials, brain motor stuck in high gear so she'd be good and pissed about nothing by the time he got home, whenever that'd be.

The ray of the thick-bodied flashlight shrank to a pinhole. He gripped the handle and thudded the back of the lamp against the ground at his side. The beam spread wide again, brighter for the dust. "So nothing, then? No news?"

"I said I'd take care of it," Paul said. "What's your assessment of this shit hole?"

"You can't leave her wandering the countryside, Paul. She ain't right."

"You'd like to think she ain't," Paul said. "Sure would be tidier."

Whether or not Mom was all there wasn't worth fighting about. Rick gripped the lamp so tight his knuckles ached. "That why you drove the pickup out? So you could take off, keep looking?"

"Unrelated." He was messing with the crossover duct. "Something went missing. Decided to keep my shit where I can see it. Feeling a little violated, I guess."

Rick absently picked at the head of a framing nail. He needed to come clean or commit to playing dumb. "What's gone?"

"Know the stuff behind the horn pad? Shit I told you about yesterday?"

A sliver of joist slipped into Rick's finger with a pinch. "Yeah? Sure?"

"Gone."

"What?"

"Damnedest thing."

Rick's heart beat hard in his chest, but he didn't say anything. He waited.

Paul seemed to be waiting, too. "Well," he said, finally breaking the silence, "guess Jensen must've took it."

"What? Why?"

"Not to worry. Nothing that can't be squared away."

"Why you think it was him?" Rick still had the pills in the van, beneath the seat. He'd opted not to throw them out, mainly in case some shit like this came up and he needed to put them back to keep Paul from being an idiot. Better for him to go to jail for possession than whatever he might like to do to that cop. Paul was like Dad that way. The kid held a grudge.

"Deduced it. Besides you and me, nobody knew it was there." The ductwork crinkled to the ground on Paul's end, and his voice came clearer. He said Jensen got in the pickup the other night, dug through the glove box, and the horn went off. Paul figured it was an accident. "But then I went to sell some to a couple inbreds from Junco last night, and what do you know. *Poof*—they're gone. And like we already established, nobody besides you and me knew they were there."

Maybe Rick could say he had to take a piss, shove the pills deeper in the steering wheel so Paul would think they'd moved. No. There wasn't enough space. "You can't go running after a cop. Not with this Mom shit going on." Maybe Rick could throw the pills under the seat.

"I had a hunch you'd feel that way. But you see, what we've got here is a case of illegal search and seizure, brother. There's principle involved."

"They probably just fell out. Landed somewhere in the truck. Like that putty knife we couldn't find for a month," Rick said. "I'll help you look when we're done."

"Oho, but I learned from that putty knife. Checked every inch of floorboard, every crack and crevice and cubbyhole. Them pills is absent."

This was no good. That cop was enough to worry about without Paul having an excuse to fly headlong at him.

Rick thought he'd best come out and say it. Say he took the pills, because wherever the hell Mom was, she didn't need a kid in jail. Not on top of another kid killed and a husband who paid her bills but wouldn't step foot in the same room with her. Rick pictured her yellow pile of curls leaning from the side of her head as she roamed the ditches, warbling on and on to some George Jones song like a little bird. Shit tore him up.

"You're awful quiet over there, partner," Paul said. "Contemplative."

"What?"

"What what? I'm waiting on you. You got a call to make here."

Rick's lamplight drew down to a speck. He slammed the butt at his side again and the lamp lit back up. He scanned the ruined tarp. The truth was they could do it in a day. He had more pride than that, but they could. They could leave the shredded insulation in, cover up the whole mess. Switch out the pipes and patch the son of a bitch with bigger sheets of tarp. It'd always stink like mildew, but hell. If they laid new carpet, the place would stink like new carpet for a few months first. Long enough for Dad to sell the thing.

On the other hand, they could stretch the job into two days if they put up a new belly, three if they did the place right. It'd mean leaving Pam overnight, frying and popping fuses till he got home. It'd mean leaving Mom out wandering around, God knew where. But an extra day might cool Paul off.

Rick tilted the lamp to the right of the clean hole he'd made. More shreds hung a few inches away.

"Just start tearing shit out," Rick said. "Nothing down here to salvage."

7 HARLEY WAS PULLED OFF THE COUNTY OIL, a road of bare, dusty gravel that hadn't been actually sprayed with black pitch since people stopped saying "macadamized." He'd watched the sun rise and waited for the volunteer fire department to finish soaking the abandoned Jipp place. The blaze had been small, contained to the house, but dry as it'd been, they couldn't take a chance on flare-ups. When they were done, he'd head over, see what started it.

There'd been busier nights, but the last one clung to his skin like sweat-damp clothes after a short, deep sleep. The last call was a one-car accident near the Oakview line. Harold Zurcher hit one of Frank Tvrdy's cows. Zurcher was three sheets to the wind, so he was loose when the grille hit. The only one hurt was the cow.

He'd been barely bigger than a calf, a red Angus. His back was broken, bony rear half nearly torn off. Harley finished the job, stopped the panicked, confused eyes and choked bawls with a shot he hadn't relished any more than Tvrdy had. Then the men cleared the road, rolled and dragged the body by its legs into the ditch. They'd done a makeshift job of driving in the downed fence posts so they at least stood upright.

Now another snatch of static sputtered from the radio and grated like a rasp. "Harley? Carol." He checked the urge to switch her off. Whenever he left the station, he forwarded calls to Carol's broom closet of an office in the courthouse. Sometimes he had to remind himself she was more than a squealing pitch through the speaker. He grabbed the handset from the cradle and said go ahead.

They needed a welfare check on an older woman in town, Doris Luschen. Her daughter-in-law from Omaha called, said Doris hadn't answered the phone in a day. Harley started the cruiser and headed for Madson.

Beneath the shade of a tall cottonwood, he knocked twice at the woman's back door, then tried the knob. Unlocked. He knocked again anyway. No answer.

He heaved a short, bracing breath and went in. He'd never grown used to it, walking into a person's house uninvited.

He called out, said who he was, hoping not to give her a heart attack if she hadn't already had one. Above a pounding in his own chest, he heard what sounded like a mewling kitten. He took a few steps and called again. It repeated, faint. Deadened by the floor. The sound came from a cracked cellar door behind him. He'd taken it for a pantry.

He pulled the door open. At the base of the steps lay a pale foot. The sight made his mouth go dry. A thick knot, one that had nothing to do with Doris Luschen, formed in his throat. He swallowed it away.

He said to stay put, not to move. She said she was planning on staying in tonight anyway, thanks, and managed a feeble laugh. Harley jogged out to the car, radioed Carol for an ambulance, and went back in.

Under the dim glow of a hanging bulb, Doris Luschen's hair looked freshly cropped, short and smart and colored like champagne, but her legs splayed from her hitched-up skirt. The bottom half of her beige underwear shone. Her gnarled knuckles worked to pinch the fabric of the dress, to pull it down and conceal herself. "I got it," Harley told her. He did his best to get her covered without moving her. "Stay still."

"Getting a little too good at that," she said and gave another weak laugh. She didn't know how long she'd been down here. She thought this morning was still last night. And she was scared she'd broken a hip. Her legs wouldn't move, she said. It was clear her left arm wasn't doing so well, either.

She strained and twisted to see the length of her body. Harley remembered the rolling eyes of Tvrdy's calf.

It'd be all right now, he told her. Paramedics were on their way. "You're just lucky you're so popular." She asked who'd called. He said her daughter-in-law down in Omaha.

"Oh, yeah," she said dryly. "Yeah, she'd be the one." Then she tilted her face and strained again to see, to survey the damage. "Don't look too good, does it?" She searched him then, studying him for what he thought. She had a set of thick, pronounced teeth that likely always made her more striking than pretty. Her eyes had a steely swiftness, a depth to them.

"Let's wait and see what the paramedics say."

"Probably say it's time to take me out back, put me down."

Harley's eyes darted to the poured-concrete floor.

She broke into a cackle that subsided to a rattling cough. "Hell of a first date."

When the paramedics from Wilton carried her out on a stretcher, she seemed to be on the mend, raising hell about leaving her breakfast dishes in the sink. She asked Harley if he wouldn't mind washing them.

It was probably the least he could do, he said, in exchange for the peep show. That garnered another good cackle as the EMTs shut the ambulance doors.

When they pulled away, Harley left the cottonwood's shade for the Fury. It sat in the morning's full sun, and already, less than two hours into daylight, the car's air was too thick. He slipped into gear as soon as the engine started, eager to get the wind running through.

He headed toward the Jipp place to see if anything could tell him who did what. Fires were common enough this late in summer. All that kept the whole county from going up were a few spindly arcs of center-pivot irrigation lines. But at the Jipp place last night, there'd been no lightning, no electricity to short, no grain-bin dust to combust. Somebody had to have gone there with fire on hand.

He sped west and rumbled over the narrow, wood-planked bridge spanning the Wakonda. The creek was low, a trickle in its gouge of dirt. Past its straggling trees, pastures rolled out and up, windmills sprouting barely taller than a man. They didn't need to be higher. There was wind enough close to the earth.

He slowed, made the right on the county oil, then a left on the old Schleswig-Holstein. The road divided the north and south halves of the square-mile section. Ziske's and the home place were to the south, and to the north all but the Old German Cemetery was now Lonny Logemann's land. The road was flanked by fences, no right-of-way to speak of. To the left, Ziske had tarnished barbwire and knotty, writhing posts. On the right, Logemann had put in T-posts and electric line, leaving a gap for access to the cemetery and the abandoned Jipp place behind it.

Lonny was the one who'd seen the fire, thanks to his unremitting dedication to closing down the Avark every night. Taking this back road to his place, he'd seen a distant glow, then sped home to call it in. He was lucky he hadn't taken out his new fence.

Harley slowed and made the right toward the deserted Jipp homestead, what was left of the house and barn and outbuildings.

As the Fury passed the graveyard, grass brushed the wheel wells and undercarriage.

Harley walked a lap around the squat, square building whose stucco kept the wood from being sandblasted away. The hipped roof was punctured with holes the fire crew had hacked to vent heat and smoke.

Around back, he watched his step, remembering a storm cellar whose doors had rotted away or been scavenged. He knew the Jipp place. He'd spent time here with the Carberry girl, Marylene, one summer in high school.

The dim recollection reminded him of running across Red's girl last night. She'd worn a wedding band but didn't correct him when he called her a Reinhardt. He opted not to dissect what that meant.

In the front room, floral paper peeled from the walls. Collapsed plaster littered the floor. A black scorch ran up the wall behind an old cast-iron stove. He passed it, into a wide, open entryway to the back of the house. The fire left the single room there untouched. Its walls' only adornment was a negative shadow of off-white where a cross once hung.

In the far back corner was the space he'd shared with Marylene. All he remembered was an image like a blurry snapshot, ruined by a finger over the lens. A patch of blue from a slip or skirt, a haze of skin—his or hers, he didn't know. The rest, the feeling or anything said, was long gone.

What was there now was a pair of Wonder Bread bags. They were stuffed with crumpled paper napkins and bits of crust. Beside them sat two gallon-sized bottles of Cutty Sark. One was drained and empty. The other held a good carton's worth of cigarette butts, Salem filters. Judging by the number, whoever left them had either frequented or holed up in the house awhile. Days, at least. And the liquid still pooled at the bottle's bottom said they'd been here recently. As recently as last night, when the fire broke out.

Harley went to the front room again. With the toe of his boot, he flipped smoke-stained hunks of plaster until a glimpse of bright yellow caught his eye. He squatted and lifted away the layer of ceiling.

There on the floor, melted into the wood, was a triangle of familiar yellow mesh. The plastic was attached to what remained of an adjustable hat brim. A DeKalb hat brim. And though a free hat from a seed company that gave away hundreds wasn't enough to connect the theft and the fire, the screw-back American Legion lapel pin that pierced the fabric of Jack Christiansen's was.

Still squatting, Harley spotted an odd dark spot on a strip of fallen wallpaper. Wet newsprint had bled through itself, but what was left of Tuesday's *Pickard Post-Gazette*'s masthead was clear enough to read.

He used a strip of lath to sift ashes in the stove's potbelly and heard a tinny rustling. He reached in, felt against powder that deadened his touch, and pulled out what looked to be a jean rivet or the base of a snap. He sifted. Buttons, zipper teeth, a pair of overall buckles. Remnants of clothing, all of it. All lit up with balled pages of newsprint and, given the stink and pour patterns, more than a splash of gas for good measure. Beneath the broken plaster, more burnt clothes. They'd been arranged in a tidy semicircle pile around the stove.

Scraps of hat in hand, Harley returned to the station. Glenn asked how the night went. Harley listed the calls: Tvrdy's cow, Doris Luschen's fall, the Jipp fire. He dropped what was left of Jack's hat on the corner of Glenn's desk. "From the fire."

Glenn's short fingers reached toward the brim but didn't touch it. He folded his forearms on the desk. "Anything else?"

Harley told him about the bread wrappers, the drained bottles, the cigarette butts. As he did, he tried to recall if he'd seen Paul smoke Salems. Or any cigarettes at all. Paul no doubt smoked. No doubt smoked more than cigarettes.

Glenn swept a hand over his shining scalp like he was pushing back phantom strands. "Don't go jumping straight to Reddick."

Harley wondered if he had a tell, like a bad poker player. "I get you want to tread light, but should we rule it out? He lives three doors down from the Christiansens', recently known to frequent empty houses—mother's history of burning trash naked?" Harley went to his desk and pulled out a blank patrol activity report. "Hell, I don't know—some fixation on clothes, setting fires. You know what they say about apples falling from trees." He said it aloud without thinking, without considering his own trees.

The phone rang. Harley steeled himself for Ziske's bark, but it was Carol signing off. She wasn't so abrasive when she wasn't sputtering from a radio speaker, though she still had an unfortunate pinched, nasal quality. She said Doris Luschen had a stroke in the ambulance, which meant a stroke was likely what'd landed her in the cellar to begin with. They'd got her to the hospital, but it was touch-and-go. Carol thought Harley would want to know. He thanked her before hanging up.

"You got enough notes to do the patrol report next shift?" Glenn said.

Harley told him he did.

"Then clock out." Glenn took his focus off the hat and put it distractedly on Harley. "Go do whatever it is you do."

The same line ended all Harley's workweeks. In better spirits,

Glenn took wild stabs at Harley's off-duty existence. Moonshining, taxidermy, running guns for the IRA. Harley never burst the bubble by mentioning groceries or yard work, though that was a fair chunk of it. He usually let himself sleep a little past nightfall, ate dinner for breakfast, and after the TV stations signed off he'd put on a record or read a book. Drink more Jim Beam than he needed to. Soberer mornings, he'd pop down to the Avark when Frank was still the only one there. The two of them threw darts.

"Just don't let me hear about it," Glenn said, as usual, but without the guesswork.

Harley paper clipped his notes to the blank report. "There's a reason he's the usual suspect, Glenn. Vern Sawyer's flipped Chevelle? Ferguson girl at the quarry? Wagner kid with the stolen snowmobile—"

"Six years, Harley. That game of chicken was six years back. Ferguson girl's been dead four. The Wagner thing—only kids we even know were there was Wagner and the brother who called it in."

"Because the rest scattered. It was eight degrees. We know more were there. We saw the tracks."

"Reddick might have a knack for giving people just enough rope. I'll grant you that." Glenn used a pen to poke the burnt DeKalb hat like it might've been a dead squirrel. "But getting people to do thickheaded, senseless things don't explain whatever the hell this is."

Harley supposed it didn't. Which wasn't a comfort.

When he left, he resolved to clear his head. Get his mind off everything. He mowed the narrow strip of fescue between the house and its chain-link fence. The grass hadn't grown since last week, but he did it anyway, to wear himself out. It was quick work, since what there was of a yard he kept unadorned, though Sherry had planted a patch of peonies the last spring she'd been around. Harley would let them go till fall, then mow over them. He'd done that the first year, thinking it would be the end of the patch. Apparently it was just an effective way to keep peonies.

He showered, poured himself a drink, and lay on the couch. *Hollywood Squares* flipped on the thirteen-inch screen. When he'd finished the bourbon with a rushed gulp that burned metallic, he shut his eyes. All he saw behind his lids was the lapel pin. Its blue enamel and brass were charred, but the ridged points and the stamped US were still plenty clear.

At the Christiansens' place, Glenn said he couldn't begin to guess why, much less who. Harley had a good notion about the who. The why was what had him concerned. But he didn't suspect a little sleep would make it any clearer.

8 THAT AFTERNOON, Pam sat at the kitchen table, the night before and trying to leave lingering like a dream. All day she'd had a sensation like the one she'd heard came before a lightning strike. She waited for it: a bolt of the kind of holy retribution she didn't even believe in.

Singer machine ready to go in front of her, she was pinning an iron-on denim patch that'd come loose in the crotch of Rick's work jeans. Work jeans. Like he owned a pair of jeans that wasn't all covered in tar and paint and chew and snot. She tried to pay attention but kept pricking herself with the pushpins. Between winces, she caught glimpses of Anna in the living room. She was uncharacteristically hyper, rolling back and forth on the shag carpet in front of the TV. Whenever a tan limb whipped past the periphery, Pam reminded herself: she had not tried to kill Anna.

Every time she sat down and tried to sew, every time since Anna was two, it was this same thing. Pam telling herself: she had not tried to kill Anna. And she'd replay what she'd seen. She'd seen Anna sitting on the diamond-patterned linoleum. She'd seen Anna's chubby little fingers pinched around that sharp, shining needle. And she'd seen Anna sitting right next to the wall socket. That was what Pam had seen. That was what she'd known. Then she'd looked down at a tangle of red thread tumbling up from the bobbin, and she'd untangled it. In the background, the deep electric thump-hum, the silence, the catching of Anna's breath, the yowl.

But that'd been it. Anna was fine, and now she knew better than to mess with the outlets. Even Babe always said there was nothing wrong with letting kids make mistakes. It was how they learned.

Pam didn't know if Anna remembered. But each time Pam snapped about the least little thing and saw that stare, she couldn't help wondering.

Pam pinched three pins between her lips and kept an eye on Anna rolling in and out of view. She'd lost her baby fat, like her legs and arms had grown into the extra bulk that used to dimple at the knees and ankles, the elbows and wrists. Her dark brown hair, nearly black last winter, was still downy and thin, but it spilled to her shoulders.

With the patch pinned in place, Pam pulled the waist of Rick's jeans over the machine's base and pressed the treadle. The needle made a hiccup of a stitch and pulled the bobbin thread up through the fabric, loose and tangled.

A skit played on *Sesame Street*. A song that was the numbers one through twelve. In the corner of Pam's eye, Anna rolled and jerked back and forth, singing it over and over.

Pam wound back the hand wheel and pulled away the fabric to find the bobbin thread a tangle.

Anna rolled and jerked, and the numbers started over: *One-two-three-four—*

"Anna." The pins dropped from Pam's lips and bounced when they hit the fabric in her lap. She maneuvered the denim slowly, tried to spot them before they fell beneath her bare feet. She ducked her head below the table and scanned the linoleum.

A brush at her elbow made her jump so she knocked her skull against the table edge. Anna stood at her side. She held out a pin that had dropped to the floor. She stared, concerned, with those gigantic brown eyes. Eyes like those paintings of the girls with huge heads and Twiggy hairdos and tiny, rail-thin bodies. Not Pam's eyes, which were hazel. And normal-sized.

Pam took the pin.

Anna looked down, eyebrows knit, scanning the linoleum for the others.

"I'll get them," Pam told her. "Go watch TV."

She went back to the space in front of the TV and sat cross-legged, no longer a flurry of limbs. Ernie and Bert, Anna's favorites, rattled back and forth at each other. Bert had a purple hand, for some reason.

Pam sifted through the denim for the pins and found them. At the edge of her vision, Anna sat too still. She wasn't pouting. She didn't pout. Of course she didn't. That would've been like Pam was when she was a kid. No, Anna was biding her time, Pam thought. Anna was biding her time until she was old enough she no longer had to live with the gathering wall cloud that was Pam.

A tear of sweat ran down the back of Pam's knee with a tingle. The tingle froze her for a second, and she waited for that bolt of lightning. It didn't come. She scratched.

"Put on your shoes," she said. "It's too hot. I need some air."

Anna disappeared down the hall. Pam grabbed her purse from the chair beside her. The bills were still there in wads, though she'd pushed them to the bottom in case Rick walked by the bag. He never dug around in there. Even if she told him to grab something from it, he'd hand the straps over and let her dig. But then, he'd never walked past it and seen wads of cash sitting there, either.

When they got to Gordon's, the air was arctic-cold. The store was Madson's nineteenth-century mercantile equivalent to a department store. The building was narrow but two stories, with brick walls that stretched high to a pressed-tin ceiling. Upstairs, in the clothing section, Pam picked through a pile of men's sale jeans for a thirty-two waist, thirty-four inseam. They were out. She went to women's.

Pam sorted through a rack of plaid blouses with mother-of-pearl snaps. She held a hanger to her shoulders and the fabric to her waist. Anna played her usual game, crawling beneath the hanging clothes and huddling at the middle of the carousel displays.

The tag on the blouse read $4.99. She looked over the lines and circles of racks for a red clearance sign. She spotted a 40% OFF across the way.

Scraping hangers against the rack, Pam flipped through halter tops and spaghetti straps. She looked through the smalls and mediums before she realized Anna was still at the other end of the department, tucked away somewhere between men's blazers and coveralls. Pam lifted her chin and opened her mouth to call Anna's name, but nothing came out.

Instead, Pam's legs moved even and slow down the stairs to housewares. She picked through a stack of thick white bath towels. She pulled them out, whipped them loose, and inspected them. She gathered up a stack of four and hugged them to her chest. She passed the pots and pans, passed the small appliances, and listened to the creak of wood beneath her footsteps toward the register.

There, she put the towels on the counter and eyed the pear-shaped saleswoman whose perm was like an unshorn sheep. She was back in the office, paging through a stack of papers. Pam tried to remember her name. Not Gordon. Nelson. Helen Nelson.

"Mrs. Nelson?" Pam's palms were slicked with sweat.

The woman glanced above a pair of bifocals. She made her

way over, using the long counter for balance. The way she moved was slow, listing back and forth. By the time she made it to the register, it was all Pam could do to keep from thrusting the terry-cloth stack at her.

"Hot out there, ain't it?" The woman didn't look at Pam. She said it to the price tag she squinted at. She nudged her bifocals up then let them slide down the bridge of her nose. She punched numbers into the register and read the total.

Pam didn't hear it. She opened her bag and rifled for what seemed like a convincing stretch of time.

"They still calling for rain this weekend?" Helen Nelson readied a bag for the towels.

"Shoot," Pam said. "I think I forgot my billfold in the car."

"Probably won't cool it down anyway. Probably make it muggy."

"Let me run out and get it." She listened for footsteps behind her or taps from the level above.

Helen said that was fine. She'd leave the towels right here on the counter. She toddled back toward the office.

Pam turned, breath held, ready to see Anna standing there. But there was no sign of her.

Pam walked. She walked the short distance to the blinding sun of the double doors and took a breath. She squeezed the handle and pushed through. Beneath her sandals' soles, she felt the unforgiving iron of the top step and the groaning boards of every step that followed. As she crossed the concrete sidewalk, the heavy heat pressed into her skin, a sudden relief from the indoor cold. The tingling sensation that lightning was about to strike was gone. The Nova sat waiting at the curb.

She got in. She watched the front windows of Gordon's. Nothing moved. No one watched. She pulled the keys from her purse and started the car. She calculated what the ninety wadded-up dollars in her purse could do. Two tanks could get her six, seven hours away, and she'd still have about seventy to spare. Foot on the brake, she slipped the gearshift into reverse.

Helen Nelson knew Babe, but she might not make the connection. Pam could call from some gas station pay phone, tell Babe or Dad where Anna was, then hang up.

A snatch of white flashed in the store window, then disappeared. Pam's foot was still on the brake. She let off slowly, releasing it. She rolled straight back into the street without checking to see if it was clear. She watched the front stoop of Gordon's recede like she was pulled away by a tide.

The car drifted to a stop on the slight rise of pavement behind her. Helen Nelson came waddling out to the top step. She threw up an arm whose underside flapped like a fitted sheet on a clothesline. Her other arm trailed down at an angle. Pam didn't trace the line to see where it ended. She knew what she'd see.

The Nova blocked the whole of Main. A mint-green pickup had slowed to an idle and kept its distance. The driver waited, no doubt unsure what to do. Helen Nelson stared. The look of panic and confusion drained from her face. She waited, like the pickup, keeping her distance. She looked through the windshield like she was trying to read Pam's eyes.

Pam put the car in drive and pulled forward into the parking space. She cut the engine and got out. Slowly, the pickup behind her coasted by, not picking up to normal speed till after the intersection.

Pam walked to the base of the steps. Without conviction, she said, "I don't know what's wrong with me." She rubbed at the top of her forehead. The gesture shaded her eyes.

"Left your billfold at home, I suppose." The woman kept her face a flat mask, her voice flatter. "Was about to go get it and forgot somebody." She still gripped Anna's small hand. Anna stood unmoving. Pam couldn't look at her, just made out her figure. "Not a mother, probably, till you've done it."

Pam tried to give an embarrassed smile of relief, but she couldn't muster one. When she finally did meet Helen's eyes, they looked away, to Anna, who wasn't staring like Pam was a gathering storm. Anna looked at Pam like she saw the wreckage of a tornado already passed. With a worn-out sadness that didn't fit a three-year-old, Anna stared like she'd seen some terrible inevitability.

The nerves itched in Pam's skin. Anna let go of Helen's hand and slowly, carefully made her way down the steps.

9 AFTER THEY'D MEASURED and cut holes for ducts and pipe, Rick and Paul put up the belly. Each worked along an opposite trailer side with a hammer. Rick had a mean cramp in his shoulder and a crick in his neck, and the work was slow. But the point was to stall Paul anyway, to keep him from going after that cop.

Paul hadn't said a word about Jensen or the drugs since morning, a good sign he was cooling off. He'd been mostly silent, outside of the occasional limerick, sometimes a jingle. He'd told a story about some kid who'd wanted to show off a snowmobile he'd stolen, show how fast it'd go. Rick had heard about it. He just didn't know Paul had been there when it happened. Kid ran straight through a barbwire fence, Paul said. Had to get an arm chopped off at the elbow. Lucky he didn't get decapitated, Paul said.

Now he called out in a girlish high pitch, "*Mister Wizard—*" He stretched the words so they sounded like they came from a ghost or the bottom of a well. "*Mister Wizard*," he said again. "I don't want to be a mobile home repairman no more."

For whatever reason, it hit Rick just right. He choked out a winded laugh. Paul had timing like that. Like he could sense Rick was ready to scream and start hacking at shit with the claw end of the hammer. Paul knew when misery was stretched taut as it got and sensed just when to pluck it.

At times like that, Rick thought Paul might turn out all right. Maybe all he needed was to get some shit out of his system. It made sense he'd have some shit to get out of his system. He'd only ever known upside down and aftermath. But maybe at some point he'd find somebody like Rick found Pam, have a kid like Rick had Anna. Maybe all Paul needed was some people who needed him to keep it together. Somebody needing him might put things in perspective. That was what Paul needed. Perspective.

Rick drove in the last couple nails and told Paul they might as well call it a day. They'd run the ductwork and water lines, put in the new floor tomorrow. Paul said that was fine. He was taking off, then.

"Help me load tools," Rick said. "I'll give you money for the motel."

"Much as a night in a motel sounds appealing," Paul said, "the thought of spending it with my brother doesn't trip my trigger."

Rick lay still in the dirt as he heard Paul shimmy. "Dad wants this shit done tomorrow." Rick's voice buzzed against the tarp. "You leave now, you won't be here at dawn. We need to lay new subfloor. Carpet."

The side of the van slid open. Tools jangled where Paul tossed them in. "Too much on the agenda, brother. Find Mom, seek vengeance, hot date with a little blond number."

"We ain't even run pipes."

"Got other pipe to attend to. Needs a good run," Paul said. "That entendre didn't work like I hoped. But suffice it to say I'll be back. Maybe not at dawn, but this piece of shit'll be here."

"Don't go after the fucking cop, Paul."

"Won't have to, I suspect. He generally comes to me. You got the pipe was a metaphor? For my penis?"

Paul's pickup door squealed open. Rick slid from beneath the trailer and yelled Paul's name, told him to hold up. He did, though the door slammed shut.

"Listen," Rick told him when he reached the open window. He wasn't sure what he planned to say.

Paul waited, head back and jaw clenched, eyes halfway lidded like he was barely tolerating the delay.

Rick weighed his options. He could tell Paul about the speed. He could go get the pills from the van and chuck them at the dumbass.

"You got something to say, then?" Paul said.

But the problem with telling Paul about the speed was this: Paul trusted him. And that said something. Paul trusted nobody. He never had any grounds to. Trust was something that came from knowing you could depend on people besides yourself.

Rick searched for something. Anything. He caught a whiff of aluminum sealant and saw the bucket from yesterday in the pickup bed. "What's the roof coat for?"

"Favor."

"It's near empty."

"Small job. You got something to say, say it."

"I was thinking," Rick said. "Maybe the cop did you a favor. Got rid of the speed without pressing charges like he did the ludes."

"What?"

"Maybe he keeps tabs so you'll stay out of trouble."

"You mean he's looking out for me?" One of his eyebrows cocked a bit. "Kind of like a father figure?"

"Sure. I don't know. Sure. Something like that."

Paul looked about as somber as Rick had seen him. Like it'd really struck him. Then he said, "That's touching, Rick. That touches my heart."

Sometimes Rick wanted to grab that head of long, stringy hair and slam it straight into whatever was hardest and closest by.

"Didn't say you had to clock out, you know," Paul said. "Work all night if you want. Hell, I'd give you that speed if I still had it. That'd keep you up." He gave a wink and started the pickup. Over the rumble of the motor, the tape deck restarted and Robert Plant screamed the first *Hey, hey, Mama* of "Black Dog." Paul threw the gear in reverse and shot backward. He gave a short wave before peeling out in a cloud of dust.

Rick stood and watched the tailgate draw down to a pinpoint.

He went to the van for his dip. He'd taken it out of his back pocket so he could spend the day lying on his back. His shoulder ached from hammering at a bad angle, and the tingle from the wad in his gum would take his mind off the cramp. It'd take his mind off wanting to knock some sense into that little son of a bitch.

So much for keeping an eye on Paul. And now Rick was committed to taking two, three days on this thing, which meant Pam would spend the night alone back home, getting all worked up about nothing. Rick pulled himself into the driver's seat and reached over to the passenger-side floor. He grabbed a Falstaff from the Styrofoam cooler and pulled the tab.

Then again, if he spent the money for the motel on gas instead, he'd still have receipts. Hell, he might even save Dad a couple bucks. Rick could run back home, not leave Pam there alone overnight. He wouldn't get as early a start tomorrow, but Paul was always late anyway.

Dad said to get it done in two days. Rick could do it. He needed daylight and Paul to get the carpet done, but the pipe was cut. The only thing left was to run the lines, solder the couplings. That and put in new ductwork. He could do all that himself. And it didn't matter a whole hell of a lot whether it was light out or dark. It was night beneath the trailer as it was.

With the speed, Paul said, Rick could work all night if he had to.

Rick set the beer in the console and held the steering wheel for balance. He reached below the seat and stretched with the arm whose shoulder cramped. He felt the grooves of the metal floorboard till he heard the crinkle of cellophane.

10

HARLEY WOKE TO THE KITCHEN PHONE clanging on the wall. The thirteen-inch set glowed from the end table past his socks, static slowly flipping with a black bar border. The glow defeated the purpose of the front-room curtains, but he still managed to knock his shin on the coffee table. It was dark out, he realized. No light bled in around the drapes.

It was Glenn on the phone. Harley tried to make out the oven clock, see how much he'd overslept. Then he remembered he couldn't have. Tonight was off. He alternated shifts with Ray Ecklund. Each worked four on, three off one week, then three on, four off the next. This was the next. Wednesday night was supposed to be off.

"Ecklund's hurt," Glenn said, voice thick from waking. "Broke his ankle, they think." Lonny Logemann had called dispatch, said somebody was driving around the Jipp place. Lonny thought it could be the arsonist. A criminal returning to the scene of the crime like in some detective show. When Ecklund got there, he'd walked around back and swore up and down somebody'd tripped him. He landed in the open storm cellar. Tripped on an animal, Glenn guessed. "Possum?" he said. Whatever it was scurried away in the grass. Any rate, he needed somebody to cover patrol.

Harley's eyes groggily fixed on the TV screen's black border as it rose, hesitated, and disappeared to reappear at the bottom. The sound of his own voice woke him. "Lonny get a look at the vehicle?"

Too dark, Glenn said. All he caught was headlamps and taillights.

"Yeah, I'll head out."

Glenn didn't answer but stayed on the line. "Carol called again this morning," he finally said. "After you left. About Doris Luschen."

"Not looking good?"

"She passed."

Harley remembered the pale foot at the bottom of the cellar steps. The breakfast dishes she didn't want anyone to see. For a second, he was tempted to go over and wash them.

"Yeah, I'll head out," he said again and hung up.

Anybody could've been driving around the Jipp place, gawking because of the fire. This time of night, it was likely a carful of bored kids, probably from town, since there weren't many in the country anymore. Still, as Harley pulled a fresh undershirt from the dryer, he pictured the red tailgate of an F-250, partly hidden by tall grass and saplings.

He drove out to the Jipps' and did a quick walk-through to see if anything looked changed since morning. Nothing he could see.

On his way back to the cruiser, something rustled. He scanned the grass with his flashlight and listened. It stopped. Probably Ecklund's possum.

Since the firebug had holed up in the Jipp place awhile, Harley checked other abandoned homesteads, ones off the beaten path on county roads. He checked the Schneider place, then the Rasmussen house. Both had stood empty since the fifties, the land snatched up by neighbors with shiny new combines no good for anything but wheat. The houses were boarded up and locked.

At the Carberry farm, when he got out and walked the perimeter, he heard a low hum like a distant engine. The house sat a ways off the gravel on a level spread. He aimed the flashlight gleam toward the road. It dissipated in a mist, short of anything there to see.

Harley's nerves were just shot, either from chronic lack of sleep or waking in a panic. Every rustle of brush, every snapping twig sent a little jolt down his neck and shoulders. He headed back to the Fury.

The home place wasn't off the beaten path, but he supposed it couldn't hurt to head over there, take a cursory glance. He made his way to County Road K and headed north to the highway.

As he drove past, in the sliver of dark between the house and barn, a red glow of flame pulsated in a jagged, off-kilter rhythm.

He pulled off the highway's edge. Where they held the wheel, his palms throbbed, steady. He made the wide turn into the drive, slipped the cruiser into the grass between the house and windbreak, and got out. Each snap of the dry wild rye beneath his boots shot another twinge down his neck. He made a pass around the back bumper, ensured the car was shielded from highway view, and grabbed the thick wool blanket he kept in the trunk. He'd use it to put out the brush fire, if that was what he'd even seen.

He listened above his breath and footsteps as he crossed the yard and passed between the house and barn to the back.

The glow came from the burn barrel near the root cellar door. The flames were low, the fire small or dying out. An acrid stink, stinging and sharp, rose from the smoke.

He swiped his flashlight across the property. He swept the beam over the back stoop, the windbreak, the pile of splintered wagon wood. Nobody.

The flames came from a smaller barrel inside the barrel, like an odd set of nesting dolls. The fire ran low along the bottom and licked up the sides. He wadded the blanket in a loose ball, held his breath against the fumes, and pushed the dense fabric in to smother the flame. He used the wool to pull out the bucket. It was a five-gallon metal can of roof coating. Harley didn't know how easy the stuff combusted or how long it burned. For all he knew, the bucket itself could've been here already the other day.

He knew he should check the house. For an instant, he pictured Paul peering from one of the windows, watching him come here again. He remembered Glenn saying Harley was jumping to conclusions. Maybe so. But burn barrels, fires, clothes and nakedness, each seemed like a pinprick of light in a constellation whose figure Harley couldn't make out.

He went around front. In the starlight, the porch roof sagged, slowly detaching itself. The pull shades in both upstairs windows were split into curls. He mounted the steps, skipping the third, which creaked, to the entry reserved for strangers. The door yawned open with a sigh that filled his head. His memory filled in the sound that'd always followed, the pats of her feet, the dry scratch of the straw broom. That was the only time this door opened, when his mother swatted a cloud of dust and lint.

He took a breath of outside air like he could bring it inside with him. He scanned the front room with the flashlight. The space was smaller than he remembered. The ceiling too high. The night's light was dampened by the trees outside, though the kitchen entryway to the right glowed bluish. He didn't look there.

A high-pitched scrape behind the door froze him where he stood. He waited. When it scraped again, he pulled the door back to see a branch drag against the front window. Below it, on the floor, two cigarette butts and three empty cans. Two Buds and a Coors.

He squatted. The cans were warm. Empty. There was no

telling how long they'd been here. And the butts weren't Salems. A Marlboro and a Camel. The Marlboro was bent, flattened into the hardwood. He pried it loose. An oval scorch melted through the layers of wax she'd worked into the boards. She'd used one of Dad's old shirts that'd passed the point of mending.

Harley always told himself the house was safe from intruders, set right by the highway as it was. When he'd done the walk-through in '60, when they'd searched for the boy's body, the place had been undisturbed. He'd reminded himself of that this morn-ing, when he'd picked up the receiver to call Loren Braasch about getting the house locked up. Harley had hung up before dialing a single digit.

Because there'd been no way to broach the subject. Harley had spent the bulk of his life keeping his distance from this place, assuring people he was as cut off from what happened here as they were. He had to. Otherwise every third interaction was June Christiansen in her bedroom, looking at him like he was a drowned puppy. People evidently needed that. They needed to know you could overcome a thing like what happened here and keep going. That or you were just broken—more broken than they'd ever be. That worked fine, too. The one thing they couldn't abide was that you just lived with it. You drank and slept and did laundry with it. You waited at the DMV and clocked in and out with it.

He picked the char. When he looked away and took a breath, it was no good. Stagnant air filled his chest, and the black spot clung to his vision. The glow of the kitchen entryway pressed at his back. Who knew what he'd find in there? What trash kids left piled in corners. What words they'd scrawled or carved into the paint and plaster. He pictured the door to her bedroom directly above. Dad hadn't ever cleared it out. He'd locked the door and slept here, where the davenport had been, the same shotgun she'd used tucked between the wood claw legs.

Harley wasn't sure what would be worse, seeing the place wrecked or his reaction if it was. Like his dad, Harley knew some doors were best left shut.

He debated. He needed to do a walk-through. Take mental inventory. But he also knew no chain-smoking firebug was here. He could tell that much from the air. Not just the lack of smoke. The staleness and weight of it.

Outside, an engine hummed on the highway. The sound was distant but nearing. He gathered the cans and butts and walked out on the porch. He dropped the debris and kicked a can that landed underfoot. He made his way down the steps to the cruiser's back bumper as the hum grew steadily louder, the roll of tires more distinct. He leaned back against the trunk and pulled a cigarette from the soft pack in his pocket. The lighter clanked. He stood, obscured by the brush, and watched the highway. After his cigarette lit, the car slowed and passed.

11

PAM CREPT FROM THE BEDROOM into the hall, purse and sandals in hand. All afternoon and evening, the image of Helen Nelson's averted eyes, of Anna's desolate stare from the store stoop had her tingling again, waiting for that lightning bolt. It hadn't struck. What had was that she'd stopped at the Mobil station on the way home from Gordon's and filled the tank.

She'd almost packed a bag. She could've done it this time, since Rick was off working in Arnold. She'd flipped through the hangers in the closet, through the folded layers in each of the drawers. There was nothing she wanted. There was nothing she had that she couldn't find a better version of in a church basement thrift store for a quarter.

The Winnie-the-Pooh night-light glowed from Anna's room. Pam nudged the door to see if Anna was sleeping. She was. She slept beneath the button-eyed watch of a denim-covered wad of fiberfill named Mr. Turtle and a brown teddy bear that played some plinking lullaby if you turned the crank in its butt.

Anna would sleep till morning. She slept as hard as Rick but for longer stretches. And if worse came to worst, if that bolt of lightning struck and Pam's car rolled and landed upside down in a field and crushed the last breath out of her before she could call Babe and tell her where to find Anna, a stuffed turtle was probably every bit as good a maternal option.

Anna's hair was wet from sweat and spiraled like it'd been set with rollers. That hair. It was Rick's, but when Pam first saw it, then just a spray of black that jutted above her dark, potato-looking face, Pam thought the baby was black or Indian. Something. Something not Pam. "That's not my baby," she told them, and she meant it.

It still didn't seem right. It didn't seem right somebody could carry a baby around in her belly for nine miserable months, baby living off the same blood she did, eating all the food she ate, then pop out and be somebody she couldn't have picked out of a lineup. Pam knew then. She knew if she'd taken a minute or two to think about what the hell it would all mean, making a person—if she hadn't let herself go to the novelty of the whole thing and treated it like that time she smoked hash and threw a big hunk of concrete at the Nova just because she realized she could—if she'd thought *Why?* instead of *Why not?*—if she'd taken just a goddamn minute or two to really think about it instead of being full of wonder at the absurdity of it all like a jackass, then no. She would not have done it.

Beneath her soft steps down the hall and through the living room, Pam felt the hollow, the give.

She pulled the door open and walked onto the metal mesh of the porch.

Maybe she just wasn't cut out for any of this. Maybe it was like how some people were naturally good at math and others were good at spelling; maybe other people were naturals at playing house and forgetting that they were going to die and that all the people they knew were going to die. Maybe other people could live with how keeping people around only reminded you of how fast you were all going and they were okay with lapsing into the dream of it, the dream of constant faces and places every day, and maybe it didn't scare the ever-living shit out of them when they woke up every once in a while, just long enough to realize their whole life was gone in a haze of vacuuming and figuring out bills and patching crotches of jeans. Maybe that was just it. She pulled the door shut behind her.

Turning the key so the engine roared, she knew that was it. That that had to be right. Because if she had some natural maternal or wifely instinct she was choosing to override, then that would make her a terrible person, now, wouldn't it? And Pam didn't feel like a terrible person. But if she were to place odds on what would make her round that corner? Maybe not make her a terrible person but make her do something a terrible person would do? She'd say the chances were a hell of a lot higher if she was doing something that didn't feel right. Something that didn't come natural.

She shifted into reverse, pulled out, and put the Nova in drive.

Anna was better off with a stuffed turtle, because mothers who killed their babies and wives who killed their husbands likely weren't the types who had a good deal of maternal and wifely instincts. They were probably people like Pam, who knew they weren't cut out for this shit to begin with but who swallowed it up—swallowed it whole every day of their lives and then went around trying to pretend they were something they weren't, against their own instincts, till it drove them crazy and they backed over their husbands' necks with tractors or laced their kids' mashed carrots with rat poison.

She made the turn onto the trailer court's main road and saw the back of the Fall Meadows Estates sign. Estates. Her manor in Fall Meadows Estates. Absurd. East or west. She made a right onto the highway. East it was.

At the blind intersection of the county road, she braked. She hadn't last night. She hadn't slowed. Maybe because yesterday it wouldn't have mattered if somebody had T-boned her and swept her clean out of this world.

Of course, she'd also been in a hurry to pass the Jensen place. Now she crept by. Now she let herself look straight back into the darkness.

There, an orange light pulsed like a wrong-colored lightning bug. Like a signal.

Though the air was hot, her knee shivered when she sank the gas. She sped across the plain, past the high stalks and tassels and over the steel-girder bridge whose narrow I-beams were graffitied with generations of initials. His face from last night, Harley Jensen's, surfaced in her head again, like it rose from that same murky water.

She didn't know it was him she'd just seen. It could have been anybody down there, creeping around that place. And there was no good reason to stop if it was.

There was no good reason for her to pull in the Lucas drive, park, and slide into her sandals. But after she did, she headed around to the trunk and propped herself on its slope. She leaned back and dared herself to close her eyes, to listen for the Wakonda, low but bubbling. With her eyes shut, the world was louder, sharper, but her skin sealed her in. Her own steady pump of blood, the chatter inside her head, the twitches of her nerves made her feel trapped in a space suit, cut off from everything by her own body, not feeling or breathing the air around her.

Then she heard it. The low rumble of the engine, the roll of radials on the highway. She opened her eyes and perched ready to bolt if it wasn't him. But it was.

The cruiser made the same broad, looping turn across the highway and pulled off the road to park. When the engine cut, the only sound was crickets. The door opened with one pop, closed with another. The lighter lid clanked. The barrel rasped, and his steps brushed the grass.

"Evening," she said. Though it was dark, she shielded her eyes with a flat hand, like a visor. Like she was sunbathing. She forced the hand down to her side.

"Morning." He didn't walk to her. He walked to the open space of the drive behind the Nova, blue smoke rising like a loosening braid. He looked out across the distance, to the dark windbreak on the other side. "Needed some air?"

"Yep."

"Wear your shoes?"

She stuck out a foot for him to see and thought hard for something to say. All she heard was the pumping of blood, its murmur in her head.

"Want a smoke?"

She said she did, and he walked to her, minding his steps in the grass. She took the cigarette from him, and he lit it. She puffed and looked up as the lighter lid shut. He edged away, looking across the valley. He was silent for a while. His silence was louder than the crickets.

She took a drag and caught a glint of starlight off her finger. Her wedding band. If he saw it, he might ask, and if he asked, she didn't know what she'd tell him. That thought alone, of saying she'd mixed herself up with that family, washed over her with a heaviness. She used her pinkie and thumb to nudge the ring loose over her knuckle.

"It's probably been a while if you did," he said, "but you ever root around any of these empty houses?"

She had, of course. Everybody who grew up out here had.

But she didn't know why he was asking. And he was still a cop, and she was still technically a Reddick. "Hung out here a few times." She tucked the ring in the pocket of her cutoffs. "House was already gone. Mom always said there were rats and rabid squirrels in those places."

He gave a low breath of a laugh. "Babe can leave an impression."

Pam took another deep drag. She felt tipsy.

"Never the Jensen place, though?"

She shook her head. "Nobody did. Not that I knew of."

He looked at her like he had last night, like he was watching for something. Getting a read. Then he let his head drop with a short nod. "Well, I hate to cut this short." He looked toward the house. "Odd question—" he said, then, "No." He waved to say he was leaving.

"What?"

He'd taken a pair of steps toward his car. He stopped and stood, quiet and considering. "Don't suppose you'd want to follow me down there."

She didn't know this man. He had a gun. And he was asking her to go to an empty, dilapidated house where his mother blew her head off.

Pam tried to hear the crickets over her pumping blood. She couldn't. "All right," she said.

"Not inside, of course. It's just—" he said. "You know, the roof caves in, might be good to have somebody know about it. Go get help."

She said she would.

He told her to follow, to pull in next to where he parked the cruiser at the side of the house.

Parked in the high grass, Pam saw the beat of her heart

through the thin white cotton of her T-shirt. Unless somebody came up the drive and pulled in right behind the cars, they couldn't be seen. Nobody had any idea at all she was here. She pictured Anna, still sleeping. She thought of the turtle keeping watch.

She felt the handle of the car door and pulled it. Then she walked to the corner of his rear bumper.

He was already at the base of the steps, back turned. One hand held a flashlight and the other rested on his belt so she could see just his thumb, like that thumb was holding him down, his body in place. She pictured that thumb on the divot in front of her hip bone. Holding her down and in place. He mounted the steps and crossed the porch. When he walked through the doorway, he left it open behind him. She watched his flashlight travel the walls.

In the brush, a few yards past the hood of her car, something rustled. A crack rang out like somebody had stepped on a branch.

Pam shot toward the porch. Before she knew where she was, she stood in the doorway.

A screech sounded, like nails on glass. She gripped his arm with her fingertips. He gave a tiny tremor.

"Branch," he whispered sharply, without looking. The flashlight beam stopped at the edge where this room gave way to another, like it'd hit some kind of barrier. "Get back outside," he whispered.

"I heard a noise."

He didn't answer. He shook his head, reached a hand back, and held her wrist. He turned off the flashlight. He was listening. She didn't know how he could hear anything. All she could hear was the rush of blood in her ears.

"Probably a possum," he said.

Blue light filtered through the other room's windows. When the leaves outside flittered with a shift of air, the light rippled like water reflecting. He angled his body away from it, toward her, but he looked above and past. Brows knit, he worked over some problem she got the feeling had nothing to do with her, even as his palm found her hip. She felt the heat of it through her T-shirt. She willed that thumb toward the divot, toward the space where her cutoffs rested low. But the thumb didn't move. And it wasn't that kind of touch. The touch felt more like he was using her hip to keep his balance.

She moved toward him anyway, feeling the pad of the thumb that wasn't there, feeling it like he'd pivoted her with the press of a button. Her sandal scuffed the floor like sandpaper and jarred him from his far-off stare. She couldn't see his eyes then. They were shadowed. All the same, she felt the shock of that downed wire. She waited. She looked at the line of his mouth, then back up at the dark space where his eyes were. She wondered if he could see her focus.

He took a short step toward her. His boot struck hard beneath the nail of her big toe. Her eyes watered, but she didn't blink. His chest was near enough to feel its warmth. His belt buckle brushed cold and hard against her belly. But he made no move to bend toward her, even as she stared at his mouth.

His hold left her hip and reached toward his pocket for a cigarette. He fiddled with the foil. "We should head out," he said, low. He guided her onto the porch and down the steps.

She felt warm and numb, and she needed to sit. She did, kicking off her shoes and pushing herself onto the trunk of the Nova. She left space between her bare knees and leaned back on the heels of her hands while he walked to his car. He dropped the flashlight through the open passenger window. Then he stood in front of her, with some distance, and lit a cigarette.

"Your dad build this house?" she asked. The words came out to fill space, to move the still air, but they thickened it instead.

"Shit, I'm not that old. Loren Braasch's grandpa Ole built it. Seems right they got it back, even if nobody wants to live in it."

She'd been holding her breath. "I'm sorry."

Another noise. This time somewhere across the yard, in front of the barn. He put up a palm, signaling her to stay put. She waited, frozen, till the hand finally lowered. She didn't speak, hardly breathed, till he took another drag. He was probably right. It was probably some animal in the grass.

The crickets chirped. He pulled the cigarette pack from his breast pocket and reached across the distance to offer one.

She tensed her legs to balance as she leaned forward. "Place seems pretty solid."

"It is," he said. He took a short drag and let it go through his nose as he took in another. He held it, only letting go as he spoke. "That was less than honest. About worrying it'd cave in."

Her heart skipped a beat she felt in her stomach. "Why'd you ask me down here, then?"

"In case I got in, saw the place trashed," he said. "Looking like that bridge over there." He took another deep drag. The bridge over the Wakonda, he meant. Spray-painted with initials, graduation years. "Didn't know how I'd feel about it."

"You thought me being here would make a difference?"

"Nope." He exhaled. "Keep me from reacting, though." He stroked his lower lip with the tip of his thumb, like he was thinking.

"Can I get a light?"

He stepped to her then, to reach her, to shield the flame from the breeze that wasn't there. He stood at an angle, body turned halfway toward the house, and she felt the cool leather of his belt. The coarse fabric of his pants brushed between her knees. She clamped them together, to hold his waist. He was still for a breath. Two breaths. He dropped the lighter back in his pocket, then turned to face her, pushing her legs wider, and stepped in. He pulled the lit cigarette from her lips with the same hand that held his own. He dropped both to the dirt and grass below and ground out the embers. One of his palms found the small of her back and pressed, pulling her down the slope of the trunk. He smelled like warm Old Spice. She felt him, held herself to him, and his mouth found hers. His fingers threaded up through her hair and cupped the back of her head.

His other rough palm and thumb found their way down the side of her neck, made a trail below her ear to her collarbone, and stopped.

There was another sound. This one was the hum of an engine. It grew louder.

His body moved away and took its heat with it. She felt the kind of chill that came with waking from a nap. The kind of chill that came for no good reason, no matter how hot the day. But her head was filled with warm water, and the skin around her lips was already raw from his stubble. She watched him. It was like she wasn't there at all, the way he focused on the hill and waited for the engine.

The world beyond him lit up in the headlights. Then they passed, disappearing behind the corn and rising against the far hill.

The dark hump speeding on the highway looked like a van. Her heart did another out-of-beat pump. Rick's work van, was what it looked like. Except it couldn't have been. He was in

Arnold for the night. And even if he wasn't, he wouldn't have been headed toward Madson at three-something in the morning.

Harley pulled out another two cigarettes. He lit them and gave her one.

Unless Rick was looking for her. Unless he'd stopped by the trailer, didn't find her there, and now was headed toward town or her parents' place.

Or unless there was somebody Rick could be headed to Madson to see. She took a long drag and felt the warm water in her head ebb away. Billie from bowling? She'd always had a thing for Rick. Pam pictured them, on what she imagined Billie's bed must look like. Red satin sheets and a shiny black comforter. Pam didn't know why, but she suspected there was a nearby shelf filled with small crystal animals. A black lacquer shelf with gilt edges. She pictured Rick taking Billie from behind, holding one of her probably varicose-veined thighs, Billie staring at the TV from behind those dewdrop glasses and smoking the whole time. Pam let the image sit there. She pictured it as clear as she could and waited for a feeling like a punch to the chest. It didn't come. Maybe because it wasn't real, no matter how real she tried to make it. Because he was off in Arnold, holed up in some cheap motel with his brother.

She took another drag, felt the tip barely wet from Harley's lips.

She pictured Rick in Arnold instead. She pictured him and his brother and a pair of slutty waitresses with little dolls' faces and perfect thighs who came to the motel room saying they needed rewiring done on their trailers.

Nope. Still nothing.

In the distance, on the ledge of world past the Lucas drive, a pair of headlights shone again. When they pointed down the incline, she saw what she knew was the same black hump of a van. It sank and disappeared into the rows. As it neared, she listened closer. This time she heard it. The rattle of sheet metal. The particular chug of the work van, the engine that always sounded like it was gummed up with old oil. He hadn't been in Madson long enough to screw Billie, but he sure as hell wasn't in Arnold.

As the van passed the end of the long drive, she swore it slowed. But then time itself had slowed. Her heart beat. Her feet went cold.

The van passed.

She pictured Rick walking into the trailer. She saw him see Anna, Mr. Turtle. And there it was. There was the punch to the chest.

"I should go," she said.

12

RICK WASN'T A PILL GUY. He was a beer guy. But by the time he'd reached Merna, twenty-five miles east of Arnold, he'd thought about the long drive ahead and felt beneath the seat. He'd grabbed one of the cellophane mounds and fished out another chalky pill like the two that helped him finish the plumbing and ductwork. That shit worked.

It'd be late when he got to town, drove down to Mom's, but he could at least make sure the house still stood. See if she'd come back on her own. See if Paul's pickup was there. If it wasn't, he'd hope Paul was out looking, not still nailing some blonde or locked up in jail for going after the cop. Either way, then Rick could turn around and head home, crawl in bed beside Pam for a couple hours before driving back to Arnold. That'd be good. To get some rest in his own bed. Keep her from frying circuits for a bit.

When he pulled into Madson, his mouth was parched, his pits were wet, and he could feel his hair growing. He scratched at his scalp and felt the cramp in each root that comes from taking off a hat that's been worn too long. When he made the turn on Walnut, the headlights lit up the locust trees around the house. For the first time it struck him the name of the street didn't fit.

The pavement gave way to gravel and curved left to avoid the house. As if the road were too good for it. As if it liked the green yards lining the other direction better.

Mom's place was on the right, as far on the bottom edge of town as a house could get and still be in town. The tamped-down, dried-up yard was separated from a field by a snowy-looking row of elderberries.

Rick tried to remember the elderberries but tasted only the acidic tinge the pills left on his tongue. Not that Mom used the berries anymore anyway. She ate bread Paul picked up from the store and whatever came in a can, when she remembered to eat. She used to make jam, though, when they were kids. She made it back when they went on those picnics. They'd gone on picnics a few times, after Dell Junior was gone. They'd wade through the tall grass of some old, empty house with a big barn and eat bologna sandwiches at the base of the front porch steps. She'd tried for a while. To make things halfway normal.

The buckling shingles of Mom's roof had a long, rusty streak from the chimney down toward the gutter, which was loose. Paul should've fixed it. Rick would come by and do it when he got a chance. Beneath the loose gutter, red glowed through the curtains of the living room window. She left the lamp on when she fell asleep in the recliner. The red was from the curtains. It was a comfort, the red. It made things look like they always did.

Rick jogged the short distance to the window. In the thin gap between the drapes, he made out the recliner's back. No sign of her yellow curls jutting out past the side. No sign of her short glass of scotch on the arm. No sign of her smoke trailing up toward the ceiling in threads. She was still gone.

In the yard, there was no sign of Paul's pickup, either. Hopefully he was out looking.

Rick was gritting his teeth. Grinding them. He made a point to loosen his jaw as he jumped back in the van and followed the gravel away from the house. He made a left on Main and sped by all the quiet two- and three-stories. They looked like gingerbread houses. Busy-looking. With hand-turned wood posts, scrollwork wood cutouts filling up every spare blank space. Like everybody who built in town back then was trying to show up the place next door. All that thin-carved wood. Just more shit to rot and break. In daytime, the houses looked fancy as ever, but in the haze of the streetlamps they were dingy, and Rick felt that same coat of grime itching on his skin. He scratched his growing hair as he pulled up to the intersection of the highway.

He made a left to head west out of town. He wanted to get back to the trailer and Anna's soft little purr of a snore. He wanted to get home to Pam, warm in their bed.

THE NOVA WAS GONE.

Rick pulled in next to where it should've been and killed the engine. It chugged and rattled like it was trying to restart, vibrating sheet metal and his skin. He scratched. He hopped down and slammed the door harder than he meant to. He crossed the dirt yard and took the porch steps two at a time without feeling his feet below him. He touched the doorknob. He turned it. Unlocked.

Three strides inside the living room, he listened, but all he heard was the buzzing sound of no sound at all. Then a tick. Or a thud. From the kitchen. His hand gripped the buck-knife case on his belt, and his head whipped toward the noise. A tick. Or a plop. The drip of the faucet.

He headed for the hallway wishing his boots made softer steps till he heard the thud wasn't his boots but his heart. It thumped loud and fast as he neared the light from Anna's room. The door was wide open, not cracked like it was supposed to be, like it always was, and he took the last few steps running, not caring about the noise he made, just wanting to see her where she was supposed to be, sleeping. Safe.

She lay behind the bars of the crib she'd outgrown. She lay there still. He watched her for movement. He listened for the purr of her snore but couldn't catch it over the sound of his head. He stepped closer, and she smacked a wrist against the bars and murmured. He gave a breath that stuttered with his heart settling.

He went to the next room, their room. At the edge of the bed, something slipped beneath his boot. Fabric, some clothes. He blinked and tried to make out the soft roll of Pam's hip against the dark. He felt the space where she should've been. Just wrinkled sheets. The flat mattress.

He didn't want to wake Anna. He didn't want her to know her mother had left her alone. He shut the door to their room before flipping on the light. Her clothes still hung in the closet. Her bras and underwear still sat tucked in the drawer.

He turned off the light. He walked softly back down the hall and out the front door he'd left open. He sat on the grate of the porch, planted his feet on the second step down, and put his elbows on his knees. He held his head, his cramped-up hair, and cursed the speed. Speed made time move slower, not faster. Speed should've made time move faster.

She'd come back. She left her underwear. Could she afford to get new underwear? He didn't know. She kept track of the money. She'd been pissed last week she'd had to put back hamburger for meat loaf. Later that night, she'd been pissed about cleaning his dead foot skin off the heat register. He felt the spongy wetness in his socks and the itch from his tingling skin. His head filled with the relief he got from rubbing his feet on the ridges of the register.

So much relief, he wanted to whip off his boots and peel off his socks and do it right this minute. But he wouldn't. And when she came back he wouldn't. If she came back, he wouldn't ever rub his feet on that register again.

The money. He knew she kept it somewhere in the kitchen. If the money was still there, he'd know she hadn't left for good.

Before he could stand and run inside to search the drawers and cupboards, gravel popped and an engine neared. The front quarter-panel of the Nova nosed past the Silvercrest at the end of the block. She made the turn up their road. She slowed to a creep and stopped short of the van, short of her parking space. He tried to see her face, to see what she might be thinking. All he could make out was the pale of it. She made the turn and put the car in park. It was idling high. He needed to adjust the timing. He kept forgetting. He'd do it tomorrow. She shut off the engine, and he rubbed the thighs of his jeans, ready to stand but not standing. Not yet. He felt like he was watching a deer. Like if he made a sudden movement, she might dart off into the darkness past the trailer court. He waited. She sat in the car. She wasn't moving, just sitting.

He waved with a jerk he didn't mean to make. Then he sat. Waited.

The car door opened. She dropped her sandals on the dirt and slipped into them. He stayed put, still scared she might dart. She walked up to the railing and held it. There was a white indent where her gold ring should have been. She was looking at his boots.

"Needed to get some air," she said.

"Couldn't sleep?"

She shook her head.

"Anna's still asleep," he said, feeling her out. She couldn't go and leave Anna like that. She had to know. That's when things happened you couldn't take back. Couldn't undo. When you weren't looking. When you weren't there to hear and see. But he still had the feeling Pam could disappear with the wind of a breath. Vaporize at a moment's notice. And he was still too relieved to have her standing here to take a chance on pissing her off.

"I figured," she said.

"Went driving around, then? Because you couldn't sleep?"

She nodded, and a long strand of her hair came spindling down in front of her face. She pushed it away and stared at the toes of his boots. It looked like she felt bad enough, leaving Anna like she had. There was no reason to make it worse.

And it wasn't her fault she couldn't sleep without him. She had trouble sleeping as it was. She'd wind up on the couch under a spare sheet half the time. He always told her, just lock the door and listen to the fan. Focus on the fan and let it drown things out. But she wouldn't run it at all when he wasn't there.

So she couldn't sleep tonight and didn't want to wake Anna with the sound of the TV in the front room. So she went driving around. That was all. Of course it was. He was just edgy because of this deal with Mom. He tried to let that settle and wash through him, but he was jumpy. Twitchy. Probably the speed.

He eyed the pale indent in her finger again. She must've taken off her ring before bed. Put it back on in the morning. He'd never noticed.

"Finish the Arnold job tomorrow. Early enough I'll be home by dinner," he said. "You can get some better rest, for once."

Her face had gone blank. No expression. It was good. It meant her brain wasn't overheating. She kept her eyes down and minded the steps as she passed him. He reached out and grazed her shin with his fingers. The touch made her jump, made her jerk a little as she pulled open the door. He rose and followed her in.

13

IN THE HOUR BEFORE DAWN, Harley checked one last homestead for chain-smoking squatters drinking Cutty Sark from gallon jugs. The Knudsen place sat tucked beneath the ridge of the county oil, right alongside the highway a mile from town. The Penkes owned the land and used the outbuildings for storage. They kept the yard well lit, so trespassers were unlikely. Then again, if the trespasser was Paul, Harley supposed he was nothing if not bold.

Harley listened. He couldn't shake the sense there'd been someone lingering just out of sight all night. He replayed the sounds: brushing grass, cracking twigs, the low hum of an engine. All he heard now was silence. It should've settled his nerves, probably, but it didn't. He'd been wired since Glenn called, more wired by the burn barrel fire. Then there'd been what happened with Pam Reinhardt. That had him tightly wound in a way he hadn't counted on.

Under the white glow of the lamppost, the brooder house was sealed up, door dead-bolted. The horse barn was unlocked and mostly empty. The stalls were stripped out. A round-rung ladder at the back led to a partial loft. Harley climbed a few steps, far enough to see two moldy bales and a generator.

At the bigger hay barn, he nudged the double doors aside to see the chrome trim of a bulbous winged Plymouth Savoy, midfifties. The plates were out of date, still stamped THE BEEF STATE, and the tag in the bottom right corner was from '60. He wondered where and when and why Penke had picked it up. Aside from the car, the barn held broken odds and ends. A pair of old tire pumps, a collection of rusted window screens.

He slid the doors shut and crossed the yard to the porch. He climbed the steps and tried the knob. Locked. Around back, above thick foundation stones, the door was stairless and closed, too high for anyone's reach.

HARLEY WAITED AT the station till dawn, when the *Post-Gazette*'s Thursday supplement thunked against the portable siding. He snatched it up and headed to Ziske's.

Ziske's spread lay between the county oil and the home place, its drive off the old Schleswig-Holstein, right across the road from the Old German Cemetery and the Jipp place. Maybe he'd heard or seen something notable the last few days. Lord knew he called the station enough when he hadn't.

The gravel drive sank toward Ziske's house and outbuildings, which were tucked between a pair of hills turned gold with parched grass.

The concrete steps and stoop sagged into the earth, sloping away from the front door. Harley leaned and peered through the latched screen. At the back of the house, a kitchen radio blared some tinny, manic accordion tune. He called Ziske's name twice before the thing shut off.

The old man scooted to the door, cursing his walker under his breath. He flipped the hook and turned his back. "You're early, paperboy."

"Figure you been up two hours already."

"Two, three. I got coffee."

"I can't stay long." Harley held the paper out as Ziske turned his back.

"You got time for a cup of coffee." He scooted down the hall.

Harley had never seen Ziske without his cowboy hat and now wished to hell he'd put it back on. The groove from the hat band was deep enough it surely never filled in, and what was left of the old man's hair ran in snaking white trails over the humps and bumps of his head. Where scalp showed through, it was tough to say where age spot ended and his regular color began.

Ziske poured Harley a cup of coffee that looked like tea. That was no doubt how the old folks drank it all day long. What they called coffee was a hue barely darker than rusty pipes.

Harley dropped the supplement on the table. "There. Now it doesn't show up, Gene won't think you're running a scam."

Ziske grunted and used his walker for balance as he sat. He told Harley to pull up a chair.

"Seen anybody around the Jipp place, last few nights?" Harley sat down. "Anybody in a red pickup?"

"Think I see that far? Hell. Jipps' is past the cemetery. My view that way's a cottonwood and some gravestones."

"There's a comfort."

"Some days," Ziske said. "Heard the fire truck up there, whichever night it was. Ask me, Logemann's the one burnt that place. So's he could plant a few more rows where it's tough enough keeping switchgrass." Lonny Logemann was a thorn in the old man's side primarily due to shared proximity. He owned everything on the north half section beside the cemetery. "Son of a bitch—waiting on me to die. Watch. He'll take out another loan, snatch this place up, lose it to the bank. Damn drunk."

"Lonny called in the fire. Doubt he set it."

Ziske gave a hard breath. An irritated concession.

"Know if he's done any roofing? Him or Braasch? Somebody

left a bucket of sealant in the burn barrel next door. Caught fire last night."

"Sealant? Hell, even Logemann's not dumb enough to have a flat roof."

"Haven't heard or seen anything over that way, either, then?"

"Can barely hear or see me. About time for a stroke of my own." Ziske took a sip from his dainty china cup. It was a cup his wife, were she living, likely would've saved for weekly card games or Thanksgiving dinners. "You the one found Doris Luschen?"

Harley said he was. That it was too bad.

"Getting old's too damn bad." Ziske pointed at the wall, to a wedding portrait. "Wife's first cousin."

Harley recognized the old Lutheran church. Ziske's wedding party crammed in the narrow room, women in front of the men, everybody scowling like it was the reading of a will. Doris was the exception. She was all teeth. So much teeth, she may not have been able to cover them. She might've had no choice but to smile.

"Thick hips," Ziske said. "Made up for them horse teeth. When's the service?" He prodded the paper at him with a thick, arched finger. "See if it's in there yet. Betty said last night. You know, my girl Betty's still an old maid. Too old to bear any honyocks, but she can keep house. Wouldn't kill you to get somebody to keep house."

While Harley paged through what was mostly classified ads, he pictured Betty Ziske's thick brown bulb of a permanent, her broad stomach tented under the frills and lace of a wedding gown. Then he pictured what Pam's midsection must look like. Long and pale, he thought. With the slightest mound of a belly between the hips.

"Think I'm pulling your leg?" Ziske demanded.

"Suspect you're not."

"You got to be, what, fifty?"

"Forty-seven."

"Fifty years old. Waiting to figure out what you want? Don't nobody know. Better that way. Don't get it, don't care. If you knew it and got it, you'd just want something else." Ziske plucked a pair of shears from a catchall basket on the table. He slid them across the tabletop. "Clip it out for me," he said, meaning the obituary. "Hear where they had a funeral for the boy?"

"I heard, yeah." The scissors were for hair, Harley thought. Or something medical. Something too delicate for his grip. He spotted Doris's obituary. "Full notice to come," it said. There was no picture for the newsprint to bleach faceless, but he imagined one anyway: Doris leaned back against an old Mercury, squint-smiling in the sun, evaporating. He read the birth date, August 23, 1893. She'd died a month shy of her eighty-fifth birthday. She'd been a year younger than his mother. She'd had him late, his mother.

"Kirschner says he cut a stone for him. Pink granite."

"Guess it's something."

"Says he was here, at least." Ziske smoothed his hands across the tabletop. The surface was gouged and worn with dips like old butcher block. "I rattled him, you know. Rollie. That morning."

"Rollie was rattled a long time before that." The old man had always felt partly responsible. He'd hired Rollie after buying the Lucases' eighty acres and securing the full southeast quarter section. Rollie'd stayed in the vacant house in exchange for work around the place. The morning it happened, Ziske drove a pickup bed of dirt down to an old caved-in cellar. There'd been two on the Lucas spread, a sturdy one up by the house and a collapsed one a good hundred yards off. Likely left over from a sod house nobody remembered. Rollie planned to fill it that day and was there waiting. He didn't notice Ziske coming, so the old man tapped the horn. Startled him. But everything startled him. Ziske blaming himself for what happened was as useful as blaming Dell Junior, who was guilty of no more than exploring, sifting for arrowheads and buffalo bones in the powdery blowouts. Ziske blaming himself was as useful as blaming Rollie, for that matter. He'd had no more control over his reaction than a backhoe would've.

"Suppose he's washed out to sea by now," Ziske said. That was what they'd settled on, that Rollie chucked Dell Junior in the Wakonda. There'd been a smear of blood on the pickup's side, a pool of it in the fill dirt, a fresh set of tracks running to and from the direction of the creek. But they'd dredged it for miles. They'd settled on the Wakonda because they'd needed to settle.

Harley finished making a jagged-edged mess of Doris's obituary. He slid it across the table. "Wouldn't have pegged you for a scrapbooker."

"What time's the service? Can't read the print."

"If you can't read the print, what the hell do you care if it comes or not?"

"I pay for the damn thing."

"The supplement's free," Harley said as he scanned the last paragraph. "Ten-thirty. Tomorrow at Zion."

"Quick turnaround." Ziske sounded impressed for once. "Planting her up the road with the rest of them, I guess. Start up that way now, I'll make it by the time she does." He meant the Old German graveyard. "Ain't been up there since the fire. Can't imagine it, Jipp place gone. Granted, house was ramshackle the day it was built. Tell you what I regret—mowing down the Lucases'. Ole Braasch could build a hell of a house."

Ziske must've been getting dotty. "Ole Braasch built the Jensen place," Harley corrected him.

The old man scowled, then barked, "I know what goddamn places Ole Braasch built. Lucas hired him. Built Lucas the same place as your folks'. Same barn, same all of it. Right down to the nail for the outhouse paper. Might've only knew the one floor plan, Ole, but he could build it. Your folks' place over there sitting empty—goddamn waste."

Harley studied Ziske's milky blue irises beneath his wild brows, trying to read if he was hinting at what June Christiansen had been, the day before last. But no. Ziske wasn't one for allusion. If he had something to say, you couldn't pay him not to say it.

"Wish to hell I hadn't mowed that place over," he said again. "Should've razed this one instead."

"You did what you had to."

"Did what was easy. Easier knocking it down than shampooing Rollie's brains out of the rug." As soon as he'd said it, Ziske stiffened and winced. "Ah, hell."

"None taken."

Ziske took a last swig of coffee. Harley used it as an excuse to stand, pour the old man another, and head out. Ziske took a sip and shook his head, looking disgusted. "Ramshackle or not," he said, "burning down them houses is like spitting on graves. Most them places, built by folks didn't have a pot to piss in. If they did, they wouldn't have landed here. Old houses is all that's left of them." He was staring at the old wedding picture on the wall again. "Indians were smart, you know. Knew it weren't no good for more than grazing out here. Or hunts. Seen arrowheads, up in that north pasture when the rain cut it up. What was it, eight years ago, we had all that rain?"

Give or take, Harley said. He told the old man he needed to go.

Ziske waved by way of raising the cup like a toast. "I'm still pressing charges, that supplement don't come."

"Imagine you'll try if it does," Harley said and waved as he headed out.

14

THE LAST THING PAM REMEMBERED about the night before was the cusp of sleep. Rick had pinned her beneath an arm and a leg and lain hot against her back. But he never did that little spasm that told her he was asleep. His breaths never slowed to long and shallow. Not while she was awake, anyway.

When she rolled her head, the pillowcase grazed her mouth. It was still a little raw from Harley's bristles. She remembered last night, balancing her weight on the trunk of the Nova. She waited for a sinking guilt, a flu-like heaviness. It didn't come.

She got up and walked to the hall. In the next room, Anna had climbed down from the crib and sat on the floor. She'd spread out pieces of paper from a notepad. Drawings, scrawled letters. She was arranging them, putting them in some kind of order. Her hair was a rat's nest, but she'd changed from her pajamas into a T-shirt and some patched-up jeans. Pam asked if she was hungry. Anna didn't look at her. Just said in a minute.

The phone on the kitchen wall rang. It was Babe. Pam cradled the phone between her ear and shoulder, opened the bread box on the counter, and pulled two plates from the cabinet. She listened warily as Babe tried to make small talk for a sentence or two.

"Then somebody went and drained the damn gas tank," she said.

Pam stopped cold, hand on the pull of the cabinet where the butter was. She acted as if she hadn't heard. She asked what Babe had said and listened close.

"Been telling your dad for years to move those tanks down by the barn."

Pam hadn't stolen the gas, but she'd sure as hell tried, and now she listened for a hint of suspicion. There was none. It sounded more like Babe was a little proud to be proved right.

"Did you call the cops about it?" Pam pictured Harley. She pictured his belt buckle, his shoulders, his rough palm. "You should," she said, weirdly thrilled. "I would."

Babe made a raspberry noise. "Like they'd do anything about it." Then she was quiet. Pam waited. "Went down to Gordon's this morning," Babe said. The surface of her voice was offhand but the underside was hardening like cooling metal.

Pam stilled, saucer of butter in hand, and said nothing. She set the saucer on the counter and wound the phone cord's coils around her finger.

"Had to pick up some *canning wax*," Babe said, like she was real angry at that canning wax. She waited, as if it were Pam's turn to talk.

The tip of Pam's index finger throbbed purple at the end of the coils. When she listened close, she heard the line click with static. She unrolled the cord from her numb finger.

"Had a chat with *Helen Nelson*." Babe had sunk in her teeth and was about to shake Pam like an old sock. "Look, I don't have all day to play cat-and-goddamn-mouse with you, so I'll tell you right now. You're lucky if Helen Nelson ain't already told half the town what happened yesterday, and if you think she really thought you just *accidentally* left your three-year-old girl in that store, you're a hell of a lot dumber than I even thought."

"What are you saying?" Pam bit back, though it came out higher than she wanted, and that goddamn morbid smile that happened whenever it shouldn't cramped her cheeks. When she said it again, her voice practically whistled. "What are you even talking about?" She knew Babe could hear the smile. Babe had hated her for it since Aunt Sophia's funeral when Pam was eight. Pam tried sarcasm and volume to mask it. "Yeah. You're right. I left Anna in the racks of Gordon's like some knocked-up teenager"— she searched for words—"dropping some bastard on a convent porch." Convent porch? She'd never even seen a convent. She didn't even know if convents had porches. Did convents have porches?

Babe spoke slow and hard. "Listen. You need to simmer right the hell down, Sis, and get ready to listen."

The garish smile straightened without Pam having to chew her cheeks. Babe was quiet. Waiting for Pam to simmer right the hell down.

She spoke again, even and low. "I'm gonna tell you this once, and I don't expect to have to say it again."

Pam listened.

"*You* made this bed. *You* did it."

Babe let that sit there and sink in, and it did. It sank through Pam's insides like she'd swallowed sand.

"You think you want out? By my math, you got about fifteen years before you even get to think about it."

The weight of it settled in Pam's gut. Her head felt light.

"Wish you'd done things different? Think you deserve something better?"

"I didn't—"

"It was a rhetorical question, Pamela Jean." She took a long breath. "You don't deserve any better, Sis. You signed up for what you got. She didn't. That's the difference. That simple."

After Babe hung up, Pam slid down to sit in a kitchen chair.

She stared, unblinking. Across the table was the purse, the Singer sewing machine. She listened for Anna. She was silent in her room. Sorting those papers and whatever they held.

Finally, Pam stood, unplugged the Singer, and wrapped the cord around the body of it. She carried it to the hall closet, thought of all the things crammed inside, and kept walking to their bedroom. She slid it between the legs of the bedside table.

Back in the kitchen, she didn't feel her hands as she dumped the purse across the wood grain. She watched her own fingers gather up the bills she'd taken from the sugar canister, one by one, straightening them into a pile. She went to the cabinet and pulled down the canister for the flour. She lifted up the bag and dropped them in with the rest like she was dropping lot rent through the main-office mail slot. Another installment on a bill she'd never pay off.

There'd be no new start. There'd be no house with a sturdy foundation and ceilings high enough to breathe beneath. There'd be no tanks of gas to take her away from any of it. There would be this and only this. In total.

She burped the lid. She put the canister back on the shelf.

15

THE CARPET WAS COMING UP EASY. So was the pad. Whoever laid it used good pad—hadn't glued it down to the plywood, either. Didn't need it. Heavy-duty stuff. Came right up from the staples, just pop-pop-pop. In one ear, anyway. Rick's other ear was plugged. He couldn't clear it. He swallowed, gave his nose a few good farmer blows, but it was no use. It made everything in his head loud and everything outside his head hushed.

Other than that, he felt good, for no sleep. He hadn't slept back at home. He'd been too scared he wouldn't wake early enough. But he felt pretty good. Real focused. And the carpet was coming up easy. They'd used real good pad.

He squatted with the box cutter and slit the rug's crosshatch backing into long strips he could roll and carry out. A sharp squeal cut through the deadness of his ear. Rick peeked up past the frame of the bedroom window screen. Paul's pickup had pulled up. The squeal was the door. It squealed again when it shut. It was near eleven in the morning. That kid needed to get his shit together.

Rick heard him climb up through the front door. There were no stairs outside. His ass or belly thudded against the floor. Rick called out, said he was in the back bedroom. He pulled another corner of the rug and tugged the pad beneath for the satisfying pop-pop-pop. He knelt down and ran the razor along the rug back. Paul's boots pounded the hallway floor.

Rick gave his nose another blow, trying to clear that plugged ear. It wouldn't go. "Any luck? With Mom?" His voice sounded loud coming out of his head. He wondered if it sounded that loud to Paul.

"You are like a goddamn broken record." Paul walked past him. He reached down to the Styrofoam cooler in the corner of the room. It sat on the exposed plywood. He pulled out a beer and sat.

"Ain't even noon," Rick pointed out.

"Duly noted, Carry Nation." Paul asked what the day's plan was. Wanted to know if he should crawl under, solder the water lines.

"Done already. That and the ductwork. Did it last night."

"Don't say. Bet you could use a nap."

Rick kept his eyes on the blade, on the carpet. He didn't know if Paul could tell about the speed. That Rick was on it. "Guessing you stayed away from the cop, given you're here and not in jail."

Paul took a long drink, ran his eyes and fingers over the bared plywood next to the strip of carpet tacks. "Jensen? Tailed him a bit." Paul said the wood looked decent. Water streaks was all.

"You tailed a fucking cop?"

He took another swallow and exhaled a low belch. "I was creeping around some old, rickety houses, he was creeping around some old, rickety houses."

Rick waited for more. "And? Anything? You even any closer to knowing where she is?"

"Yeah. Renovating her vacation homes. Finished one already."

"You fucking high again?"

"Nah. You?"

The box cutter's tip ran off track, out from between the straight lines. "Shit." He was sweating. He nudged the shoulder of his T-shirt against his brow to keep the sweat from dripping in his eye.

"I recall telling you to keep shit normal," Paul said.

"Think I'm tearing up carpet for shits and giggles?"

"You drove into Madson last night."

How'd he know that? Rick focused on slitting the carpet backing. "Yeah? So? You got one real job, Paul, keep an eye on Mom. You don't do it, it's my problem, too."

Paul gave a half laugh. A thud of air. "You got problems enough, buddy."

"The fuck does that mean, I got—" He looked up at Paul and held the box cutter like a pointed index finger. He punctuated the air in front of him with the tip. "You're the one needs to get his shit together. Find somebody like I did and settle the fuck down. Get your priorities straight."

Paul stared back. Those floating silver irises were halfway lidded. His mouth bent in a slight smile but stayed silent, like he was holding something back. Their whole lives, Rick wished Paul would be quiet. Now that he was, the shit was nerve-racking.

God, Rick's pits were wet. He scratched his scalp.

Paul rested his head against the wall behind him. But he kept looking. Rick felt like he was being peered at through a rifle sight. "You're real good at seeing what you want to, you know that? Always have been. Like Mom and those picnics. Her wandering off with Dell Junior's shit."

"Don't start that. She don't know where he is, Paul. She tried doing something nice, tried making shit normal, and you turn it into something else."

The picnics she'd taken them on after Dell Junior was gone were about the last good times Rick remembered with Mom, and

Paul wouldn't even let him have that. In the tall grass of some dilapidated house in the country, she'd lay out an afghan and Tupperware and talk about buying the place. Fixing it up. The place was in rough shape, the front porch roof coming loose, but it was still nice, her saying what colors she'd paint the rooms, what drapes she'd hang in the windows. All Paul harped on was how she'd tell the boys to stay put and go off by herself a bit. "She probably wanted some quiet. Hell, she probably had to pee."

"And all the toys? That silver rocket?"

It'd been Dell Junior's. Paul insisted on bringing it once. Mom got sick of him and Rick bickering over it and snatched it away before she wandered off. Rick didn't know what she'd done with it. Probably put it in her purse. On the way home, Paul sifted through the wadded-up mound of afghan and Tupperware, and it was gone. After, Paul noticed other stuff that'd disappeared. An old iron locomotive. A ball and jacks. A spinning top with a plunger you pulled and sank to make it turn. Baseball cards and comics.

"You probably took it. You probably took his shit to school and traded it."

"God, I admire that," Paul said. "The way you see things. The way you don't. That's a goddamn gift, friend."

Rick wanted Paul to stop talking. "Help me tear up this floor."

"You don't look too good," Paul said. "You feel all right?"

"What?" Rick's chest gave two, three loud knocks. "I'm fine," he said. "It's just this thing with Mom. We need to keep our heads. Stick together right now." He changed the subject. "Be good to get out of here early today." He told Paul to measure and cut the new plywood.

Paul said the wood looked fine. Didn't need to replace the plywood.

Rick supposed. He supposed the wood was fine. He gave his nose a good snort. The plugged ear popped with a loud rush of air.

"Out of sight, out of mind, anyway," Paul said, voice piercing, it was so clear.

They worked in silence. The silence made time slow. Not like last night at the trailer, when Rick was waiting on Pam. This time was like sludge. Like sludge needing to be snaked from a pipe. The only sound was the boom of his knee hitting the carpet stretcher. When Paul went outside to take a leak, Rick fished two more pills from his pocket. He downed them with half a watery beer. He needed to stay awake just a few more hours.

THEY DECIDED THEY'D meet back up at Dad's, hopefully get paid on the Wilton job. Rick showed first, of course. Rick brought the receipts. Five pieces of crinkled paper. Dad eyed them through the bifocals. His skinny mustache rode high, like the receipts smelled bad. Rick wondered if he smelled bad. He needed to change his shirt. The pits were soaked and they felt too small. They were pinching his armpit hairs.

Dad typed on his adding machine. The machine sounded like it was chewing as it spit out the roll of figures. "No motel," he said. "Sleep in the van like a couple hippies? Van's got my name on it, you know."

"I had to drive back. Pam—" Rick stopped and thought. He thought for something Pam might've needed him to drive back for. All he could think was the timing needed adjusting on the Nova. He hadn't done it, and that wasn't enough to justify driving back.

Dad was already talking again anyway. "That accounts for all the gas. Next time that van needs service, it's on you. Company vehicle. Think I pay insurance and maintenance so you can joyride?"

Paul gave two knuckle raps and came in. The door opened with a rush of air, though it wasn't windy out, Rick didn't think.

Dad said, loud—too loud—apparently to Paul, "Tell your mother I paid the property tax. Not like she'll know what the hell that is. Not like you know what the hell that is. You two got a pretty good deal going on, you and your mother living free on my dime."

Paul let out a burst of breath. Like something was funny.

Rick let out a breath, too, meant to sound like *No kidding*, but it came out too hard and quick and loud. Everything was too loud.

"Something funny there?" Dad eyed Rick.

"No, no—just—I know it," Rick said to make his intention clear. "Kid don't know how good he's got it."

Paul pulled up a chair.

"Yeah?" Dad said. "Maybe she can move in with you, then. Save me on property taxes."

"Nah, no." Rick's voice rang in his ears.

"Didn't think so," Dad said. "You try living with that woman."

From where he sat, Paul stared at Dad with that dead-eyed look of his. It was deader than usual. He didn't blink. Rick didn't know how Paul went that long without blinking.

"No, I know it." Rick laughed a short laugh, but it didn't sound right. Two quick hehs. Heh-heh. Did he always laugh like that?

Dad's eyes rose to meet Rick's again, though his head stayed put. "Something wrong with you?"

"No?"

"Thought earlier he looked like he was coming down off something. Coming down with something, I mean," Paul said, loud and steady.

Dad stared. "Sweating bullets and look like you seen a ghost."

"No? I don't know. Just tired is all."

Dad went back to his notebook. "Any rate, she's your mother. A man don't speak of his mother that way." He scrawled and muttered, "*You know*. You *think* you know. Losing Dell Junior might've knocked the screw out of the hole, but it was pert-near stripped to begin with." He turned to a clean page. He carved the fresh sheet with his ballpoint, writing big enough Rick knew it was directions to get to a job. "All the same, she's your mother."

Paul was looking long and hard at Dad again. Rick had seen the look. Not on Paul, but it was just as familiar. It reminded Rick of something he couldn't place.

Dad's words echoed in his head. *Pert-near stripped. Losing Dell.* He stuck on that. Losing Dell. Dell Junior: pair of needle-nose pliers set someplace nobody could remember. Dell Junior: putty knife misplaced so long everybody eventually quit looking. Now Mom was the putty knife. Misplaced.

Mom. That was the look Paul was giving Dad. Their eyes were different, Paul's and Mom's. His were silver, hers were blue. But that was Mom's look coming straight from Paul's eyes.

Rick rubbed the dull tips of his fingers against his scalp, quick. Too quick. Everything was to and fro. Slow and quick. Quick and slow. He needed some sleep. What with the heat, the job, the crick in his neck—Pam and Mom—Rick needed some sleep.

"Picked up a single out by Seneca. Old ranch hand's place.

Fire job," Dad said. The guy he'd bought it from said first it was the wiring, then slipped it might've been a cigarette-in-bed deal. "Salvage it if you can. Otherwise, we'll part it out." He tore the page from the notebook, metal rings tearing through each hole like a lit string of Black Cats. He slid the paper across the table-top with a loud *shh*.

Rick pulled the page down into his lap to fold it.

Dad's eyes were on him. The whites and irises were swollen big, bug-eyed. From the bifocals. Rick could see the veins—the little red—they were capillaries, Rick thought.

"Boy, you look like shit," Dad said.

Seneca. Dad wanted them in Seneca now. Another job more than three hours out. Rick would ask if they could wait till Monday. If they could wait till Monday, he'd get a couple days home with Pam. Pam couldn't take all this out-of-town work. She needed some decent sleep, too.

"Monday might be good," he told Dad. "For this one. Monday would give Pam a break. She could use the break. From the out-of-town jobs."

Rick felt Paul looking at him now. He'd had enough of Paul's looking. Rick glared back, was about to ask him what the hell he was staring at.

But Paul wasn't looking like Paul. Or Mom. Paul wasn't an-gry or bored or dead-eyed, for once. For once he was just looking. If he hadn't been Paul, Rick would've thought the look was con-cern. Or pity. Paul stared like somebody who'd seen a deer hit and flung from the van grille, now lying on its side in the ditch, still trying to run.

"*Pam*," Dad cut in like a duck call, and Paul snapped out of it. "All I hear out of you. *Pam*. Want to do something for your wife, take good work when you can get it." Dad muttered, "Monday. Must think you're a banker."

Rick made a windy grunt. "Shit, no. Banker."

Paul said, "My guess is a banker wouldn't be living in a trailer." Paul looked like Paul again, and he was staring down Dad.

Dad didn't care for it. He stared right back. "You're sitting in a trailer, son."

"Well, now," Paul said. "This here's a double-wide. Double-wide's the mark of a whole different rank of people."

Rick didn't know what Paul was doing. Why he was trying to piss off Dad, who'd planted his bulbous eyeballs on him. The old man's snakeskin boots grazed the Berber carpet as he leaned into the table. "This double-wide's where your bread and butter come from, in case you forgot."

"Even got a spare room," Paul said. "Instead of paying taxes on that place in town, how about I get an apartment? Bring your old lady up here." He threaded his hands together behind his head. Leaned back in his chair like he was getting comfortable. "Could save you a pretty penny."

Across the table's veneer, Dad stared hard at him.

"I can head over, pick her up right now, if you want," Paul said.

Rick shot him a look.

Dad's mouth drew tight. He leaned back in his own chair. "Touché, kid."

Paul asked about pay on the Wilton job.

From the back of the notebook, Dad pulled two envelopes. One for Rick, one for Paul. He slid each across the tabletop with another pair of loud hisses. He said not to spend it all in one place. And he wasn't fronting any money to get there this time, since he didn't know what the hell he'd bought. No idea how long it would take. He was counting on Rick, he said, to call him tomorrow and let him know how it looked.

That had to mean something, Rick thought. That their old man trusted Rick's judgment. Rick appreciated that. He stood and yawned. He tried to, anyway. He needed some air. He needed a dip, too. He'd left it in the van's console.

Outside, Paul walked with him down to the van and asked to see the directions.

Rick dug the paper from his pocket and unfolded it. "Meet up here, what? Four? Four-thirty?"

Paul was reading. He said he'd drive separate again. Had some shit to take care of tonight. Might run him a little late in the morning.

It sounded like bad news. "Don't go tailing that cop again. You need to stay away from that cop."

Paul didn't look up. He was still reading, though there weren't more than four lines on the paper. Rick's sense of time must've been getting sludgy again. "Go get some sleep," Paul said, folding the paper and handing it back. "Ol' Dell Senior's right about one thing. You look like shit."

Paul patted Rick on the shoulder, once. He gripped it, then let it go. That wasn't like Paul, that pat. But it was a good sign. It was a good sign he'd calmed down. He must've figured out they couldn't let this Mom thing get to them. He must've finally figured out family needed to stick together.

16

A QUARTER TILL ELEVEN THAT NIGHT, Harley was driving around Junco in circles, trying to spot a dog at large in the four hundred block of Jefferson. Driving anywhere in Junco wasn't his favorite. The town was like a shirttail relative at a reunion, a cousin everybody avoided because he stared a little too long or had an uncontrollable habit of flicking his tongue in and out of his wet mouth. Why Junco was like that was anyone's guess. It was small, and it was poor, and it was "country," as some put it. But all those things could be said for Wanahee, not thirty miles north. Different. Junco was different.

Carol sputtered across the radio. There was a disturbance at the Avark, she said. Harley took the spur north to the highway and turned east. After he passed the trailer park and the blind intersection at County Road K, he glanced at the home place, for once his thoughts not on Paul or stolen clothes or any burn barrels.

All he'd hoped last night was that Pam being there would make a walk-through easier. He'd see what he'd see, spray paint, kicked-in plaster, and he'd keep his head because someone else was there, watching. That was what made his job a decent fit. He'd signed on for a steady paycheck, no staunch beliefs in upholding the law. The job fit because he'd had a lifetime's practice at keeping his head in the company of others. It had never felt like a weakness, since it took a fair amount of work to cultivate. Now, though, he wondered.

He also wondered what Pam was after, since Ziske was right. Harley wasn't exactly a young buck. And there'd been the wedding band she wore that first night. As likely as not, Harley was a brief distraction. He just didn't know from what. He didn't know if she was a recent divorcee on a tear or a bored young housewife. Not that he necessarily minded either way, so long as Babe Reinhardt didn't find out. Babe Reinhardt would skin him.

After he crossed the county oil, he glanced at the Knudsen place and thought he caught a dim shine through the picture window. But before he could brake, the window was dark again. Likely a reflection from the headlamps.

Harley slowed as much as he needed to whip left on Main, blowing the stop sign. Streetlamps lit the business district like a stage set ready to be rolled away. Everything past the high facades was black. Even the shadows looked flat, painted on, where mortar dipped between brick and where names and dates were chiseled into storefronts. The one before him read 18 SCHMIDT 83.

He got out and passed the blue-and-red Old Style sign, the dim gold of a perforated lampshade glowing in the Avark's window. The bar's glass-and-steel door sent a wink across the pavement, and through the entryway, raspy syllables mingled with muted music. No shouting, nothing that sounded out of the ordinary. Loren Braasch emerged, waving farewell to someone inside. Harley thought to mention the home place to him, about locking it up. Harley could mention the Jipp fire, tell him there'd been signs of a transient holing up in empty farmhouses.

"You're not the one I'm down here for, are you, Loren?"

"Depends," Loren said, smiling beneath his horn-rims and his net-backed seed cap. He held out his hand for a shake. Like a church greeting, he planted the other on Harley's arm, which gave a twitch. "Come to take me off to the poor farm?"

"Heard somebody was raising hell. Figured it fit your description."

"That's right. That's right. Live fast, die young, leave a pretty corpse's always been my motto. I'll live up to it soon as I get the pretty part down." His laugh trailed off on a high sigh. "No, you know, that youngest Reddick. Come in three sheets to the wind and rowdy, but he's pretty well subdued now. Passed out cold in a booth. Never seen anybody drop that quick without a punch." He said Frank, the Avark's owner, must've called for the infantry. "Shouldn't have no trouble with him, long as you got a wheelbarrow."

Harley asked if he had one handy. Loren wished him luck and gave Harley's arm another pat. Then he weaved toward his parked Chevy, not drunk, just favoring his bad knee.

Harley pulled a cigarette from his pocket, went for the lighter, then remembered he'd left it in the glove box. It needed fluid. He had matches. He bent one down around the edge of its book and flicked the flint. Between the strike and the shot of flame, he took a deep drag of fortification. He shook the book out and headed into the dimness. The place smelled like flat beer and stale smoke.

"Harley," Frank said in terse greeting. He pulled the dish towel from his shoulder and shooed it toward the booth farthest back.

Paul's long, dirt-colored hair spread wide across the table, but his head wasn't turned. The forehead lay level. If anybody had ever passed out that way in the history of booze, Harley hadn't seen it.

Frank skidded an ashtray across the bar and rested his forearms on the solid, round girth of his stomach. "Come in twenty minutes ago, blitzed out of his gourd, shouting nonsense."

"Catch any of it?"

"Nah, gibberish. Just hollering." With the stubs of his nails,

Frank scraped at the raised and bled-together blotch of an old USMC tattoo. "I'd have thrown him out myself, been done with it, but that one, who knows? Might come back and Molotov-cocktail the place. Figured a night in the drunk tank wouldn't be the worst thing."

"Think he was just drunk?"

"Sure as hell hope he don't go around sober talking gibberish and passing out on tables. Jackass."

"No, I mean you sure he wasn't high on something else?"

"Ah, hell if I know. All I care is you pay your rent before you pass out. Little shit didn't buy one beer."

Paul's arms sprawled like a U around his head. Harley asked for a pitcher of water. Frank filled one, slid it to him, and busied himself wiping down the bar.

Harley went to the booth, knuckle poised to nudge Paul's shoulder, which looked like it might rip the thin black T-shirt he wore. Instead he gave Paul's boot a kick with his own. Limp as a rag doll. "Reddick," he said, sharp. No response. Paul wasn't passed out, Harley was certain. But he was bent on playing this whole thing out anyway.

Harley grabbed a fistful of hair, lifted, and splashed the cold water in Paul's face to rouse him. His mouth chomped open and shut like a fish gulping at air. His lips formed a faint, shit-eating grin. He peeked through one eye like a kid cheating at hide-and-seek.

"Harley," he said in greeting. His eyes were clear and clean, without even the slightest layer of lacquer. His pupils were the same little pits, not dilated. "Been meaning to bump into you."

"Wish you'd get a new hobby."

Harley kept Paul in front of him, where he could see him. Paul slid into the cruiser's back seat with no trouble, and they drove the three blocks east to the courthouse, the tall square of brick on Third and Spruce. Harley pulled the Fury into the alley entrance. Before he got out, he finished his smoke and checked the time. He'd need it for the arrest report. The final digit of the dashboard clock, the 8 in 11:38, rolled into place with a thin electric hum and a dull click. He eyed Paul in the rearview. On the drive over, Paul had rested both arms along the back of the seat like it was his couch. Now he leaned in close to the window, fogged hot air on the glass with his breath, and drew a heart.

"Cute," Harley said. He stubbed his cigarette out. "I don't know what shit you're trying to pull. I gather you're after a night in a cell. Need an alibi or general distraction?"

"Any bail? Guess I should've checked rates in advance."

"No bail." Harley wondered where the truck was. He'd scanned Main when he first pulled in and hadn't spotted the F-250. "You can call whoever you need to in the morning, unless you're parked nearby."

Paul didn't offer up the Ford's whereabouts. Harley walked him through the back door of the courthouse and down the steps to the basement. The holding cell was old and small. The brick room of the former sheriff's office was mostly claimed by the assessor's secretary for storage. Piles of brown cardboard boxes with scrawled-on dates and codes lined the walls and made the already small space smaller.

Harley saw to it Paul was bedded down in the narrow cell. He looked too at ease there, took too quickly to the shelf bed's tick mattress.

Harley gripped the cell door. It was old-fashioned, with thick steel bands riveted in a weave. The open squares between the strips were small. The place was claustrophobic as it was, so he left the cell open. That way Paul was in plain sight of the desk.

"Say, long as I got you here," Paul called.

"Just full of cute." Harley pulled an arrest report from the dusty paper tray on the desk and tried to remember the date. Too many shifts in a row was wearing on him.

"Didn't get much chance to catch up the other night, back at your home place."

Harley breathed deep to conjure some patience. If Paul could be counted on for one thing, it was that he'd talk, albeit cryptically. With any luck, maybe he'd drop a hint or two about why somebody would steal a dead man's clothes and set fire to them in an abandoned house. Not that Harley wanted to sift through the chatter to get there.

"Any big cases you're working on? Tracking down any hot leads?"

Harley filled out his personnel number. "Why? Anything you want to confess to? Long as you got me here?"

"Nope. You?"

"Those quaaludes were your mother's." Paul mentioned them a few months back, during one of the routine searches of the Ford's glove box. He'd insinuated Harley must've enjoyed them, given no charges came of it. "That why you were at my folks' place? Thought if I messed with yours, you'd mess with mine?"

"What? Eight ludes? Nah, I let that one go."

"Thanks."

"Besides, if I wanted to mess with yours, why pick that place? You wouldn't care if somebody leveled it, I bet. Hell. After that search for Dell Junior, I bet you steer clear of all them houses right around the old Lucas place."

Harley replayed last night's sounds, the brushing grass and the distant engine. The roof sealant in the burn barrel. Trailers had flat roofs. Paul worked for his dad, repairing trailers. Harley pictured Paul peering from a window of the house again. Maybe the vision wasn't all that paranoid.

"I heard about the Jipp place, up by the cemetery," Paul said.

"Yeah, don't suppose you know anything firsthand."

"I know it's too bad somebody didn't torch the old home place instead. Maybe then you could shake it."

"Shake what?" Harley said, not so much asking as daring Paul to say what he had in mind.

"Same old deal." The shelf creaked beneath his weight. "Same old deal you took so personal out at the water tower."

The goddamn water tower.

About the time Paul should've graduated high school but didn't, he climbed up the tower and teetered around drunk and buck-naked. In itself, there was nothing notable about that. Kids scaled and spray-painted it seasonally. Usually they'd mark it with their initials, proclaim some undying love, though in Junco some numb nuts once painted a swastika. They did it backward, of course, like everything else in Junco.

Harley had been driving past and saw Paul's truck, saw somebody naked on the catwalk, and radioed Wilton for an ambulance. The Ferguson girl had been dead two months. Calling an ambulance wasn't an overabundance of caution. It was a matter of precedent.

The cruiser crept up the long service road to the base of the tower till Harley made sense of what he was seeing. Paul was alone and apparently had nothing to proclaim with a can of spray paint. He'd disrobed, climbed up, and then hung upside down, knees hooked over the catwalk rail. Not swinging, not seemingly having a good time, just dangling, his twig and berries aimed toward the dirt. The only thing not aimed toward the dirt was his twelve-gauge Winchester.

Harley had gripped the handset where it clipped to the radio again, but he didn't slide it from the cradle. He didn't call for backup. That was protocol—an armed suspect in a standoff, you called for backup. But Harley didn't.

The twelve-gauge was the same one Paul still kept in the rack, a Model 24, double-barrel side-by-side. Not exactly a sniper rifle. The thing was for potshots. It could do some damage, but Paul had it propped one-armed in the crook of his elbow, butt against his ribs. He was also upside down and drunk. Harley was less worried about where the shot landed than where Paul would. The kick alone might've dropped him headfirst. And if he kept hanging upside down, he was surely going that way anyway.

Harley parked at the base of the tower, sidearm out and aimed for precaution. He yelled from behind the cruiser door. He told Paul to slide the gun onto the catwalk. "Come on down, kid," Harley told him. "Feet first."

Paul said no thanks. "How good a shot are you?"

"Fair to middling."

Paul drifted the barrels closer, in the direction of Harley's voice.

Harley realized then, by the drift of the barrels, Paul couldn't make him out. Not past the flood lamps.

Paul closed his eyes. He smiled out at the night air. His naked chest expanded with a deep breath. Harley yelled again for him to slide the gun onto the catwalk.

"I'm not dropping it, Harley. But you go ahead and ask one more time. I believe that's protocol, right? Three?"

It came clear then, what Paul was after. The implication felt like a hardened seed or kernel lodged at the base of Harley's sternum. It swelled like heat behind his ribs till it broke open. It flooded through bone and muscle and skin.

"You want to die, Paul? Let go."

Paul opened his eyes to the night and blinding flood lamps. The smile stayed. It broadened like he was glad Harley understood. "I thought it'd be poetic. Bad taste?"

The distant whine of the ambulance siren floated from the highway.

Paul heaved a loud, irritated stage breath. He slid the shotgun onto the catwalk. Then he swung himself upright like he'd been hanging from a set of playground monkey bars. When he climbed down, it was easy and nonchalant, and when his feet were planted on the dirt, he didn't resist. Harley didn't even bother to cuff him.

After the ambulance loaded up Paul and his clothes and left, Harley climbed the tower for the gun. The safety was on. He slid the lever and broke open the breech. The barrels were empty. He'd pulled Paul over dozens of times. He'd opened the breech nearly as many. There was nothing illegal about a loaded gun in the rack, and Paul was always one to exercise his liberties.

Harley climbed down, Winchester in his grip. Then he walked to the Ford and slid the shotgun back in the rack.

The shelf in the cell creaked again, and Harley glanced up. Paul was situating, adjusting the wool blanket. "'Feet first,' you said. 'Come down feet first.' I'd say that indicates a fixation."

"'Fixation.' Overnight in a psych ward teach you that?"

"Beg your pardon—it was two nights."

Two nights. Then they transferred him to North-Central Juvenile Services till his court date. Harley testified that the nakedness and Paul's dangling from the catwalk qualified as erratic suicidal behavior. The judge was unconvinced. He issued a ticket for trespassing, deemed no further evaluations necessary, and released Paul into parental custody.

"Middle initial," Harley said. He needed it for the report.

"Come on, Harley. You know by now. *D.* For Dell. My brother's middle name, too. The live one, of course. Not the one you Keystone Kops never found. You know my brother?"

Harley didn't. Harley didn't even know the other brother's name.

"He's got a kid, pretty young wife—" Paul stopped, like he was waiting for Harley to cut him off.

Paul was no doubt trying to fill the air, eat away time, which likely meant Harley needed to be someplace else, preventing something Paul didn't want prevented.

"He's why I ran into you tonight," Paul said. "My brother likes to see the good in people, bless his heart, and he thinks maybe you've been looking out for me. Looking out for my best interests. Is that it, Harley? Is that why you flushed those ludes?" He gave a dramatic pause. He had a flair. Then, as if it'd just struck him, though it surely hadn't, he said, "Is that why you put the shotgun back? Never told another soul about it? Half-assed the report and testimony that could've put me in prison? Am I just the son you never had?"

"Nope." Harley slapped the clipboard against the desk and walked to the open cell. He pulled the door shut.

It wasn't generosity that kept him from calling for backup that night. It was because Harley knew what prison did to somebody like Paul. If he was dangerous going in, rest assured he'd be worse coming out.

Harley didn't report the standoff because the whole world's best-case scenario for Paul, Paul included, was a psych ward. Or at least juvie. Once you called an ambulance for something like that, juvenile court got involved. In juvie, there was at least half a chance somebody'd realize Paul could benefit from a goddamn psych ward. Harley had suspected as much before the standoff. After, he knew it.

"Something I said?" Paul called through the door's metal strips.

Harley left for patrol.

JUST SHY OF two in the morning, after tracing a fair portion of the county road grid, one-mile-by-one-mile squares, Harley was back at Highway 28. He parked in the Lucas drive and dialed through AM hiss for a station that'd already signed on or never signed off. He found one out of Vermillion. He kept it low enough he could hear Carol over the radio if he needed to. He sat there through Hank Snow and Connie Smith and an old Ray Price song, through a station ID and a weather report and the droning of grain futures. One truck passed in that time, slowing to the speed limit when the driver must've seen the cruiser parked on the hilltop.

She never showed. Which was just as well. He was no doubt a fool for waiting.

WHEN HE CAME back to the courthouse, Harley opened the cell door to silence. The wool blanket was wadded up between the wall and Paul, who slept on his back. His rib cage barely rose and fell beneath his thin T-shirt. Harley now saw it bore the white outline of a naked, sexless angel, either soaring upward or plummeting, wings outstretched. He made out the words above and below it, LED-ZEPPELIN and UNITED STATES OF AMERICA 1977.

Eyes closed and expression washed from his face, he looked younger. His mouth had fallen open in an O that resembled a figurine Harley's aunt Mae had. A Hummel, he thought. Her boy had sent it home from Germany.

Shortly after dawn, Harley heard a stretching grunt from inside the cell. He told Paul to come out when he needed to make his call.

Harley paged through a copy of the supplement he'd found upstairs by the DMV window. He avoided the second-to-last page but could still picture Doris Luschen's smiling teeth there.

A pair of boots brushed the concrete floor of the cell, and Paul emerged, rubbing the sleep from his eyes. Harley pushed the rotary phone toward the desk's edge. The movement clanged the ringer.

He listened as Paul made his call. "Rick take off already?" A voice murmured in response, a woman's voice. "Nah, down in

Madson." She said something. "Jail," he said. "Listen, I know you got your hands full with Anna, but my pickup's in Wilton." He looked to Harley and winked for seemingly no good reason. There was silence, then a mumble on the other end. "No, no bail. Need a ride is all." Another pause, then something curt, inaudible. Paul hung up.

"Figure something out?"

"Yeah, my sister-in-law." Paul yawned, grasping toward the ceiling like the angel on his chest. "She'll be down in a bit," he said cheerfully. Then he walked back to his cell and lay down on the shelf to wait.

17

OUTSIDE THE REAR ENTRANCE of the courthouse, a tear of sweat tickled the back of Pam's neck. She gouged at it with her chewed-down nails.

Paul said there wasn't any bail. If there wasn't any bail, she didn't see why she needed to go in. Maybe he'd hear if she honked. She honked.

She'd spent last night trapped in the trailer with Rick, who'd lost his best quality, his ability to sleep. He'd pinned her in place again, though he hadn't needed to. She'd felt too weighted down to move since Babe's phone call. The prospect of Helen Nelson running her mouth about that day at Gordon's was nothing. What people thought of Pam, what people thought of her as a mother or a wife, might've mattered to Babe, but Pam didn't give two shits about that. What sank her was the rest of it.

Babe was right. Anna didn't ask to be, just like Pam didn't, just like Babe didn't, just like nobody in the history of the world ever had. Which was really something. Because people kept doing it, didn't they? Making more people who didn't ask to be and who, often as not, didn't want to be. And Babe was right that Pam didn't deserve better. After doing a thing like that, Pam deserved a hell of a lot worse than she'd ever get, given in the end everybody got the same goddamn thing.

In the passenger seat, Anna knocked the soles of her sandals together with a dull thud, over and over and over.

Harley probably wasn't even here. On TV, jails always had bailiffs. Fat men dressed in khaki who guarded cells and didn't get any lines except when they yelled at prisoners making a ruckus. Sometimes you never even saw their faces. Sometimes all you saw was their fat backs as they opened and closed the cells or ran their batons across the bars.

She honked again.

He could've been off work by now. It was daylight, and she couldn't imagine him in daylight. She couldn't imagine him any other way than how she'd seen him, black-and-white in the trophy case photo or tinted gray by night or lit up red by the Zippo flame.

Leave it to that fuckup Paul. Leave it to another Reddick. They were all hell-bent on ruining her life. Though she supposed she'd done a decent job herself.

"Wait here," she told Anna.

No, Anna said, it was too hot. She was right. It was too hot. She grunted and pulled at the chrome door handle. When it wouldn't pop open, she leaned back to mess with the lock plunger, which was already up.

Pam walked around to Anna's side and lifted her out. "I'll carry you." If Pam had to go in there, she'd at least make it quick.

No, Anna said, she wanted to walk.

Pam set her down, took Anna's balled fist, and crossed the gravel lot to the back door. It was marked by a plain, painted sign on a stake: JAIL ENTRANCE. No need to dress it up, Pam guessed.

They took the stairs to the basement one at a time, the most Anna's legs could manage. When they reached the bottom third of the staircase, in the space beneath the sloping overhead wall, Pam saw. Beneath the glow of the fluorescents, his black boot was planted on the concrete floor. It was the boot that ground out the burning cigarettes the other night. Another pair of steps, and she saw the other boot propped on his knee. She scooped up Anna.

No, Anna said.

Pam looked at her. At the way her thin brows drew together in little puckers above the bridge of her nose, not like a child anymore but like a tiny old woman. For an instant, Pam missed that wide-eyed look of alarm. Now it was almost as if Anna knew everything that had gone on and was bent on punishing Pam for it. Making her go through this whole thing in slow motion.

Anna arched and pushed away, but Pam clasped the squirming body to her side. She took a breath that tingled in her hands. The air was cold and damp and she wished she was back outside where the heat already hung thick in the air. She took the last step.

At first he didn't seem to recognize her. Like being someplace other than out in the country, out in the dark, made her somebody else. Maybe one of her sisters. Another one of Red's girls. But then she saw it. His lids dropped a bit. The thin lines of his forehead flattened. His eyes sharpened to a warmer brown. They were brown, she now saw, and she realized she couldn't have known before. He looked at the girl propped heavy and squirming on her hip. The corner of his mouth rose in something like amusement. He shook his head. He looked away.

"Reddick," he said.

She opened her mouth, then closed it. He meant Paul.

Who of course took his sweet-ass time. Even in the cold air, beads of sweat formed at the backs of her knees. Somewhere beyond the open cell door, he scuffled. She reached toward Harley's shirtsleeve, felt Anna watching, and pulled back. He didn't look at her. His pen tip sat motionless in a crossword puzzle square.

Paul emerged and sauntered out, smiling big and broad. He reached for Anna. Pam struggled against the pull of Anna's weight before giving in. "Take her," Pam said, handing her off, then wishing she hadn't. She wished she had something to do with her empty arms. "Need me to sign anything, sir?" He could've at least looked at her.

"Nope. We're good." He scribbled some note in the margin of the newspaper. She eyed the thin loops of his writing, wondering what it said.

"There's no bail?" In the periphery, Paul bounced Anna on his hip. He wrapped Anna's small fingers around one of his own.

"Nope," Harley said.

"So? Is that just it, then?" The strain in her voice was like a thin, tense thread yanked out of her.

Harley finally looked, one brow cocked to say she was a twit for asking. She felt like one of those dead butterflies on a board, pinned by the blacks of his eyes. She bit the insides of her cheeks.

"Yeah. That'll be it, then." He went back to his crossword.

"I guess we're through here," Paul said. Too chipper. He bounced Anna on his hip. "Ain't we," he said. "Ain't we done here, Anna."

PAUL SAT WITH Anna in his lap while Pam drove. She held the wheel and kept her face blank as they passed the Jensen house and the blind intersection. She needed to keep Paul where she could see him. Till she knew if he suspected anything. Till she knew what came next if he did.

"How'd you get arrested?" she asked him.

"Easier than you think when a cop's got it out for you," he said. "Just a few well-plotted antics."

Her eyes darted at him, then back at the road. "You did it on purpose?"

"Enough about me," he said. "How long you two known each other?"

"What?"

"Chemistry's thick. Palpable."

Pam pulled a strand of whipping hair from her eye and tossed it back where the rest flew through the open window. "You're messed up," she said. She wouldn't acknowledge it. Any of it. "Probably eating pills again like candy."

Anna asked about candy.

"No. No candy," Pam said. The wind, the tires' roll on the pavement filled her head so she couldn't think. She'd change the subject. "Don't suppose you found your mother yet. Rick says you're really giving it your all. Says you'd just as soon let her wander around drunk, batshit crazy and yammering."

"She's got a right," he said matter-of-factly. "And she ain't crazy." He pursed his lips and squinted like he was pondering. "Unless real, real, justifiably pissed is crazy." He seemed to mull it over. "I guess a certain degree of justifiably pissed could be crazy. But so could a certain degree of happy or stupid, then. You go parsing that sort of thing, meaning just falls apart, don't it?"

While Pam had wondered, too, recently, if Virginia was the sanest of them all for bolting, she tried to keep Paul on goddamn track. "You know, Rick's scared she'll die out there, drunk in the heat."

"She'll die somewhere at some point. Not sure it matters if she's indoors."

It seemed like a fair point.

"And for the record, I've been looking. Maybe not searching, per se. More like watching." His focus was out the window, on the passing pasture grass. "I was watching out at the Jensen place, for example. Night before last."

Pam's breath went shallow, like the open window sucked the air from her chest.

"Pam, I'm no paragon of morality." Paul cupped his hands around Anna's ears. She tried to pull them away, but he held them there and lowered his voice. "People fuck up. All I'm saying is don't fuck up with Harley. Specifically. Not now that he's connecting dots. Whatever you feel about my brother, he does his best." He let his hands drop from Anna's head. "He does his own idiot best better than anybody I know. And if anybody can stumble good-intentioned into cross fire, it's that jackass."

Her head buzzed as she tried to connect her own dots. She couldn't. Not right this second.

"Meantime, stay away from empty houses," he said.

She asked why his truck was in Wilton. It was all she could think to say. She asked if he'd been looking for his mom there.

"No," he said, drawing out the word so it ended higher than it started, like the answer was obvious. Like Pam was slow. "That was so I'd need a ride this morning."

Anna was pinching a toe. She asked Paul which one it was. The one that ate roast beef, he told her.

Pam needed to stall. She needed to figure out what it all meant. What the cross fire was and what came next. She said she couldn't take him to Wilton right now. She'd left a load of towels in the dryer and the timer didn't work. If she didn't get back, it'd burn the place to the ground. And she needed to feed Anna and put her down for a nap. She'd take him to Wilton after.

At the trailer, Pam warmed leftover tuna casserole in the oven, which left the place so sweltering she might as well have turned the oven on and left the Correlle dish on the counter. It would've heated as quick.

Then she put them both down for a nap. Pam wanted Paul out of her sight. She couldn't take the sound of his voice anymore. She put Anna in the crib she was too big for, and she sent Paul to her and Rick's room. Alone, she tried to get the dark tacks of Harley's eyes out of her.

Instead of dragging out the sewing machine, she patched Rick's jeans by hand. While she sewed, the tumble of towels in the bathroom vibrated every layer of plywood and sheet metal and linoleum and the tips of the orange shag in the living room until she was numb with it.

When she did feel something, it was panic. The dryer. She'd forgotten the reason she'd needed to get back to the trailer in the first place. She'd left the dryer going since early morning. She sprinted to turn it off. When she did, her first thought was she was lucky the element hadn't gone out. Her second thought was how much the electric bill would be. Her third thought was if she'd just left the thing going, left the towels tumbling, maybe they would've caught fire, which would have taken care of the whole goddamn everything. If it hadn't burned the trailer to the ground, at least it would've burned up the goddamn towels, which had woven together at the frayed edges.

She pulled half the load to the top of the dryer, each terry-cloth rag knotted to the next. The other half spilled up from the open door like a magician's trick handkerchief pulled from a gaping mouth—like the thin, tense thread of her voice yanked from her at the station. She felt the black pins of his pupils again. But instead of feeling like a dead bug, she remembered the pins of his five o'clock shadow and the thumb she'd wished to the divot of her hip bone. And tracing it all back there, she felt a heat that had nothing to do with ovens or dryers left on too long or a trailer baking under a late July sun every day so the heat never left it, no matter how many box fans you propped in the windows.

She went to the kitchen for scissors to cut apart the towels. She pulled open the junk drawer. The bottom corner of the phone book peeked from beneath a layer of spare fuses and random screws that'd lost their holes and whose displacement was probably why every single thing in her life didn't work. There sat the screws and bolts to every single thing in this trailer that stayed broken while Rick ran off to Arnold or Bayard or Burwell to fix the same things all day for people he didn't know. She pulled the thin book from the drawer and set it on the counter. She flipped to J.

There were Jensens in Wilton, in Wanahee, and there, in Madson. *Jensen, Harley: 513 N Linden, MADS 68596. . . . . . 6462.* He was right there. She left the book flipped open. She slipped it back in the drawer, covering the screws and nuts and bolts.

18

RICK HAD STILL NOT SLEPT.

He hadn't slept the night before last because he couldn't. He'd needed to get back out to the trailer in Arnold. But last night, when he could've slept, he'd decided he wouldn't. Not with the smell of Pam's hair like warm soap and the sound of Anna's purr of a snore from the next room. It was so loud she could've been right there nestled in his ear. Rick's skin had prickled up all night like a plucked bird's, but it was nice. Warm. They were all right there. The three of them. He may not have known where Mom was, he might never know where Dell Junior ended up, but he knew where he and Pam and Anna were. All he wanted was to stay like that. That was the way things were supposed to be.

Now, though, he did wish he had slept. The sun was too bright. It was drying out his eyeballs. And he swore the highway wasn't up to code. It was too thin. Almost too thin for the van to fit.

Then again, it could've been the road wasn't too thin but the hills were too thick. Big, rolling, then lopsided, jagged shapes. They hid the highway from anybody not on it. They hid all sorts of things, those hills. They hid rivers that looped and twisted so much they looked fake. Scooped trenches made fancy on purpose. The hills hid ranches. Lakes. Whole towns. In grade school, he'd heard a story about two sisters lost in the hills. They'd been chasing wildflowers. One wandered off for help and wound up baked like a pot roast.

In fourth grade he heard that story. He sat up front, and the teacher got nervous halfway through and hurried the end. She hadn't looked at him. Rick felt bad for her. He wanted to tell her it was okay. Dell Junior didn't get baked like a pot roast in the sandhills. Or if he did, it wasn't till after he got killed with a shovel.

At the trailer Dad bought, the fire was not from wiring. Sure as shit, it'd been a cigarette in the back bedroom. Insulation hung down like dirty pelts, like in some old western he'd seen. Some mountain man outfitter's store in an old western. The cowboy must've drank till he forgot the cigarette. Till his hand went limp to the mattress. Somebody must've caught the fire quick, but not quick enough for the cowboy. Everything in the other rooms looked normal, just smoke-stained. Couch, table and chairs, books, some eight-tracks. Everything looked right in every room except this one, where there was no bed frame or box spring or even the coils of a mattress. The only thing in this bedroom was a bubbled black and cracking nightstand. That must've been why the owner lied the first time. Thought Dad wouldn't buy the place if he knew somebody'd been cremated here.

Dad would just be glad wiring wasn't the problem. The place needed gutting, but Rick could salvage it. He drove into town and used the pay phone outside the post office. He called and told Dad what he thought. Four days. Rick didn't know where he came up with it, four days. He didn't know if that was right or not. Dad said do it in three, then. After they hung up, Rick called Pam. She said she was in the middle of sewing his jeans and doing laundry. She was pissy or distracted. Whatever she was left him with a feeling like beetles in his stomach, all scattering around. When the operator clicked in and told him to deposit more change, he said he'd call back later.

That afternoon, he was pulling out the bathroom paneling.

His leather-cased transistor radio kept him company. It blared an AM station out of Valentine.

The sink was fine. The paneling wasn't bad, either, but it had to go. It was stained with smoke and had a reek no amount of bleach could ever get out.

The screen door slammed. It sent a vibration through the place. Footsteps pounded. He gripped the crowbar as they neared, shaking the floor.

"Rick."

Rick took a long breath. It was Paul. That settled the swarms in his stomach.

"Nice place." Paul dropped a twelve-pack of High Life on the bathroom vanity.

"I know it." Rick pushed the sharp wedge of the bar between the panel and stud. "Went into town, called Dad. Says get it done in three days."

Paul looked around. "You know, trailers are temporary by nature. Think it's safe to let this one go. Think it's safe to part this one out."

"Nah, we can salvage it. But three days. Seems tight." The paneling pulled back with a shriek that made Rick's eyes pulse. Paul's aftershave didn't help.

"I see you slept." Paul was staring at Rick in the smoky mirror. Rick caught a glance of himself but didn't look too hard. He was pasty. Bug-eyed. He looked like shit.

"Can't leave Pam three days," Rick thought out loud. "Shouldn't have left her this morning. She sounds riled already this morning."

"You talked to her?" Paul said.

"Yeah?"

Why was he asking that? Of course Rick talked to Pam. Rick always talked to Pam after he got to out-of-town jobs. Why wouldn't he have talked to Pam?

Paul tore open the thin cardboard of the twelve-pack and grabbed a bottle. He asked if there was another pry bar. Where it was.

"Why'd you ask me that?" Rick said.

"What?"

"If I talked to Pam."

Rick watched him in the mirror. He looked blank. Paul never looked blank, but now he did. He stared down the hole in the sink. "Saw her this morning is all. She came and got me from the drunk tank. Thought she probably mentioned it. Pickup was in Wilton, she gave me a ride." Paul shrugged. "Nothing." There was something he wasn't saying.

Nothing. The beetles in Rick's stomach scattered and swarmed. Nothing was something. Rick didn't know what nothing was, but he knew it was something.

"She probably thought it'd piss you off. The drunk tank thing." He asked about the crowbar again.

"You eat yet?" Rick asked.

"What?" Paul said it like Rick wasn't making sense.

"I need a break. I need some food." He knew he must've needed some food, though he didn't feel hungry. When did he eat? Last night. He'd picked at the tuna casserole Pam had made.

"You need some fucking sleep is what you need."

They took the van to a highway diner in Thedford. There was a pay phone in the lot. Rick told Paul to go on in. Rick said he'd call Dad about the trailer. See if he wanted them to strip it instead.

Rick shut the accordion door of the booth. The sun glared

through the glass so he felt like an ant under a magnifying glass, like the hairs on his arms might catch fire. He slid the door open. The ring signal purred through the earholes. Six rings. Six rings before Pam picked up and said hello. Like she was curious. Like she wasn't sure who it would be.

Who else would it be?

She asked where he was.

He'd told her this morning where he was. "Thedford," he said. "Getting a bite to eat."

She sighed hard. A pissed-off sigh. "If you'd reminded me, I would've packed sandwiches."

"No—I know. I picked up some bread and bologna." He hadn't. "Paul needed something to eat. Paul showed up." He waited.

"Yeah?"

Why'd she take so long to say it? Was her voice higher than usual? Anna babbled something in the background. He was glad to hear her but wanted to hear Pam. He thought he heard somebody else. A voice in a tunnel. "You got the TV going?"

She said she did.

"Yeah, Paul showed up finally," he said again.

"That's good," she said. "Should help you get done sooner, won't it?"

Nothing. Nothing about picking Paul up from jail.

"Coming back tonight?" she asked him.

"He said you picked him up from jail this morning." He tried to force a little laugh behind it, like it was funny somehow. It should've been, probably. The sun glared through the glass. The glass blocked the air. He stepped partway out of the booth to feel the air move. To catch a breath.

Please insert twenty-five cents, the operator said, clicking in and out on the line. He dug in his pocket for change. He cradled the phone between his ear and shoulder and sifted through nickels. Something in the background squealed. The TV again.

"You there?" He fed the slot five nickels and a dime and hoped Pam couldn't hear them. He also hoped it counted the dime. It didn't sound like it counted the dime.

"I'm here."

"You sound winded."

"I'm trying to—" she spat out and stopped. She went on, "I'm rolling dough."

"All right."

"For noodles."

"Okay."

"For tuna casserole."

"Okay, I said." Wait. She made tuna casserole last night. "Didn't you make tuna casserole last night?"

"Yeah, and then your brother ate it, and it's all I got to make." Her voice was getting tight. Wound up.

Paul ate the leftovers. Did Paul spend all morning there? She picked him up from jail, and he ate there. Was he there already when Rick called earlier? Why wasn't picking up Paul from jail and him spending all morning there worth mentioning when Rick talked to her earlier?

She was on a rant now, and he could picture her like she was right in front of him. That tendon in her neck stuck out, right above the knob of her collarbone. He knew that tendon, and in a way, knowing it comforted him. But there was something else there, too. Something he didn't know. Something he couldn't picture. He could only sense it. She was still ranting. She was listing every ingredient she had in the house. "Oh. And a stick of fucking butter," she said. "I guess me and Anna could share a stick of fu—"

A click. *Please insert twenty-five cents.* No way they counted that dime. The operator sounded so close. Like she was right there in the glass box. While Pam and the trailer and Anna sounded so far away. Another click. Something hissed from the TV. Applause. He dug in his other pocket. A quarter.

"You there?" He shouldn't have asked. He knew she was. He could hear the TV. "What's Anna doing?"

"She's fine," she said, though it wasn't what he'd asked. "She's right here." That wasn't what he'd asked, either.

There was a space of quiet. The distant hiss of TV applause again.

"You staying out there, then? Tonight?" she asked him.

He looked to the windows of the restaurant. He tried to see where his brother sat inside, but the glass was set too high in the brick. All he saw was a reflection of the gutter on a house behind him. It was the old U-shaped kind, the gutter.

Something was wrong. Something right there in front of him. Something that was too big or too near to see. As if he were standing midway up a sand hill and couldn't see the dune, just the dirt and grass and flowers that grew up in spikes. He looked to the diner windows again. He couldn't see himself in the reflection. He couldn't see even the top of the phone booth.

"Yeah," he said. The lie came out spent and thick. "Yeah, gonna stay the night in Thedford."

19 LATE MORNING, the middle of Harley's night, he stretched on the couch, head resting on the crook of his elbow. The TV screen flipped but all he saw was Pam with the girl on her hip. It took an extra two fingers of bourbon to put the warm buzz between his ears, another for him to stop piecing everything together.

First he thought she'd been covering for Paul. She'd been messing with Harley to keep him off Paul's trail, for whatever purpose. But the Avark bit and Paul's jail cell ramblings about his brother's wife cleared things up. If they hadn't, the look on his face would've. Paul was tickled as could be, getting Harley and Pam in the same room. Paul had been the reel-to-reel that played in Harley's head on endless loop the night before last: the cracking twigs and rustling grass, the distant engines. Paul was Ecklund's possum, and Paul set fire to the roof sealant. Which meant the vision of Paul getting his jollies watching Harley come and go from the home place wasn't paranoid. Paul had seen his sister-in-law and Harley get acquainted. Which also meant Harley might now have two Reddick boys to contend with.

The rest of it, the theft, the fire, the why of it all, Harley had no idea.

The TV picture rose, lowered, and flipped. In between, two Phyllis Dillers filled the screen. At the bottom was her head, at the top her shoulders and chest. He set his glass on the end table, made his eyes shut.

The ring of the phone jerked him from sleep. An anchorman

on TV wore a thick necktie and thicker hair. Harley's heart raced. He thought he'd slept to the ten o'clock news. Then he checked the window. Sun glared around the drape like a solar eclipse. He made his way to the phone.

"It's me," she said.

"Jesus Christ."

"Meet me where we were the other night?"

The burst of a laugh came before he could stop it. "Hell, no."

She said nothing for a bit. Then, "I'll be there anyway. If you want to know, that's where I'll be." She hung up.

AS SOON AS he walked in the portable, Harley saw Glenn's mouth ringed in a thin, perfectly round white line. The bottle of antacid sat on the desk like a mug of coffee might have, within reach of his thick, short fingers.

Glenn's job had been killing him since he was a deputy. He wasn't suited for it. Never was. He'd never wanted it and never asked for it. He'd inherited it. Half the people saw the last name and thought they were voting his dad in again. The rest checked him on the ballot because he'd been put up unopposed.

Harley made his way to the coffee maker. "You need to goddamn retire, Glenn."

"Doris Luschen's place got hit."

Harley stopped, mid-pour, and kept his back turned. "When?"

"Services were ten-thirty, went till, I don't know. Noon? The daughter-in-law called. Same one that called in the welfare check. Doris probably died to get away from her. Said it happened during the funeral or church reception or—I don't know what. Harley, that woman knew every bobby pin in the bathroom drawer. Every chicken leg in the icebox. Probably had those little colored-dot price tags stuck on every one of the old lady's things before she so much as sneezed."

Harley went to his desk with a cup of coffee not brewed black enough. He needed something stronger to help him to get his bearings.

"Came in and stole some preserves, a loaf from the bread box, gas can from the garage, and then, what do you know, all of Doris's damn clothes. Her goddamn clothes."

Harley pictured Doris leaned back against the Mercury, evaporating. The sight of her foot at the bottom of the stairs. There was a lot to tell Glenn, but right now he needed defusing. "Hell, Glenn. I don't know."

Glenn gave a muted, airy burp, and the words that followed were windy. "We get another fire call, find another empty farmhouse burnt, this time Doris Luschen's clothes—weirder it is, worse it winds up. I don't need to tell you. Look at that thing down in Junco."

"You got some stuff—" Harley gestured with a finger, let Glenn know about the Mylanta.

Glenn's eyes roved the office like some corner might hold a pile of Doris Luschen's underwear. He opened the pen drawer of his desk, pulled out a napkin, and dabbed it with his tongue. He worked it around his mouth. The paper blew up in little gusts like a bird's broken wing. "This is the kind of thing escalates. Like that thing down in Junco. Starts out somebody breaks in places, paints public stalls with his stool, ends with somebody drowned in manure." He looked like he was on the verge of a cardiac arrest.

"Before you get any more worked up, remember that's Junco. This is Madson."

Glenn took a pause for breath and considered it. "I guess," he admitted. "Guess a few more branches on the family tree down there would help."

"We'll figure it out." Harley took a sip of weak coffee, contemplating what was next. "You already been down there? Doris's place?"

"Couldn't have dusted for prints, for all the good it'd do. Would've been all smudged up by that damned daughter-in-law. Just into everything." He made the low, airy burp again, put his stubby fingers to his sternum, and rubbed. "You've got to feel for Doris's boy. Married to a woman like that."

THAT NIGHT, HARLEY'S attention never strayed far from the rearview as he drove through town. He patrolled north to south, then east to west. As it happened, that left Virginia Reddick's place for last. No sign of her son's truck.

Outside Madson, he made the rounds of the empty homesteads. The Schneider place was quiet. The Rasmussen house, quiet. The old Carberry farmstead, quiet.

Harley walked around the Knudsen place again. The front door was still locked, same with the brooder house. The horse barn held only the moldy bales and generator. The hay barn with the old Plymouth and discarded window screens looked no different than before.

All that left was the home place, which was the last place he needed to be. He'd try to get in and get out before she showed.

But when he turned down the drive, it was already too late. He saw the shine off the back bumper and the angle of her legs, not hidden deep enough in the grass.

20

PAM PERCHED ON THE TRUNK OF THE CAR, her once-cold beer now only cool. The can sweated where her thighs pursed to hold it. As she'd sat here, hovered above the brush, time stopped, then slowly ticked on again.

At first, each creak of a tree limb, each flutter of a leaf, seized her muscles and made her nearly dart across the highway. But she'd forced herself to stay put, like stoners in high school trying to outdo each other, seeing how long they could hold a palm to a lighter flame. Then, at some point, she sank in. She sat and listened to the crickets, the soughing of grass and leaves whenever the air moved, the occasional moan of the house's boards bending against each other.

The air was warm but not hot, and a brief, wet breeze lifted off the nearby corn and grass. Above, the sky was so clear and the stars so many they looked like lit-up gauze, the Milky Way a fold where the tossed-down fabric doubled over on itself. If life were only this, Pam thought, it could've been halfway livable.

Maybe fifteen more years could be like that. A matter of sinking in. Maybe she'd sink in and naturally stop trying to dart off. All she had to do was hold her palm to a flame for fifteen years.

A car slowed on the highway and blood thrummed in her ears. Stars sparked off the unlit cherries on the cruiser's roof. Her chest ached. She didn't know if it was fear or dread or what. Just a burning kind of ache.

He turned in the drive and stopped, headlights blinding. When he rolled past, he swung into the space closer to the house. The gear shifted into park and the engine cut to silence.

"You're not why I'm here," he called from his window.

She could feel the beer. She wasn't drunk, just a little bold. "Thought you'd have a thing or three to say to me."

He was quiet, like he had to think about it. "Cute kid. Where's your brother-in-law?"

"They're out in Thedford. Should be a few days." She'd heard Paul in the background earlier telling Rick to get some fucking sleep. Rick called from the motel. She didn't bother saying motel phones cost as much as the rooms. She was still too relieved he was there and she was here.

Harley's door opened with its loud pop. His footsteps raked the grass as they passed toward the house.

He asked how long she'd been here. About two beers, she said. And she hadn't seen anybody? Heard anything unusual?

"Wouldn't still be here if I had."

"Well, you got that much sense."

He checked the barn, then ran his lamp across the windows of the house. He disappeared around the side. When he'd made a full circle, he walked to the porch. He hesitated, then went up the steps, skipping the third. He opened the door, and his flashlight wavered through the room they'd been in the other night.

When he came down the steps again, he stood with his back to her, facing the house. "Not sure what you think can happen here."

"I didn't mean for you to find out like that." God. It sounded like a line straight out of *As the World Turns*.

"You meant for me to find out?" The Zippo lid clanked and the barrel rasped.

"I hadn't thought that far ahead." She wished he'd turn around and offer her a cigarette. "I was young," she said. "When I got married."

"Was, huh?"

He was calling her dumb and naïve. But he also had a point. She was only twenty-four. For a second, she pictured what she'd do if she could tweeze herself out of the life she'd slivered herself into. She'd get a job, her own money. An apartment in town. The one above the laundromat next to Ohrt's Bar & Grill. Once a week she'd order a takeout burger and fries. She'd have her own place, quiet at night and clean, smelling like detergent and Downy. Maybe some nights he'd show up, slip in when he was supposed to be on patrol, then leave. She'd sleep till morning glowed through the curtains and woke her.

"I'm sure there was a little more to it. At some point, anyway," he said.

There had been. There'd been a time when everything about Rick she now couldn't see or stand drew her in. That look of his that wrung her out—yearning and sadness all tangled together. It had a mystique, she guessed. About five months into being pregnant, she remembered where she'd seen that look. In a cat out at her folks' barn who'd gotten into some antifreeze.

"You ever married?" she asked him.

"Yeah, tried it." He used a thumb to scratch his eyebrow.

"What happened?"

"Wasn't exactly one event," he said. "Know how I asked you down here that night, to keep me from reacting?"

She said she did.

"That kind of disposition doesn't make for a great spouse."

She wondered if they'd had kids. The thought stilled her so she scarcely breathed. She rethought Helen Nelson's tendency to run her mouth. There must've been something illegal about leaving Anna in a store and driving away. Endangerment. Abandonment.

Pam had left her back at the trailer again. That must've been something. Neglect. If he asked, she'd say Anna was at Pam's parents' for the night.

"I don't feel bad about it, you know," she said. "What happened."

"Not much happened to speak of." He quit staring at the house and turned around, coming closer. Her stomach throbbed with his steps. They stopped at his trunk. He leaned back, propped a heel on his bumper, and looked out the same direction she did, at the vacant highway. "Think Paul said anything yet?"

"I don't know." She leaned forward, elbows on her knees. She'd wondered all day. She'd wondered what it would mean if he had. But she hadn't connected any dots. She asked Harley for a cigarette. He held one out without looking and passed her the lighter. "What's the grudge between you and Paul, anyway?"

"Mainly? He's headed to the pen or worse."

"Pretty sure we're all headed for worse." She lit the cigarette.

"True enough," he said. The burning paper of his cigarette gave a quiet hiss. He exhaled blue. "Imagine most of it goes back to his brother's body we never found."

The mention of Dell Junior made her drag a hand through her hair and scrape her nails against the scalp. For being dead almost twenty years, that kid had a way of being everywhere, all the time. The ever-present reason Pam was supposed to be grateful. The reason she wasn't supposed to get upset about putting butter back at the store or not being able to replace a crappy pair of shoes Anna wore out in a month. No, Dell Junior was always there to remind Pam she should have a goddamn party because none of them was dead yet. "Think people give that kid a little too much credit," she said. "Paul wasn't even old enough to remember him."

"Might be worse, never knowing anything halfway normal."

Pam pictured her dad under the dim lights of the kitchen, the hum of the cattle futures on the radio, the tall ceilings and sturdy block foundation of the house. "If all you ever know is miserable, maybe you don't know it is."

"I suspect Paul's got a pretty good idea."

"Ask me, they've milked it. Eighteen years. At a point, you move on."

Harley gave a short, curt breath. She couldn't tell if it was agreement or a mean laugh.

"Something funny?" she asked him.

"Moving on." When he said it, she felt his voice nearer. He was looking at her finally. "You get where we're standing, right?"

She did. And she knew then what drew her here to begin with. Harley had a mystique, too. It wasn't a great omen, mystique. "Saying you never moved on?"

"I left. Turned thirteen, took work as a farmhand south of Junco. Been through the place once since, when we searched for Dell Junior. But no, nobody moves on from something like that. Or anything else, probably. What's happened is who you are."

"Yeah, well. At least you tried. The Reddicks didn't. And they never let you forget it."

"You can bet nobody lets them forget it."

She took the last swig of her beer and slid down the trunk to round the side of the Nova. She wasn't leaving, but if he thought she was, he made no move to stop her. She reached in and grabbed the third beer she'd brought, tossing the empty on the passenger floor before she walked back to her perch.

In the moonlight, his shoulders were broad, nearly twice the width of her own.

Half the times she'd seen him, Harley had his back turned to her. That was what was different about his mystique. Harley might've been a wreck in some way, but there was nothing he was trying to wring from her. What made Harley different, what made her still wish that thumb toward the divot of her hip bone, was there was no need in him.

"You know much about their mother?" he asked.

Pam wondered if she should tell him. About Virginia taking off. But even if Virginia was a liability to herself, part of Pam now rooted for her. Paul had at least one good point. Virginia had a right.

Pam shrugged. "She's pretty distant."

He dropped his cigarette in the dirt and ground it out. The house made a groan and shudder.

His neck straightened and his arm bent, hand reaching near a dark mass she realized was his gun. He didn't touch it. Finally, he moved. He headed for the steps.

Pam thought to tell him it was all right. The place did that. She'd been hearing the same sounds since she'd come out here. She made a stride to tell him so, but he reached back a hand, fingers spread to say stay put. It was the same gesture he'd made the other night, when the animal in the grass had been Paul.

He went up the stairs. His boots kept tight to the edge, near the railing, and again he skipped the third. When he crossed the porch, only one board made a short creak. Otherwise his steps were silent. The same way hers were when she'd walked down the hall of the trailer before coming out here. It was the kind of silence that came from knowing every spot too soft and weak to take weight without sighing. He opened the door and his back disappeared into the black space of the entryway.

She waited for the movement of his lamp beam across the front room walls. It didn't light.

Time stopped again. A pathetic breeze, not cool, lifted the air. He was still in there, still with no light.

She walked to the base of the steps. Then she slipped upward, skipping the third, and crossed the threshold.

21 RICK WATCHED PAUL SLEEP. He didn't know how long he'd watched Paul sleep. They'd gotten a room with two full-sized beds at the Broken Wheel. Paul stayed out at the job for once, said he was too tired from laying carpet to drive back. Rick knew there was something more to it, but he didn't know what. It was that something that was too big, too close to see.

While they'd worked, Rick caught Paul staring at him. Watching him. He'd watched him all night, whenever Rick messed with the TV antenna, trying to stop the high-pitched whine. The set had whined through the news and through Richard Pryor on *The Tonight Show*. It'd whined through the national anthem, pitch rising each time the screen flooded white with one or another building in Washington. Like the marble buzzed with its own sound. Every time Rick got up to adjust the rabbit ears, he turned around to Paul staring. Watching. Paul wanted Rick to go to sleep. He'd kept saying it. Get some fucking sleep. So Rick pretended to. He'd pretended to sleep till Paul drifted off. Then he'd sat up. He clutched his knees at the edge of the full-sized mattress.

Full. The bed felt empty as hell. Rick stared and waited, like Paul might talk in his sleep. He didn't. He just lay there and snored, all ropy and golden. His skin looked painted on. Shiny like brass. Probably the light from the parking lot lamppost.

The phone sat on the nightstand. Next to a rubber Snoopy soap holder. It'd been in the bathroom of the dead-cowboy trailer. Rick didn't know why. He didn't know why some ranch hand had a rubber Snoopy soap holder. But there it was.

He wanted to call her again. He wouldn't. He'd spent four dollars and seventy-five cents between all the calls earlier. Pam would likely waste the call fighting about how much it cost.

The van's tank was near-empty. No place would be open to fill it. He'd be running on fumes by Halsey. The pickup's tank was full, though. Paul had filled it on the way to the motel.

Paul's keys sat on the nightstand beside Rick's. Rick would leave his own. He had a spare key to the trailer in his wallet anyway. He picked up Paul's keys slowly, so they didn't jingle. He grabbed Snoopy.

Two hours in, the pickup's headlights made a hole of yellow light above the pavement. The road was even thinner than it'd been on the way out. Tighter fit. The pickup couldn't fit between the lines. There was no way in hell the road was up to code.

Something streaked past him. A pair of bright white legs, it looked like, walking in the knee-deep brush. He let off the gas. He leaned forward and watched the passenger-side mirror. No legs. He braked and checked the mirror again. Still no legs. He threw the gearshift in park.

It could've been somebody who needed help. Shit. It could've been Mom out wandering, combing the ditches. Then again, it could've been somebody up to no good.

He'd play it safe. He lifted the shotgun from the rack, opened the door, and hopped down into a squat. He waddled the length of the bed to the tailgate. His heart pumped hard. The pump made his arms shake. He slid the barrel out first, then looked, quick, around the bumper. The road and grass lit red in the taillights. There was nobody. Nobody he could see, anyway.

He put his back to the pickup bed's side and stayed low. "Mom?" he yelled out.

Nothing.

"Mom, that you?"

No answer. Not even the sound of legs swishing in the grass. Whoever it was had hunkered down to wait him out. That, or nobody was there.

He rose just high enough his head was still hidden by the pickup bed. He ran back to the door. He jumped in and put the gun in the rack. He breathed out the shakes. Then he squealed the tires against the pavement.

22 IN THE DARK FRONT ROOM, the blue glow of moonlight from the kitchen entryway burned at Harley's side. There was still no one here he could sense. Surely no chain-smoker. What he'd heard was settling. The settling of a place grown old and tired, turning to dust. It was the sound of a house doing all somebody had opted out of doing with a shotgun shell, not twenty feet from where he stood. He wished the house would go on and get the lead out. Collapse. Let the grass claim it.

He heard the pats of Pam's feet cross the boards of the porch. When she stood behind him, he could feel her. The presence of a person with blood coursing through veins. A body with thin electric signals firing inside.

"It's just the house," she whispered. "The sound. It's been doing it all night."

"Get outside anyway. Get in your car and drive home." He waited. She didn't move. "Nobody's here," he told her. "Still need to do a walk-through."

She made no move to leave. She'd go with him, she said. There was a finality in the way she said it.

He felt for her wrist. He gripped it. Where he could feel between the blank spots of his calluses, her skin was warm and dry.

The number of paces from one wall's edge to the next seemed fewer, as though the house had shrunk. At the kitchen entry he made a hard left so all he saw of the room was the back door. The filmy panes that looked out on the yard were dull in the moonlight. He made three paces he was sure were once five. He took another hard left into the narrow, steep stairway and felt a pull from her.

Not hard, not meant to keep him from moving forward. The resistance was slight. She was dwelling on the space at his back.

In the stairway, he switched on the flashlight. The railing had fallen off and lay diagonal across the steps. It was a fair indication nobody'd been up here, not in a while. He pushed the rail aside with his boot. Near the top of the steps, he nailed his head on something. He looked up and saw the spindles of the banister, fallen over like the bars of a cage. A coolness washed through him. A feeling like relief. It was another sign nobody'd been up here in a while.

"Hold on," he said and let go of her wrist. He pushed the banister upward and leaned it against the hallway wall. When he took another step, her hand held his forearm. She kept it there and followed.

Upstairs were the two bedrooms and bathroom. The door to his folks' room was closed. He passed it. He made his way down the hall, her trailing behind him, and checked the bathroom first. Plaster lay in chunks in the pedestal sink. The basin tilted from the wall like it was trying to work itself loose from the plumbing.

Across the hall was the room he'd shared with his sister till she'd done the smartest thing she could've, got knocked up by Carl Shumway and moved to Oregon. The room was empty. What furniture there'd been was sold or given away. The hole under the loose slat of floorboard was empty, too. He knew without looking. He'd cleaned it out when he left. There'd been an old, clear marble with a white sulfide cow trapped in the center. There'd been an old cigarette card like nothing he'd seen before or since. A picture of a red fox on a table, paw on the chin of a skin-colored mask. He'd found it in the root cellar out back. He wondered what he'd ever done with those things.

He stopped outside their room, his parents' room. He turned the knob. Locked. He reached above the doorframe and pinched the skeleton key. He jostled the lock till it popped. He felt Pam's presence at his back, the warmth of her breath behind him. He opened the door.

The bed was still made. The spread was still in place, draped over the sags their bodies had worn in. The wardrobe, a chifforobe, she'd called it, stood between the bed and the window, closed. What few things she'd had were no doubt still there. On the bureau lay the thick-backed brush and hand mirror, the bowl of powder and the perfume bottle, doilies. All of it was there, caked in a silt of cobwebs and dust. He remembered what he'd heard about dust. This was the first place he'd considered it. That motes of her were there in a fine coat on the dresser top. Motes of her that weren't her any more than the perfume had been. He'd snuck up once and sprayed it. He'd learned a perfume didn't smell like the person unless it was layered in, dulled by what came from their own pores.

He pulled the door to, locked it, and slid the key in his pocket. He felt its weight there. He pulled it out and put it above the door again.

Pam had said nothing this whole time. He was grateful.

He led her the short distance to the stairs. A third of the way down, he pulled the banister so it rested like a grate on a sewer. At the second-to-last step, he switched off the flashlight. He slipped his forearm from her hand and took hers again.

In the kitchen, he let his eyes adjust to the grainy dimness and tried to keep from breathing. To keep from inhaling the air of the room.

There was no table. No chairs. No stove between the mudroom entryway and the yawning dark of the open pantry. There was no sink, though the pipes still ran up the wall. He saw the sharp line of white space where it once attached. The old paint. They'd had to change it. They'd scoured the walls but still had to paint. They'd scrubbed the floorboards. Painted those, too. Dad had gotten a deal. A slate-blue color. Just a hint of gray, mostly blue. They'd painted the whole room with it, he and his sister and Dad. Walls and ceiling and floor. So the only way you could see where wall ended and ceiling began was by shadow.

They'd had carbide gas lighting. The fixture had burned too bright against the slate-blue. It made the three of them paler, their eye whites larger. So they were all locked in an expression of shock. Not surprise. Shock. Like after a compound fracture or a car wreck. It got so none of them could stand the sight of each other because of that paint.

His father had busted up and burned the chair. She'd sat in a chair. To push the trigger with her toe. Her chair, although it was no different from the others.

She'd pulled it back from the table, which was set. Steam drifted up from the boat of tan gravy. Like a window sheer, he'd thought. A sheer he'd wished were thicker. The gravy had already formed a puckered skin against the ladle. He'd been the first inside. He smelled the powder, the spent shell, and a scent like iron. A scent so thick he tasted it on his tongue. Her chair had a high, slatted back. A woven cane seat. Not comfortable. It'd blown over. He saw the gray dirt on the soles of her feet. That, of it all, was what he remembered clearest. That gray dirt, the soles of her feet.

She was just a thing. Not only then but all along. They all were. Things. He hadn't known till then.

It'd struck him in that moment, a sharp, simple thought that'd always been in him but shadowy and dull. A sharp, simple thought that would never leave him, not when he was with others and not when he was alone: What she'd done was something a person could do. There had been, always, and would always be that.

He breathed.

23

PAM DIDN'T KNOW WHAT HE WAS SEEING and didn't want to. What she wanted was air. What she wanted was to not be here, standing in this room she shouldn't have known about but did, a room she'd pictured in her head because she couldn't help herself, any more than she could keep herself from picturing the pickup tire on Pooley's neck and how she imagined the pressure of it blew up his head, like a balloon, till it popped. Worst of all, she'd pictured this place different. A place airy and sunny yellow with white curtains billowing and everything past them blinding green and a blue sky with those flat-bottomed and cottony clouds that looked fake, that looked painted on. Not a room so dark and closed in she couldn't breathe.

When she could, she moved. She touched the cool wall behind her and felt for the edge of the other room, the space where he held her hip the other night. She shrank in that direction, but he had her wrist. She shrank that way but kept her arm still so he couldn't feel her inching. When she couldn't reach any farther, she tried one more inch. He moved then, fluidly. He turned to follow her as if he'd seen nothing. As if he hadn't been standing there frozen in place and seeing whatever it was she didn't want to know.

"You all right?" he asked her, as if she were the one with a goddamn problem. As if she were the one with all the misery and craziness and heaviness that filled the air like that thick, oily dust in the Oldsmobile. Was she all right. She was the only one who was partway all right. Out of everyone she knew, she was it.

She pulled him toward the heavy wood front door, which was

still cracked, leading out to air that would be thick but not half this thick, when it shut. Right in front of her it shut, sucking its thin gap of light and air from the room, and she thought for half a second, pins and needles all through her, that it shut itself. Then she saw his arm above her head, palm flat against the wood. His armpit was level with her temple, and that warm Old Spice smell filled her head with a sharpness. She felt his hand hot on her waist and he turned her body to face him. The belt buckle, hard and curved, grazed her belly.

"Let me go out first," he said.

She didn't move and she didn't speak.

"You all right?" he asked again.

Words came, words like, *I need some goddamn air*, but they stuck in her throat and she didn't say them. Instead she did what made no sense. Instead she did the least sensible thing she could. She pressed herself to him, length and breadth. He took a breath, expanded. His arm slipped down her shoulder and arm, but not to touch her. He grasped for the doorknob at her back. She reached up then and pulled his neck, pulled his face down toward hers. He was stone when her cheekbone found the edge of his jaw. He wouldn't bend any more, so she stretched on bent toes up to find his mouth a taut line. She brushed her lower lip against his and he tried to pull the door open behind her. But there was no space. Not with her there. Then she felt, finally, the pad of his thumb. It made a single stroke down the inside curve of her hip bone. He was trying to move her aside. But like a lever pushed or a string pulled, she ran her bare leg up the coarse fabric and held him.

He was motionless so long her thigh cramped from holding it at the angle. But she didn't let go. His palm left the doorknob and touched the small of her back.

Then there was only breath. She held him with her legs when the two of them slid and crumpled down, and she didn't jump at the clunk and patter, the cartoon boing of the flashlight's fall to the floor.

What followed was slow, the sliding of fabric, then warm palms and fingertips clutched on the ledges of collarbones. It was all the weight of him, pressing, and the thickness of his shoulders. The dip in his back where her calves wrapped and rested. Inside her was all warm silence.

In the stillness after, she felt the grit of his stomach's trail of hair against her belly. Her knees straddled his sides and she felt the hard floor beneath her back, beneath her heels and toes. She felt the air again, a heat not from bodies.

She waited. For the other weight. The sinking weight of what she'd done. Or the punch to the chest. Or the drain of sand through her throat and into her stomach. Or the itching nerves of a lightning strike. But there was only warmth. Not numbness but a soft, constant buzzing.

He slipped out of her and stood, pulling up his pants. The glow behind him cut him clean as a flat paper figure she traced for detail. The thin, curled hairs beneath his arms as he pulled on his undershirt. The edges of his holster. By the slight downward tilt of his head, she could tell he buttoned his uniform shirt by feel. He watched her body. Her skin rose in bumps.

He bent down, picked up her underwear and cutoffs, then stopped.

"What?" She pushed herself up on her elbows as he reached to crack the door open. Starlight cut across the floor in a narrow line.

Static. A voice called out tinny, from a can. His CB. He

handed her the clothes and disappeared around the door. His boots whispered across the grass. He spoke, but she couldn't make out what he said. She slipped on her underwear and cutoffs and covered her chest with her T-shirt before she peered out.

At the base of the steps, he called up, quiet and stern. "There's a fire," he said. "Get home. Now."

She pulled on the T-shirt as the cruiser roared to life. She'd put the shirt on inside out. She pulled it off, righted it, and pulled it on again. He was at the end of the drive by the time she shut the door behind her. She stood on the porch and watched him turn left, in the direction of Madson.

She didn't want to go. She could still feel him, still feel the floorboards at her back. She wanted to curl up in the Nova and stay here. Never leave. Or at least never go back.

But from behind the house came a sound like wind. Past the clapboard corners of the house, a cloud of brightness filled the air, a glow like a distant town's streetlamps lighting the sky. The sound neared. Light seeped and sharpened around the edges so the yard was black with the house's shadow.

She sprinted down the steps to the car. She got in, turned the key, and slammed the Nova into reverse. The tires skidded back across the grass. She weaved out onto the highway.

24 IN THE DARKNESS TWENTY MILES FROM HOME, Rick saw streaks of light in the corners of his eyes. They were what he'd mistaken for legs alongside the highway. He'd seen them again and again till he figured out they weren't legs. He knew he just needed some sleep. He hadn't slept since Wednesday night, and it had to be Saturday morning by now. All the same, he half wondered if the streaks had always been there and he'd never noticed them. Now that he had, they sure didn't seem to be going anywhere.

He made the turn into Park Meadows and coasted to the end of their road. The Nova was gone. Where it should've been was an empty space of crabgrass patches and dirt under the streetlamp fog.

He idled. She'd been skittish last time, when she came back and saw the van. If she came back and saw Paul's pickup, he didn't know how skittish she'd be. Rick played it safe. He pulled back a block and parked behind Evelyn Mueller's place.

The road closer to the highway ran along an embankment. From where he parked, Rick had a clear view of the trailer. Anna was inside, he knew. Sleeping. No idea she was even alone. Not alone, he supposed, now that he was here to watch over her. But if she cried out in her sleep, if she woke scared from a dream about werewolves—he never should've let her watch that show about werewolves—nobody could hear. And she was still in the crib she'd outgrown. She might try to get out. Climb up over the bars. One of her pajama footies could skid and she'd fall, crush her windpipe on the rail.

The thought made him jump from the truck and scurry down

the embankment. The high grass, tan and sand-colored, streaked past and blended together. He squeezed the rubber Snoopy soap holder in his fist as he jogged across the road and up the trailer steps. He turned the knob. Unlocked. Pam had left the door unlocked again. He went through the living room and down the hall to where Anna slept. He set the Snoopy down beside her, on its back, like it'd float in a tub of water.

He threaded his arms beneath his girl, beneath her heavy head and limp knees, and lifted her to him. He cradled her like a baby. She didn't wake. That unsettled him, that he could come in here and pick her up and not wake her. She must've known it was him. She must've known it was Daddy. He told himself that was it. He carried her to their room. He laid Anna where she would have fit between them if Pam were here.

Without pulling off his boots, Rick lay down, too. He still wouldn't sleep. For one, he needed to be awake when Pam got home. He needed to be awake to tell her she couldn't leave the damn door unlocked. And she couldn't up and leave Anna alone in the trailer. That was when things happened you couldn't undo. When nobody was there to see.

For another, Rick apparently didn't need to sleep anymore. He hadn't popped any speed since yesterday, but he hadn't needed to. It was like he'd caught some twelfth wind that never stopped blowing.

He'd close his eyes, though. They felt dried like the paper skin of onions.

He bent his head toward Anna and smelled the top of her hair. She had a clean sweat smell. But another scent crept around the edges. It was sweat, too, but something else. A smell that stung like charred trailer paneling. The smell rang in his ears. Not warm soap but just as familiar.

It was aftershave. Brut. There on his own pillow.

The swarm of beetles scattered against the walls of Rick's stomach. The nothing that was something was here on the sheets. It was why Paul brushed off seeing Pam yesterday morning. It was why Pam wouldn't say Paul had been here. It was why Pam had snuck out in the middle of the night and come back looking guilty, an indent where her wedding band should've been. The same night Paul had a hot date with a blond number. It was why, back at Dad's place, when Rick said Pam needed him home, Paul had looked at Rick like he was a hit deer hurled in a ditch, knocked on its side, still trying to run.

Rick had a gift, Paul said. A gift for seeing only what he wanted to see.

Rick stood and scooped up Anna like the bed was hot charcoal. This time she opened her eyes and looked cross at being woken. She settled when she saw him. Her arms circled his neck. He was tempted to spray her down in the sink. Wash away any trace of the sheets. He wanted her out of this room. He wanted her out of this trailer.

Clutching her close, he half sprinted down the hall, through the door, and across the road. The gravel bled past the corners of his vision in streaks of white light. She woke enough to ask where they were going as he climbed the embankment. His boot slipped. His knee hit the dirt but he kept Anna up, kept Anna off the ground. Grandma's, he told her. But she needed to nap first. Up here in Uncle Paul's pickup. The name left a tinge of bile at the back of his throat. When he got her in, she tucked into her little egg shape on the seat.

He went to start the pickup and checked the gas gauge. Bottomed out. It'd taken the full tank to get here. He might not even make it to Mom's before running out. He'd need gas. He'd need to feed Anna.

Anna. Where was Anna when Pam was fucking his brother on Rick's own sheets? The thought rose through him and swelled his skin tight. Could Anna hear what they talked about after, slick with each other?

He shut the pickup door and saw the gun in the rack. He couldn't leave Anna with the gun in the rack. He grabbed it, ran back across the road, and propped it inside the front door. Pam kept the money in the kitchen, but he didn't know where. He dug through the drawers first. He pulled loose folded towels. He dumped the junk drawer in the sink.

The cupboards. He thumbed through rims of plates and bowls. Nothing.

The Tupperware. He pulled down containers, popped them open. He pushed his fingers through the sugar, sifted the grains. Inside its plastic bin, the sugar was still in the bag. Maybe she'd hid the money underneath. He upended the canister and dumped it in the sink. Nothing. Just sugar.

The flour was still in a bag, too. He dumped it.

The bills fluttered out. Plenty of them, it looked like. Plenty enough, for all the pissing and moaning she did about money. He snatched them up and shoved them in his pockets, trying not to crush what was left of the pills, just in case. He smeared and patted the flour dust, the white handprints it made on his jeans.

Jeans. Clothes. He went to Anna's room. He grabbed her blanket and Mr. Turtle from the crib, then opened drawers. He'd made built-in drawers for Anna's room. Real nice built-ins. He grabbed fistfuls of clothes and wadded them in the middle of her blanket. He cinched it all into a bundle.

At the front door, he snatched up the gun and headed outside.

Gas. There'd be no place open to buy gas this late.

Their hose sat coiled around the side of the trailer. He'd never used it for anything but spraying mud off his boots. He'd never had other cause to use it. He'd never put down sod or seed for a yard. Just as well.

He laid down the shotgun and the mound of Anna's things in the weeds and took out his buck knife. He worked the blade against the hose. He cut a length of tube he could run from a gas tank.

From this side of the trailer, he wouldn't see Pam pull up. In his head, he pictured what he wouldn't see. The Nova swinging into the empty space, her slipping into her sandals and crossing the dirt and crabgrass, looking disappointed. Disappointed Paul was a no-show, wherever they usually met. She'd walk inside and down the hall and lie on the bed—Rick's bed. Rick's mattress. Rick's sheets. She wouldn't even see Anna was gone. Pam would go straight to the bed and bury her head in his pillow that stank of Paul. She'd breathe deep.

He pictured her knuckles braced on the edge of the mattress. Paul's sickly pale white ass rising and falling on top of her. Rick pictured it again. And again. Not because he couldn't not. He did it because each time he saw it, the sink in his stomach set solid and deadened. He did it because it was like saying a word too many times. Till it didn't mean anything anymore. He knew it'd all flood back when she got here, when the Nova pulled in. It'd flood back till he felt his skin would split. But for now he let it play in his head and numb him as he sawed the hose. He'd already cut the length for siphoning. Now he was cutting to cut. To do something with his hands.

A hum. From the highway. It grew deeper and louder. He

heard the engine, the roll of radials on the trailer court's main road. He squatted where he was, buck knife in his grip.

He checked himself. He folded the blunt side of the blade against the thigh of his jeans and slid the knife into its sheath. His head beat with his heart like his ear was pressed against a pillow. A pillow that now stank of Brut and sweat.

The blood rushed hot to his ears so they rang with it. The car idled high before the engine cut. He ground his teeth against the sound of each step she made toward the trailer. His chest seized once at the screen door opening, and again with the slap when it closed.

He listened for scurrying. Scuffling. A scream when she saw Anna wasn't where she'd left her. He listened for the frenzied patter of footfalls. Another slap of the screen door.

Rick listened. But nothing came.

THE DRIVE INTO Madson was like sleep and waking. Spaces of time gone like pavement between yellow dashes. In his head, in the hollows above his eyes, gasoline wafted. He'd tried the hose on Evelyn Mueller's Mercury and a shitty Datsun before he finally managed to pull some from Les Bowman's Dodge Ram. The gas barely hit the tip of his tongue, and he'd spit. He'd opened a beer and swished it, but the fumes were still there. He supposed gas was better than Brut.

In case Paul got out of Thedford and came looking for his pickup, Rick parked in the gravel alley northwest of Mom's place, on the far side of McKinney's. The mechanic's sprawling graveyard of cars and trucks and buses blocked any view of the pickup.

Rick carried Anna toward the locust trees that ringed Mom's place. When he came close, he saw something wasn't right. About the house.

The lamp didn't shine red through the drapes. The lamp that was always on. Always. Day and night.

When he carried Anna inside, the darkness was too thick. He remembered the overhead. They'd never used it. Mom always used the lamp. He swept his arm up and down the wall till he felt the switch and flipped it.

The light blinded. It sparked off the vinyl recliner and the end table and the Zenith. It lit the red drapes too red. He switched it off. He squeezed his eyes shut. Anna was awake now and wriggling. He was clutching her too close. He loosened his grip and opened his eyes to the dark. He stood still and blinked till he could see.

Somebody'd switched the lamp off. The only person who should've been here was Paul. But Paul wouldn't have switched the lamp off. Paul said to keep shit normal. That lamp being on was normal. Mom? Maybe Mom was here and went back to sleeping in her room again.

He settled Anna in on the couch with her wad of things. He pulled out the turtle and handed it to her. She rubbed her eyes with her fists, then curled up against the arm of the couch. He ruffled her hair before he walked down the hall.

The house stank like rotten vegetables. Like old books and wet cigarettes. He walked through, checking and rechecking all the rooms till a streak of light in the corner of his vision stopped him in the hall. The picture hung there. Behind the glass, Dell Junior straddled the Schwinn in the yard. The frame was old. Oak. After the cops called off the search, she'd taken out a yellowed picture of stiff, unsmiling dead relatives and put in Dell Junior. Dell Junior, swapped in for dead people Dell Junior never knew.

Maybe that explained Mom up and disappearing. Maybe she was somehow swapping herself in with Dell Junior, too. Mom wasn't anywhere, and Dell Junior wasn't anywhere. Rick didn't know what it could've meant. But the thought itched through him.

The thought itched through him until it radiated. Until it glowed. Then Rick knew.

The knowing shimmered like light. Like the streaks. They were in the same place, Mom and Dell Junior. The same place that wasn't anywhere. The thought settled him. The thought somehow made sense. It was somehow all right.

He turned the switch on the living room lamp. The bulb was shot. Rick supposed that made sense, too.

Instead of digging around for a new bulb, he sat on the floor by the couch in the dark. He sat by where Anna held Mr. Turtle. Rick wouldn't sleep. He didn't need to anymore, of course, but he also knew he couldn't. Even if it was good Mom and Dell Junior were together, wherever it was that wasn't anywhere, he didn't want Anna wandering off there, too. Not without him, anyway. Not alone.

He reached back to hold her ankle. To keep it there. He held her ankle in the dark.

25 HARLEY WAS PARKED ALONGSIDE the drive of the Knudsen homestead. He'd left room for fire trucks passing to and from the highway. The volunteer crews
from Madson and Wilton both worked to keep the blaze contained to the house and windbreak. Leaning against the cruiser
in the dark, he watched the flames wave up in short-lived streaks.
Above, smoke billowed white like fast-moving clouds, though
Harley knew the smoke couldn't have been white. It'd been a
trick of contrast, the black night sky above the red glow. Through
the plumes and above, against the dark, embers shot up, glimmered, and died out like meteorites. Shooting stars headed the
wrong direction.

When it came, morning was hazy in the blackened ruins. They
steamed. He was thankful for the way the vapor softened the
edges of day, made the morning look like fall instead of summer's
peak. He could imagine this was some fall morning far away from
the jarring, competing pictures in his head: the pale haze of her
hips rising from the floor, then gray dirt on the soles of feet. Some
fall morning months from now, there'd be routine again.

The Wilton crew had left, but a few of Madson's boys were
still inside. They clomped around in their heavy rubber suits and
yelled to each other in voices just as weighed down. Whatever
they said was tired and winded, deadened by what was left of the
walls. They were checking for hot spots, ensuring the place was
soggy enough it wouldn't flare up again.

While they worked, he passed the brooder house. The building
was still dead-bolted, still sealed up tight. He went to the horse

barn with the stalls stripped out to see what he'd see, kill time before he could get inside the farmhouse and find what he knew he would: buttons, snaps, zippers. Ashes of newsprint and the stink of gasoline. Empty booze bottles filled with cigarette butts.

Something was different. In the horse barn. Something was off. From where he stood in the open doorway, he made out the tops of the molded bales and the generator in the loft. He stood and stared but couldn't place what was different.

He walked to the bigger hay barn and pushed aside one of the doors.

The Plymouth was gone. He hadn't taken down the plates. He hadn't thought to. He'd figured it for an auction buy.

Who knew how long it'd take to track plates from '60? They'd need to dig through file boxes, sift through the paperwork for all the Plymouth Savoys. On his way to the cruiser, where he'd radio Carol, ask her to start digging, he passed the smaller horse barn again and glanced, still nagged by what was different.

The ladder to the loft. It was gone. He wondered if it'd been here last he checked, hours before. Tracks from the posts ran across the dirt and hay and disappeared in the grass at his feet. There were enough tracks he wondered if some of them hadn't been here the other day. If they were, he should've noticed. His eyes fell to trace them.

Nestled in the sparse hay, something orange shone like colored glass. He walked to it and squatted. A prescription bottle. He rolled the cylinder to see the script. Quaaludes, thirty count with two left. Made out to Virginia Reddick.

Pam said the brothers were both in Thedford. Before a vision of her hip bones rising from the dimness could flash in Harley's head, he replayed the moment he'd yelled up to her. When he'd told her to get home. She'd stared back blank, unknowing. She hadn't been covering for anybody, hadn't lied to him about Paul's whereabouts. At least not on purpose. She'd really thought Paul was in Thedford. She'd just thought wrong. Paul no doubt drove back after Pam talked to her husband on the phone. Paul drove back knowing he had a reliable story for where he was.

Harley walked, tracing the ladder trails around to the back of the house, where the rock foundation rose to the stairless entrance. The door above was open. He called up, asked the fire crew how it looked.

One of them, the oldest Braasch boy, who wasn't a boy at all but a huge, nearly middle-aged man, poked his face around the doorway. His skin was stained with char and smoke. "If you can float, come on in. But I wouldn't trust what floor's left. Pretty much gone in front. We're tiptoeing joist to joist like big ballerinas."

"Anything left of an old barn ladder? Wood? Round rungs?"

"Yeah, right here across the floor," he said, like it was nothing notable. "This whole thing'll come down in the first stiff wind. Penke's gonna need to raze it quick." He rubbed his forehead with the thumb of a thick glove. The ash smeared in a streak. "It's out, though. Best we can tell."

Harley thanked him, told him and the boys to be careful in there.

AT THE STATION, Glenn didn't have a sheen. If anything, he looked too dry. And pale. He needed to goddamn retire, was what he needed to do.

Harley asked if Carol had called with the records on the Plymouth.

Glenn shook his head. She'd called, he said, but no luck yet. He stared absently at his desk calendar, at the chicken-scratch notes there.

"Paul Reddick. Been into his mother's ludes again." Harley tossed the prescription bottle onto Glenn's desk. He told Glenn what he knew, about the ladder, about the front door being bolted the other day. Paul must've used the ladder to go in back and pulled it up after him. Then he must've set the fire and gone out the front. Looked like he'd been there multiple times, given the tracks.

"Harley." Glenn was grave. "You and me need to talk."

"Don't say I'm jumping to conclusions."

"You didn't mention you picked him up, night before last."

"You want the truth?" Harley said, then realized he couldn't tell it. Not the truth about Pam. Not if it could be avoided. She was a married woman with a kid. He couldn't tell a sheriff, even if the sheriff was Glenn, that he'd given Pam's husband grounds for divorce. While on duty. And if he couldn't tell Glenn about Pam, all the rest would sound insane—Paul following him on patrol, Paul setting the fire in the burn barrel at the home place, Paul getting thrown in the drunk tank on purpose. "You looked like you were about to die. Doris Luschen's place'd just got hit." He went to his desk and flipped open the phone book. "Check Carol's log if you want. I got a call to take him in, I took him in. Put him in the drunk tank. Turned him loose the next morning. In plenty of time to steal Doris's clothes."

Glenn turned the pill bottle with a finger, distracted. Slow and quiet, he said, "Pills don't put him at Doris's. Don't even put him at the Knudsen place." He slid open the pen drawer of his desk. He dropped the bottle into it. "Besides, it's Virginia's name on the prescription."

"Sounds like some weird wishful thinking on your part," Harley said. "Why is that, Glenn?"

"Paul Reddick's got a Ford." He leaned back in his chair and rubbed his bald hairline, like he was rubbing away an ache, his eyes closed. "You're looking for somebody drives a Plymouth."

Harley flipped the phone book on his desk to the Rs. There were three listings for Reddicks. Dell Senior, Rick, and Virginia. Rick. Harley scribbled the trailer park addresses in his notepad. He'd drive out to Fall Meadows first, see if Paul was at his dad's or brother's. Harley tore loose the paper. He tucked it behind his cigarettes.

HE PULLED UP to the end of Pam's block. There was no red F-250, but the Nova sat outside the trailer. He wanted to stop. He had a good enough excuse. But it wasn't the brightest idea. Not with the places out here being so packed together. Not given neighbors' tendency to talk. He wondered if even considering it meant his judgment was getting spotty. He needed some downtime. He needed to get some space from the pictures that flashed in his head like slides in a projector wheel. One moment was the thin, downy hair on her skin. The next was the bottom of a cane-seated chair blown over. So much for afterglow.

Harley drove across the court to Dell Senior's. Paul's truck wasn't there, either. Harley pulled up anyway and parked.

The place was a double-wide version of a grand estate,

propped on a bright green hill of yard twice the size of the surrounding lots. Harley strode up the turf grass, walked by a concrete fountain where a fat and naked boy stood at the center of a scallop-edged bowl, pissing.

The most time Harley had spent in close proximity to Dell Senior was in that district courtroom after the water tower. He'd had the same glad-handy grin he wore in his Midwest Speedway bulletin ads for trailer repair and sales. In the flyer for stock car races and demolition derbies, he smiled a set of hard, white, squared-off teeth below a thin Douglas Fairbanks mustache. The judge ate it up. Dell Senior could've charmed him into buying half of Fall Meadows if he'd wanted to.

Harley pulled open the screen door and saw a brass knocker, a lion's head with a ring in its mouth. He rapped his knuckles three times on the wood below and waited.

Rumor had it Dell Senior was a drinker and a son of a bitch. Harley didn't like him, but he took rumor with a grain of salt. There'd been plenty of talk about the Jensens, too. Affairs, alcoholism. Whispers about Dad beating her. A theory she'd had a miscarriage. That she'd gone crazy from menopause. None of it was true, but people needed it to be. Otherwise it was a problem, that somebody no different from themselves could go and do what she did. And problems have solutions. Questions have answers. So people rooted around till they found one to settle on. What they never got was there was never any problem or question to begin with. Just an event. Same thing with Dell Senior, probably. One of the man's kids was killed. People couldn't abide something so senseless. They needed to believe he'd somehow earned it.

Dell Senior wasn't answering, though his well-waxed Lincoln sat beneath the carport. Harley glared at the lion's head, took a breath for patience, and used the brass ring to knock. The clack was quieter than his knuckles, but steps thudded behind the door. There was silence before it opened.

The man's eyes looked a touch glassy, a little red. Evidently, it was true he was a drinker. "Ah," he said, with a force behind it. A force that made his chest pop up and out a hair. He was shy of Harley's height by an inch or two. "Jensen. Suspect you're looking for Paul, as usual."

"Got any idea where he is?"

"You know, I had this other one I asked you people to find, oh, about twenty years back." He smoothed his mustache, though it wasn't going anywhere. "Ran into Glenn last week, week before. Good people, Glenn. Shit sheriff, but good people. Told him maybe his deputy was confused about which boy I meant."

Harley wondered if the conversation accounted for Glenn's wishful thinking.

"See," Dell Senior said with an easy laugh, "you keep finding the one that ain't missing. And as for the other, well—" He took on a mock note of triumph that rang of Paul. "You can call off the search! Had the funeral without him."

Harley stayed even, neutral. "I heard."

He shot back, "Oh, did you heard?"

Harley's jaw tightened. He hooked his thumb through his belt loop.

"Hell of a thing, way it works. You can be dead eighteen years, but it ain't official till somebody signs a form." He leaned in a bit so his head poked from the doorway, and he shifted his glassy eyes left to right. "You hear we did it to collect insurance?" He held the back of his hand to the edge of his mouth, like he was telling Harley a secret. He whispered, "I heard that, too."

"Any idea where Paul was last night?"

Dell Senior took a measured pause before he spoke. "Maybe you don't mean to come across the way you do, Jensen. But chasing my son, searching him, throwing him in the drunk tank, the loony bin—makes me think you doubt his raising. How he was reared. Is that it? Think I don't deserve Father of the Year?"

Harley said nothing. He gripped the belt loop with one hand, the cheap storm doorframe with the other.

"I give my boys homes and money and work. Hell, I keep the electric and water running for that cuckoo Daffy Duck wife down in town," he said. "I provide for mine. Don't recall your folks winning any awards in that category."

Harley kept his temper checked, his mouth a taut, thin-lipped line.

"Tell me something, Jensen. I know you think my boy's crazy. Made that clear getting him locked up that time. But you ever consider, pulling him over every ten minutes like you got no other job, that you might be the one? You ever stop to think you might come by it naturally?"

Harley looked Dell Senior dead in the eye. Then he dropped his head to let a quarter-sized dollop of spit fall on the man's welcome mat. He rubbed it in with the toe of his boot. "Where's Paul?"

Dell Senior's eyelids tensed low behind his bifocal rims. "You got a warrant?"

"Don't need a warrant to ask a question."

"Don't need to answer your question, neither. But I will, since

I know it'll burn your ass. On his way back from Thedford." He looked satisfied, smiling those square white teeth. "Where he was all last night. Want proof, I got a Western Union receipt from this morning."

HARLEY SPED THROUGH the blind intersection at County Road K, past his folks' place and the Lucas drive, past the county oil and the burnt remnants of the Knudsen place. He lit a fresh cigarette off the one he finished. He crossed the wood bridge spanning the Wakonda, tapped his brakes at the four-way stop, and hung a right on Walnut. Dell Senior could eat his goddamn Western Union receipts. The money could've as easily been wired to the son who really was in Thedford.

When Harley got to Virginia's house, he put the cruiser in park but left the engine on. He walked to the door, lit cigarette in hand. He wasn't out to impress anybody, not after last night and this morning. Not at this point in the day.

There was no sign of her son's F-250 as Harley pounded the door. Not a peep from inside. If Paul was in there, he wasn't answering. Harley didn't know why he thought Paul might. Probably more spotty judgment. But Paul was nothing if not cocksure.

Harley leaned from the small concrete porch far enough to see the house's far side. The burn barrel sat centered in the dead yard. That was no doubt the connection, right there, the barrel Virginia Reddick had stood before naked, burning trash. The connection to Jack Christiansen's and Doris Luschen's clothes being lit up in abandoned houses was no doubt plain as day. A fixation on clothes and fires passed from mother to son like a cleft chin.

Without willing it, he pictured the bottom of a cane-seated chair and a boat of gravy in the kitchen, skin puckered around the ladle. Then Pam's willowy legs.

He banged on the door again. No answer. He decided he was glad. He'd had enough Reddicks today. He also liked to think people were a little more resilient than Glenn gave them credit for. Including Virginia. The last thing Harley needed was for her to open that door, prove him wrong.

26

RICK HAD STILL NOT SLEPT.

In the gold of the morning, Rick sat on the floor of Mom's living room, still seeing those streaks of light in the corners of his eyes. He could make them out better now, see they had colors and shapes. A curl of black hair streaked left. A short, striped shirtsleeve, red and blue and ivory, streaked right. Then a streak of skin like Rick's own. Like Anna's. A streak of skin a few shades darker than dirt.

They were Dell Junior's—that hair, that skin, that shirt he'd worn the morning he'd gone off and got killed. Which was weird. Rick had wondered last night if the streaks had always been there at the corners of his eyes, if he'd just never noticed them. But this should've been the sort of thing you'd notice and remember, Dell Junior streaking around after he got killed.

The only thing weirder than the streaks was Rick seeing himself on the floor in front of him. Rick felt himself in his grown body, the couch at his back, but there he was, lying right there on the living room carpet, near six years old.

It must've still been the morning Dell Junior died, then. That was about as weird as the streaks, but there it was. Eighteen years later, and it was still that morning.

Rick watched himself tinker with the toy train engine. He wondered whatever happened to that toy train engine made of cold, sharp metal. Or the chrome rocket. Or the spinning top. Or Dell Junior's stockpile of baseball cards and comic books. The picnics, Paul always said. Mom wandered off with Dell Junior's stuff when they had those picnics at the old, dilapidated house with the front porch roof coming loose.

Part of Paul was there in the living room, too, a streak of him kicking the bottom block in a stack he'd made, just to watch them fall. That was all there was of Paul. That foot kicking the block. Which was fine. Rick didn't want to see the rest of Paul right now.

Streaks of Dell Junior glided, yelled something.

Mom shouted from the kitchen. A short honk. Not words but a honk. So she was here, too, just not all of her. Only a short honk from the kitchen, making a big deal out of something that wasn't.

The streaks of shirt and skin and black curl crossed the floor and the door sprang open and shut. Dell Junior's Schwinn didn't scrape against the clapboard like it usually did. That was where he always leaned the Schwinn. He'd been told not to. That day, he'd left it there. Months after he was gone, Rick asked about getting a bike. Mom said to use his older brother's. It was out in the shed. Paul wound up with it when he was big enough. Rick wouldn't ride it. Didn't feel right about it. But Paul didn't mind. Paul didn't even remember Dell Junior.

A bang at the door. Three bangs. Then the streaks were gone. The short honk was gone. Anna gave a quiet grunt behind him.

Rick's head spun back to look at her. He was holding her ankle too tight. He loosened his grip. She rubbed her eyes with balled fists. Rick put a finger to his lips. A shadow darkened the drape by the door.

Three more bangs. Then the shadow shrank. It got smaller. Rick crawled to the window. He pinched and lifted a corner of the drape.

A cop. He was leaving. But he was a cop. He might be back. Cops did that.

Why were the cops looking for him? Rick needed to think. The pills? He didn't need them anymore, and there were only six left. He could flush them. But he'd stolen the gas, too. And Paul's pickup. Paul?

Rick could call the motel. Paul's was the last voice he wanted to hear, but Rick could feel him out, see if he'd called the cops. Rick crept across the floor toward the phone and kept low so his shadow wouldn't bleed through the drapes. In case the cop wasn't really gone. In case he was on a stakeout.

Rick got the number from information and called the motel. He asked for Paul's room.

The clerk asked if Rick meant the kid with the van. The skinny kid with the hair. That was him, Rick said. Gone, the clerk told him. Missed him. Turned the key in already and left.

Rick hung up. He'd thought Paul used all his money from the Wilton job to fill the pickup. That was right—they'd got paid on the Wilton job. Thirty bucks. Rick had forgotten the money in the envelope behind his wallet. He'd forgotten it before he dumped the flour container. Well, now he and Anna had a little bit more.

Maybe Paul went out to the job, to the dead cowboy trailer in Seneca. No, Paul was worthless. He wouldn't do any work on his own. He'd be on his way back here. Not here, not Mom's, because he'd been too worthless for that, too. If he'd looked after Mom like he was supposed to, if he'd done the one real job he had, Mom would still be here. Would Paul go to Dad's? No, Dad would be pissed he wasn't at the trailer in Seneca. Then again, Dad never got too pissed at Paul.

Pam. Paul would head right for Pam. Paul would head right for Pam and ride her like he rode that bike of Dell Junior's.

Rick dialed his own number. Seven rings. Eight rings. Fine. He'd let it ring.

She answered. She sounded like the phone woke her.

His voice came out a wordless croak. He hadn't used it above a whisper in what felt like days. It might've been days. How long had he been awake? Three, four days? Across the way, Anna stretched.

He cleared his throat. "What are you doing?" he asked her.

"I'm—" she said and stopped. "I was getting ready to clean the kitchen."

Clean the kitchen. Her way of saying she knew he'd been there. That she knew he'd taken the money and Anna. That she knew that he knew every goddamn thing there was to know.

But she couldn't know. Not for sure. She just thought she knew. For all she knew, somebody could've come in there and stole Anna and the money. That was why you couldn't leave the door unlocked, Pam. That was why you couldn't go off and screw Rick's own brother in the middle of the night and leave your baby girl alone to wake from a nightmare about werewolves and crush her windpipe on the crib rail, Pam.

He kept his cool. "Where's Anna?" he said.

She was quiet. That's right. Where's Anna, Pam? Thought you knew, didn't you?

"She's taking a nap. In her room."

His eyes shot to Anna. No, she was still here, sitting up on the couch. That was Anna. Were parts of her back at the trailer, too? Was that how things worked and he just never knew it? Like the streaks? Anna had to be hungry by now. Rick would find her something to eat. There had to be a can of green beans or some-thing in the cupboard. He put his finger to his lips again.

"How's the work going?" Pam asked. "Be out there much longer?"

"Shit," he said. "Operator just came on. We're about to get cut off."

"All right," she said.

All right, she'd said. He hung up.

Rick needed to think. He needed to figure out why the cop was after him. The cop might come back. Rick needed to get him and Anna out of here before the cop came back. He wondered if the cops wanted him for the pills. He'd ditch the pills. But maybe it was the stolen gas. Or Paul's truck.

Paul. He was on his way back. Paul was on his way to Pam. Well, that was fine. That was just fine. Rick would park on the embankment where he did last night. Wait to catch that backdoor son of a bitch on Rick's own front porch.

27 PAM SAT AT THE KITCHEN TABLE, where she'd propped the Snoopy on its feet so he stood at attention instead of lay like a corpse. It was just the two of them. Anna was gone. The money was gone. Rick had just called, he was off in Thedford.

Her brain vibrated with tiny pops and pulses she couldn't keep track of. She wanted to make a list. She wanted to make a list to help her put things in order. But Babe always told her, unless it deals with money, don't put it in writing. That seemed right. That seemed like the right advice right now.

When Pam had first gotten home last night, she'd rushed inside to call Harley at the sheriff's office. She needed to tell him somebody'd driven up behind the Jensen place before she left. Then she walked in and saw the kitchen wrecked and wanted to call him again. She stood there, looking at the bolts and nuts and phone book and flour in the sink, the ratty dish towels unfolded and thrown across the counter. She'd stopped and stood by the phone, listening for any sound in the trailer. But there was only the box fan in the window down the hall. God, she hated that goddamn box fan.

Instead of calling anybody, she'd grabbed the wood-handled knife. The one she used for meat loaf. It wasn't a butcher knife. She didn't own a butcher knife. The thing was more like a machete. She didn't know what it was for. She'd gone down the hall with it clutched in her fist. Then she'd seen the empty crib. The Snoopy.

He lay there with his arms flat, straight at his sides like nobody ever lay on purpose. Coffin arms. He had no mouth and looked waxy. His stomach was concave, meant to hold a bar of soap. It looked scooped out, like it'd been gutted in an autopsy. Pam imagined the opening of *Quincy*, Jack Klugman at the crib's edge, disemboweling the cartoon dog while a line of rookie cops went pale and dropped one by one to the floor.

Her cheeks cramped. Her sternum quivered. She could've cut loose, there all by herself. She could've grinned broad and ghoulish and tittered away. But she hadn't. She'd seen the open drawers in Anna's room. The missing blanket and turtle. And she'd brought Snoopy to the table and sat while the light outside went from the white of the lamppost to the gold-pink of dawn to the scalding yellow it was right now.

The phone hung on the wall, right above her head. There was a good, solid, practical reason not to pick up that phone and call the police. If she did, it wouldn't take fifteen minutes for the incident at Gordon's to fly through town, if it hadn't already. And the man she'd screwed, only a room away from where his mother blew her head off, in the light of day, would surely have no trouble believing Pam was the kind of person who'd chuck Anna down a well. Pam would be the first and only suspect.

And there were also less solid, less practical reasons for not calling. Reasons that might've been just as good but that nobody would get, much less buy.

A drug-deprived nutcase wouldn't break in and steal money armed with a rubber dog bath toy, and a pervert who wanted to have his way with Anna and drop her in a cistern wouldn't have taken her clothes and a turtle and her blanket. Whoever took her wanted her. They wanted her clothed and warm and happy. Or at least content. At least entertained.

Pam stood and walked to the sink. She grabbed the junk

drawer. She put it back on its tracks, dropped the Snoopy inside, and shut it. She wouldn't clean the mess. For one, she couldn't feel her hands or feet. For another, she wasn't sure it was necessary. She wasn't sure what came next.

She picked up the phone.

Babe answered on the fourth ring. She sounded almost human when she answered, when she didn't yet know who was calling. She even sounded kind. Pam held the tone tight in her chest before she spoke. She tried to make small talk, mentioned Rick was off in Thedford. She tried to quip that it was easier cleaning up after only one kid while he was gone, but then her eyes skated across the dusting of flour in the sink. Her voice halted and caught. She was no better at small talk than Babe. Pam asked where Dad was, hoping by some off chance he was there and her mother would hand the phone to him. He wasn't, and Babe wanted to know why Pam was calling.

"We're in a bind," she said, shocked at her ability to say it. Shocked at the level way it came out of her, so sturdy and clean and deep. "Lot rent's due, and we don't have it. Dell Senior can't pay, I guess. Says his money's tied up till next week."

Babe was a clicking silence on the line.

"It'd be a loan till next week," Pam said. She felt bad about that. She had no intention of being here next week. "You know I wouldn't ask."

There was no softness in the words that came next. There was no softness in Babe, so far as Pam knew. But there was a neutrality to them. A sincere neutrality Pam recognized as surprise. "No," Babe said. "I know you wouldn't."

"It's a good amount." Pam wouldn't push it. She wouldn't ask for more than lot rent actually was. "We'd need fifty."

Babe made a short list of numbers under her breath. "Yeah, we can swing it."

Pam's eyes stung at her lower lids. "I don't like to ask."

"I know you don't." There was still no harshness, only a clipped way of putting the conversation to rest. A signal to let it go. Babe said she'd be around the house another hour. After that, she needed to run to town, take care of a few errands. "Come by now, I got a box of kids' clothes left from the church rummage. Arlene Penke thought some might fit Anna. Looks like a few pairs of jeans she'd have to grow into, some shirts. Those might be too small already. Bring her over, try them on. What you can't use I'll give back next year."

"I think—" Pam searched for something. She saw the knife shaped like a machete on the counter. "I've got a meat loaf in the oven. Another forty-five minutes."

"You're cooking meat loaf in the morning?"

Pam spoke, hoping the right words came out. "Figured I'd get it out of the way. Before it gets too hot. Anna won't care it's re-heated. I lucked out. She's not too picky." She forced a laugh. She shouldn't have said Rick was in Thedford. She should've said Rick was home. If she'd said Rick was home, she could've gone over there and said she'd left Anna with him. She could've made up some excuse. She could've said Anna had a cold. That she was taking a nap.

"All right," Babe said with some of her usual impatience creeping back in. "So come by after, about noon. Wanted to get some more cabbage planted before it got too hot, but what's another day, I suppose."

Pam's head felt like the bulbed end of an antenna. Like she could feel all the signals and radio waves passing through the air at once. Everything in front of her looked too close and everything behind her eyes sank. "All right," she managed to get out. "See you then," she said, though she knew she wouldn't. She wouldn't, because she couldn't think of one single excuse for showing up there alone. Not one single explanation for where Anna would be besides with her. She felt the receiver's weight as she rested it in the cradle.

28 WHEN HARLEY WALKED IN FOR HIS SHIFT, he didn't so much ask as loudly state, more to himself than to the somber, bald man in the portable: "Why are you here, Glenn." Harley had been working twelve-, sometimes fourteen-hour nights going on a week straight. The one thing he expected on a Saturday evening was Glenn would be home with Miriam. Harley went to the coffee maker and grabbed the weak, day-old brew. He'd dump it in the bathroom, make new. "Carol get back with the records?" At the sink, he called out, "Could've left a note."

"Don't need Carol or the records," Glenn said.

Harley stepped from the bathroom with the empty coffeepot. "What?"

Glenn's eyes looked faraway and glazed. "The Plymouth," he said. "Belongs to Virginia Reddick."

Harley watched him. Glenn looked grayish. Gray pallor was heart. It wasn't good. "You knew this morning?"

He nodded.

There was something more to Glenn's look than being crest-fallen over the general state of the world. Something other than his usual bleeding-heart sympathy. Snatches of the past few days' conversations littered the air between them. Each was like a pin-prick of light in a constellation waiting to be drawn. When Harley said he'd seen Paul at the home place, Glenn said to tread light. When Harley'd eyed the locust trees in the rearview at the Christiansens', when he'd found the DeKalb hat, Glenn said don't jump straight to Reddick. He never specified which. Glenn's reaction to the quaaludes earlier today—the script was Virginia's, he'd said. And now the Plymouth. Glenn hadn't been doing any weird wishful thinking. Glenn had gone straight for some much weirder worst-case scenario.

"You think she's the one. Virginia."

Glenn didn't look at him. Just nodded.

"Paul lives with her, you know. Has access to her car." Harley remembered the F-250 was nowhere along Main that night at the Avark. In the morning, when Paul called Pam, he'd said it was in Wilton. It could've been. But the old Plymouth was in Knudsen's barn. And that barn wasn't but a mile walk from the Avark. "Don't it seem more likely? Paul?"

"Think that'd be better?" Glenn said. "That boy's all she's got."

More glimmers pierced the air. Glenn flushing those first quaaludes. Glenn being touchy every time Harley pulled Paul over. Glenn wanting to brush off the water tower deal as drunken teenage antics.

Glenn didn't take his eyes off a faraway spot across the room. "Just left her there that night. Burning trash naked. Moved the barrel so she could go on ahead."

Harley wondered about Glenn's pallor. If he should call Wilton for the paramedics.

Glenn kept talking. "I let her be so she could go on down that dark hole she was digging. I just made sure she did it out of everybody's sight."

A heat surged beneath Harley's skin. "All right. So if it is Virginia, which it's not, what do you think? Think if you took the barrel, threw it in your trunk, and drove away, it would've changed everything? Think a night in the drunk tank would've snapped her right out of it?" He reached for the foil in his pocket. He wouldn't smoke one now. Not with Glenn's grayness. "Wouldn't," Harley said sharply. "Likely wouldn't have made one iota difference."

Glenn looked at Harley then, eyes rheumy like June Christiansen's had been. "You believe that." Harley didn't know if it'd been a question or a statement. Glenn looked away again.

"People do what they do," Harley said. "They do what they do for a whole lifetime of reasons. Not any one thing."

"That's all a lifetime is. Whole lot of one things." Glenn's chair scooted against the linoleum tile and his keys jangled. He'd pulled them from where they hooked to his belt. "Change one thing, might change the whole course."

"Yeah, well, you can't know. You can't know, and you can't live your whole life wondering if you'd done one thing more or less, some one tiny thing, everything else would've spun out differently. True or not. You can't go through a life like that." Harley took a steadying breath. "You said yourself we did all we could." Glenn was crossing the room toward the door. "Listen. I'll go by there. Do a welfare check."

"Already did. No sign of her or the car."

"Then I'll keep looking."

Glenn nodded before he pulled the door open and walked out on the landing. The daylight was softening. Air filtered in, cooler than it had been. "That poor goddamn woman."

"Glenn."

"Yeah. I'll see ya." He pulled the door shut behind him.

Harley filled the pot and went to the coffee maker. While it brewed, he absently traced the section lines on a Pickard County plat map framed above it. The map was old, from the 1936 atlas, useless and framed for posterity. Ziske's name hovered above Lucas's and below Jipp's, which was catty-corner to Knudsen's. *I bet you steer clear of all them houses right around the old Lucas place,* Paul had said. Harley read the squares of names westward, right to left, as they rose and fell along the abandoned railroad tracks. Knudsen. Jipp. Ziske. Lucas. Jensen.

The only one still there was Ziske, whose property was separated from the Knudsen place by the county oil. The old man couldn't see or hear worth a damn, but he was still alive. It was something. It was worth checking.

If Ziske was surprised to be on the receiving end of a phone call from the sheriff's department, he didn't sound it. Harley warned he couldn't talk long. "You seen or heard anything out of the ordinary? Since I was out there?"

"I don't know what counts as ordinary and what don't no more. That son of a bitch Logemann finished mowing the Jipp place down yesterday. Sitting in piles all over the place. Bet he'll pick the windiest day of the month to burn off what's left, take us all out. Still say he's the one that burnt that old house, like it weren't no more than clearing trees."

Harley tried to picture the Jipp place gone completely. The property lines you could see in an aerial picture looking like faded scars, fully erased. Harley didn't like Logemann eating up everything only to lose it, either. But for now it was his, and if he wanted to make a living off it, he needed more space to keep up. Nobody could fault him for that. Fault Henry Ford. Fault the commodities market. "Logemann didn't burn down the Jipp place," Harley said. "Have you seen anything? Heard anything?"

"Seen that drunk son of a bitch sneaking along my fence line middle of the night, naked."

A sweeping, like a weak electric current, passed over Harley's skin. He pictured Paul Reddick hanging from the catwalk, lit up in the water tower flood lamps. He saw Virginia glowing in the flames of the burn barrel. "Wasn't Logemann." Harley wished to hell it was. "What are you talking about?"

"Don't know who else'd be up along the property line. And he's a drunk. Assume drunk accounts for the nakedness. That or he got my gas all over his clothes—drained my damn gas tank—Betty tried filling up when she left twenty minutes ago, tank was bone-dry. Son of a bitch wants to burn me in my sleep with my own gas. Even took the two-gallon can from the garage."

The stolen gas can reports. Harley told Ziske to slow the hell down. Harley needed the old man to slow the hell down and say what he saw. In order.

Ziske gave a huff of a breath. Rankled, he started again, voice full of angry composure. "First some car passed on the Schleswig-Holstein. Woke me up. Laid there I don't know how long. Finally went to take a tinkle, if you don't mind, and up towards the Old German, I seen something white. Moving. Couldn't tell what the hell it was. Thought my time was up, want the truth." He cut himself off and barked, "Don't give me any garbage. You see something all white, moving up by the Old German where half your people are planted, you think things. But then I saw it walk, not—Hell," he said, frustrated. "Hell if I know what goblins do, but I don't bet gravel troubles their feet, and this one was having a hell of a time. So I grabbed the Chuckster by the barrel and went on the porch—"

"Christ, Ziske—you can't—"

"Goddamn twenty-two," he barked back. "Peashooter. Thing wouldn't stun a ground squirrel. Took it out there for the noise, get him back on his property. And I didn't shoot it, did I?"

"You ain't said."

"Well, I didn't. I stood there and watched whoever it was—now you're telling me it wasn't Logemann, so I guess some naked gypsy-hobo—cranking my water pump."

"What?"

"My damn water pump, I said. Up by the road. Need it if the power goes out. Power goes out, you know, I got no water. There's progress. Hook it all up to a fuse that can blow—"

"Then what?"

"Then? Took a drink, looked like. Turned around and walked. Direction of Logemann's and your folks'. Right along the Schleswig-Holstein. That back property line."

Carol squawked from the radio across the room.

"What time was it?" Harley had left Pam alone there, at the home place. But this morning he'd seen her car. He'd seen she'd gotten home all right.

"Hell, I don't know. Late, early. Still dark."

Carol squawked again.

"Stay indoors. I'll head over, have a look around."

"Fair warning, I find out whoever stole that gas's been stealing my paper—some naked gypsy-hobo-ghost—I'll get out the goddamn twelve-gauge."

Ziske's paper. The balled-up remnants of newsprint. Doris Luschen's obituary in the supplement, telling everybody who read it exactly when nobody would be at the house. Jack Christiansen's death notice had run in Tuesday's paper. Later that night, Wednesday morning, was the Jipp fire. Granted, the *Post-Gazette*s could've come from anywhere. But Ziske's proximity to the Jipp and Knudsen places made his mailbox awful convenient.

"Did the supplement show?"

"No, and of course that goddamn Gene—"

Carol squawked.

"You hear that?" Ziske demanded. "What the hell's that racket?"

"I gotta go. I'll check it out." Harley hung up.

By the time he got to the radio and said go ahead, Carol was irate. Babe Reinhardt had called. She wouldn't say why. She'd asked who was on duty, and when Carol told her Harley, Babe said get his ass over to their place now.

He sprinted down the stairs to the cruiser. He needed to get out to the old Schleswig-Holstein road. He needed to get there while there was still some light, which was sinking. Babe's call had priority. But he'd make it fast and hope whatever the hell she wanted had nothing to do with what he feared it did. He couldn't see how it would. Not unless Pam went and told the woman herself.

He sped that way with a twist in his gut. Harley didn't know if the breed of women Babe Reinhardt belonged to were everywhere. He didn't know everywhere. But they were as native to Pickard County and the surrounding hills and valleys as leadplant. If they didn't know you, you were suspect, and if they did, they were very slow to warm. The coldness wasn't caution, since caution meant fear, and women like Babe had no fear. What they had was the unshakable conviction you were about to prove their worst expectations right. They sized you up and waited for your follow-through. And Harley was fairly sure he'd followed through.

He wasn't eager pulling in the gravel drive, and he was less eager when he saw Red's pickup wasn't there. Harley needed to get in, get out.

She was on the front porch when he pulled up. He left the engine running, the door wide open. He avoided her sharp watch as he walked to the base of the steps.

"Harley," she said.

He felt like a field mouse in a hawk's sights, and there was no time for pleasantries. "Heard you called. Carol didn't say why."

"She don't need to know. She's got enough dirt on everybody as it is, back from listening in on the party line." Carol was switchboard operator before coming on as a dispatcher. "Besides, it's probably nothing," she said.

"Doubt you'd call about nothing."

She took a loud, hard breath through her nose and said, "It's our youngest. Pam."

He toed a shard of limestone gravel. He held his hips with the webs of his hands and glanced at the windbreak. He wanted a cigarette.

"She called earlier. Something wasn't right. Then she was supposed to come by hours ago and didn't. She won't answer the phone, so I drove over. Her car's outside and the front door's locked. She never locks it. Still thinks she lives out here."

A dark, unformed thought shot through him. But he'd seen the Nova. He'd seen she'd gotten home safe. He'd told himself she had. "I'll check it out." He turned back toward the Fury's open door.

"There's more." The words were laced with a reedy warning tone. "She asked for money. Fifty dollars."

Harley didn't know how to take it. "What do you make of it?"

"She's got some pride. She doesn't ask for money."

"Could be all it is," he said. "She felt bad asking, now she's avoiding you. I'll go by there, check it out."

She rushed the words that came next like she was irritated having to say them. "Helen Nelson says Pam left her girl in the upstairs of Gordon's. A few days ago. Tried to drive off." She added just as quick, "Before you go jumping guns—it's Helen Nelson. Went in once for a pot lid, she kept me there an hour. Seen some show about cults. Convinced everybody was a Moonie."

"What do you think?"

"What do I think?" Babe's voice bored in, direct. "I think Pam's rash." She stopped, and when she started again, she was more tentative. The sound of Babe being tentative unnerved him more than the boring in. "I need to ask you something that doesn't go past this porch." She waited for his acknowledgment, his agreement to terms.

"All right," he said.

"If Pam thought she was in a tight enough spot, there's no telling what she'd do. I like to think she wouldn't hurt that girl. Lord knows she's too squeamish to bleed a chicken. Herself, I don't know," she said. "I guess I don't know what to watch for. When it comes to that."

Harley studied Babe. He wasn't looking for whether or not she knew anything about him and Pam. He was looking for confirmation of what was implied. That Babe thought he'd have some kind of insight. Know some telltale signs a person was about to eat a load of buckshot.

In truth, he'd gauged every single person he'd met over the last forty years for that inclination. And every once in a while he thought he saw it. That someone was the type to end it. He thought he saw it on Paul that night at the water tower. But you looked hard enough, long enough, you saw there wasn't one type.

There wasn't any connection between one person doing it and another. Every time was different. Each and every time. In the end, for all the gauging and watching, Harley didn't know what to look for any better than Babe did. In the end, all Harley knew was it was a thing a person could do.

She watched him, waiting. Her eyes were as earnest, as free of judgment as he'd ever seen them or suspected he'd ever see them again. Not unless he was the one to take the call, the one who'd one day find her at the base of a cellar's steps. The look cramped in his throat. He hated to do it, but he shook his head.

"No," she said, almost too quiet to hear. "No, didn't figure. Guess it's the sort of thing where signs pop up after. Trick of hindsight."

"Seems that way," he said. "Lot of times."

She gripped the pillar of the porch like she was holding it upright. She rubbed the wood with her thumb.

"I'll head over now." He walked back to the open cruiser door. "Let you know what's going on soon as I can."

"Harley," she said. Her eyes stayed on him, still searching but no longer earnest. They were guarded. Scrutinizing. "You know where to go, then?"

He looked up at her. Blank, he hoped. "Figured I'd radio Carol. Get the address."

She gave a quick, sharp nod. "Just see they're all right." She kept her eyes on him, face setting in a hardened sag. She dropped her hold on the porch pillar, crossed her arms against her chest, and watched him as he left.

He smoked and bottomed the needle on the Fury. Whatever Pam might've done, or might've been doing, he'd been a party to it. He thought of Glenn's grayness. That burn barrel. One thing

Harley had always been good for was not being a party to much. That'd been why his marriage fell apart. He hadn't been a party to it.

Out at Park Meadows, her Nova sat in what should've been a yard. After his first knock, he felt the knob. Locked, like Babe said. In what light was left of the day, he walked the perimeter of brush and dirt. He passed a spare, half-buried cinder block and a cut-up garden hose. He saw nothing through the windows. They were set too high to see anything besides drapes. He rounded the side and walked up the mesh steps again. They were the same as the ones at the sheriff's office portable. He supposed that was all a trailer was, a portable. He thought of Dell Senior, bloodshot and smiling those squared-off white teeth, selling what amounted to slipshod shipping containers with windows. Telling people the things were practically houses. Houses they'd have to pay to move or leave behind if the lot rent spiked or the land ever sold out from under them.

He knocked again, harder, and called out her name. After he said it, he knew his tone sounded too familiar. Thankfully, none of the neighbors had come outside when the cruiser pulled up. Most were probably scrambling for some nook to stash their pot in.

When he called out again, he said he was Harley Jensen, sheriff's deputy. The formality brought a blush of warmth to his skin. He pictured her white hips rising from the floorboards. He tried to hold the image there without it lapsing, without seeing the bottom of a cane-seat chair or gray dirt on the soles of stilled feet. But even as he saw Pam naked and willowy, he felt the night-blue glow of the kitchen at his back. He pounded the wood hard with the side of his fist. He told her he needed her to answer.

Silence. *Pretty sure we're all headed for worse*, she'd said last night.

He pounded again. A V of slim wood splintered in the flimsy veneer of the door. It pierced the meat of his pinkie. He kept pounding. Told her if she didn't answer, he was coming in.

Then the pat of footsteps pulsed the porch beneath his boots. A tension running up from his shoulders to his clenched teeth gave.

She opened the door enough to fit the width of her head. She stared out at him, lips parted in what he supposed was justified shock at him standing on the landing, wrecking her door.

"Is he here?" He said it as low as he could muster while he caught his breath.

She shook her head and blinked, like she was blinking away a daze. He didn't know if he believed her. He thought he'd seen that look once, when Darlene Wulf called about her drunk, no-account prick of a husband. Darlene had signaled. She'd pointed with a twitch. She'd darted her eyes to say the man was right next to her. Harley had waited till her grip relaxed, so she hardly touched the wood. Then he'd kicked the door and knocked the man senseless. Harley watched for any sign now from Pam. For any twitch. Any dart of the eyes.

"Your mother called," he said and watched her. "Says you were supposed to come out. Says you didn't sound right on the phone. Says she came out here and you wouldn't answer."

She looked distracted. "I'm all right." She appeared to will it true, to get her bearings. "You shouldn't be here, probably."

That relieved him some, at least of the worry her husband was within earshot. "I broke your door a bit."

"Good." She gave a short, tired smile. "It'll match everything else around here, then."

"Any reason you're avoiding Babe?"

"I believe you've met her."

What tension was left loosened. He breathed. His glance traced down her neck, where a tendon rose. Her bony shoulders in her thin T-shirt leaned in slightly toward him. He remembered what Babe had said about the daughter, about Pam leaving her at Gordon's. "Just you and the girl, then?"

Her eyes flitted to the space behind his left bicep. He turned to look. There was nobody. She must've been paranoid about who was watching. Listening in.

"Got her down for the night," she said.

He stood, not knowing what to say. "Don't suppose I should come in."

She looked at him then. She looked at him fully, first one eye, then the other. Her lips tightened. The edges curled a bit, in a strange, brief grin that left as soon as it came. The girl was fine. Pam wanted him to come in. That much was clear.

"Somebody was there last night," she said, barely above a whisper. "After you left. Somebody pulled up behind the house."

Ziske's naked hobo-ghost, likely one of Pam's own in-laws. Harley thought about telling her. He decided she'd be safer not knowing. "I'm headed that way, soon as I'm sure you're all right."

She said she was.

"I need to know it," he said. "I need to know you're all right."

She smiled again, not happily, and shifted her weight from one skinny leg to the other.

He had half a mind to reach out, take her hip in his palm. "Be a good idea if you stayed in tonight. Stay out of harm's reach." The streetlamp behind him flickered on. "I mean it. At least tonight."

"I will."

"I need to go," he said.

"I know." She looked hard into his eyes again. First one, then the other. He wanted to ask her again was she really all right, but he didn't. He'd get this thing taken care of tonight, get whoever he needed to—likely Paul—hauled in and processed for the thefts and arson. After that, he'd call. Make sure she stayed all right.

"There'll be other nights," he said.

She looked down past his waist and nodded. Then she shut the door.

29

BELLY DOWN ON THE BRUSHY EMBANKMENT by Evelyn Mueller's mobile home, Rick watched and waited for that backdoor son of a bitch Paul to show up on Rick's own front porch. Rick hadn't meant to bring the shotgun. Once it was clear Dell Junior's streaks and Anna wouldn't stay put in the pickup, he'd meant to leave the gun in the rack. But he kept it safe off to one side. Anna lay on the other. Meanwhile, Dell Junior zigged and zagged all over the place. Kept saying over and over again in a low, twangy buzz like a mouth harp but deeper: *hambone-hambone-hambone-hambone*. Irritating. Didn't make any sense. Drove Rick about nuts.

Dell Junior could've taken a lesson from Anna. She was cranky, all right, but she was quiet. Rick told her they had to be real quiet to surprise Uncle Paul. She'd had to pee once, and he'd shimmied with her down the hill a ways. He'd shown her how to go outside best he could. He got her to squat so the stream went downhill and didn't get on her shoes. If she'd been a boy, it would've been a father-son moment. But it was the sort of thing a girl's mother should've shown her. How to pee outside. There had to be some trick to it he didn't know.

A streak of Dell Junior's striped shoulder flew through the edge of Rick's vision. Rick swatted. Told him to shush. Anna swatted, too, giggling. Rick told her to shush. He wished Mom were here, but she didn't seem to be. He'd bet Mom could give a good honk, shut Dell Junior the hell up.

Anna said she was thirsty. Soon, Rick told her. She was quiet again. They waited. She scratched and fidgeted in the grass.

When he heard tires rolling down the main road, Rick put a hand on Anna's back. She stilled.

The long front end of a police cruiser, a Fury, pulled past the edge of Evelyn Mueller's trailer. The cop. The same cop that was at Mom's place earlier. He parked, went up the steps, and knocked. He came back down and circled the trailer. The hose. He'd see the pieces of hose Rick had left when he cut the tube for siphoning. The cop went back up the steps and beat the door. He yelled out Pam's name. Then he said who he was. Said he was a sheriff's deputy. He said she needed to answer the door. He kept pounding.

What was he yelling Pam's name for? Wasn't he looking for Rick?

Rick saw her. Not the whole of her. Only her knee. It bent white and thin from inside the trailer. His blood pumped hot through his limbs. His whole body hurt. Felt sick with his own blood. It was all he could do to stay put.

Anna asked if it was a policeman. Rick nodded. He put a finger to his mouth. She whispered, asked why Mama called the policeman.

Rick thought hard. Why would Pam call the policeman?

Of course. Rick would be damned. Rick would be goddamn. That was it.

Pam called the cops. Because Anna was missing. Of course she did. But why hadn't she said anything on the phone, then? Why'd she lie about Anna being there when she wasn't?

Dell Junior's shirtsleeve swept through Rick's line of sight and *hambone-hambon*ed.

Rick swatted. Shushed him. Anna swatted, too, but didn't giggle.

Dell Junior. The shit with Mom being missing. That was why Pam didn't say anything. She knew what it'd do to Rick. What it'd do to him if Anna went missing, too. Pam couldn't put him through that. She'd been protecting him.

The sick ache of pumping blood lightened a touch, then a touch more. And then that feeling like light radiating through him came again. She'd fucked up. Pam had fucked up, and that'd have to be dealt with. But something was there still, on her part. She still felt something for him. Which meant there was something to salvage.

He wanted to stand right up. He wanted to call over and wave. Show them that, here—Anna was right here. Anna was fine. Pam had fucked his brother, but everything was going to turn out fine. He could almost march down there, squeeze Pam off her feet till her back cracked. But there was that damn siphoning hose. And Paul's stolen truck. Rick would wait.

What Pam and the cop said was too low for him to hear, which seemed impossible. Everything else was so loud. Loud like the chug of an engine. The rattle of siding and skirting.

The van. He heard the van. It passed on the highway behind him. Down on the other side of the embankment. He waited for it to slow and make the turn into the court. He waited for the roll of tires on the main road and held his breath. The sound didn't come. But it'd been Paul, all right. Rick knew the sound of his own van. It'd been headed east. Rick would deal with him in a bit. Right now he'd focus on that bare knee in the doorway.

It'd disappeared. Pam's knee. Rick blinked. The knee was gone. His heart stuttered. The door was closed. She hadn't disappeared. She'd only closed the door.

The cop walked to his cruiser. He made a U-turn and headed

back to the main road. Rick held Anna low to the ground until he was sure the cop was gone. Then Rick stood.

Let's go, he told Anna. Change of plan. They'd surprise Uncle Paul later. Right now, they'd go surprise Mama. Anna asked if she could say surprise. Like a party. Like on TV. He said sure. Sure, she could yell surprise. He could've yelled it himself right now. He took Anna's hand tight in his own. Too tight, Anna whimpered, and he tried to loosen his hold a bit. He remembered the shotgun and bent, grabbed it. They walked down the embankment. Dell Junior streaked to and fro like he was celebrating. Like he was fireworks. Streaks of light. The sky was deepening blue, the stars starting to shine. Rick felt weightless. Pam had fucked up. And that'd be dealt with. But there was something more important now. Something he could salvage.

The door was locked. Good. She'd finally figured out she needed to lock the damn door.

30

PAM WAS AT THE HALLWAY'S EDGE when the work boots clomped heavy up the steps. The van hadn't pulled up. She would've heard the van pull up, the shudder and rattle when he shut the thing off. It hadn't pulled up. But those were his boots. Those were his boots on their way inside, where Anna wasn't. And Pam still couldn't be sure whether or not Paul had told Rick about Harley. Even if he hadn't, even if Rick knew nothing about her having an affair or her leaving Anna at Gordon's that day, he was sure to find out once he called the cops to say Anna was gone. And none of it would play in Pam's favor.

Her purse was loaded with the change she'd dumped from their "savings account," the old Butter-Nut can by the bed. Mostly nickels. A lot of pennies. The strap skidded down the bend of her elbow to her wrist, where she clenched the tied-off end of a pillowcase. She'd stuffed it with two changes of clothes, her birth control, some tampons, a toothbrush, a motel soap, and the knife shaped like a machete. The blade was so dull it hardly sliced through meat loaf, but it looked intimidating. She hadn't even needed to wrap it in one of the towels that were no good for anything else, but she had.

The knob clicked twice—back, forth.

Before the key scraped the lock, she slipped from her sandals, snatched them up, and moved soundlessly down the hall to the back door.

They'd never used the back door once Rick finished putting up paneling, so there were no stairs. She opened it and dropped her things to the dirt. His boots crossed the floor at the trailer's other end. He called her name.

She sat, then slid down, bare foot landing on a nest of burrs. She gritted her teeth, reached up, and pushed the bottom edge of the door as far as she could with her fingertips. She balanced on one foot and pinched two burrs from the thin skin of her arch. She stepped into her shoes and gathered up her things. The bags whispered against the weeds.

She hadn't relocked the door behind her. He might not notice. She slipped around to the trailer's short end and flattened her back against the skirting and siding. She steadied her breath, the hammering in her chest. He called her name.

The plan was to drive till the Nova ran out of gas. Get as close to the interstate as she could. When the tank dried up, she'd hitch a ride east to Chicago or west to Cheyenne or south to a place with a name like Nacogdoches or Tishomingo or Natchez. She'd say she had a sister there. Some family emergency. And if she had to ride with a trucker, she'd keep one hand in the pillowcase, fingers folded around the wood handle of that knife.

Her big brass P key ring had shifted in her pocket when she made the jump down from the back door. It dug into her groin.

If she started the Nova now, he'd come running out and want to know what was going on. He'd want to know where Anna was, and Pam would have to say why she was carrying a pillowcase full of toiletries and a knife shaped like a machete and why she'd dumped all the pennies and nickels from the Butter-Nut can into her purse. He'd run back inside and call the cops, call Harley, and that'd be the end of it. That right there would be the end of everything.

No. She wouldn't have to tell him anything. She'd start the Nova, he'd come running out, and she'd gun it.

She felt his steps at her back. They vibrated through the thin wall, through the insulation, through the siding molded to look like clapboard. She heard the knob of the back door turn. As it sighed open, she darted around the front of the trailer toward the car, toward the road.

Surprise!

Anna's yell, the squeal that followed, knocked the wind from Pam's stomach. She stopped cold, not ten paces from the Nova's door. Anna stood on the landing, hands cupped over her mouth with excitement.

Surprise, Mama, she said again, this time a little annoyed Pam hadn't reacted the way she should've.

Pam stood where she was, purse heavy in one hand, pillowcase dangling from the other. She closed her open mouth. It'd gone dry. Her head was light. Dizzy. Like the whole world had tilted.

Behind Anna, past the open storm door that swung loose against the railing, he surfaced from the dark pit of the trailer entrance. He stepped into the light of the lamppost.

He looked wrong. The shape of his limbs, the worn and patched jeans streaked with silver swaths of roof coating, the now-thick Fu Manchu in a sea of stubble—those were all Rick's. She understood they were his. But nothing else was right. She couldn't put this body and Rick together.

His T-shirt and jeans sagged. His weather-worn skin looked drained of blood so the tan was a yellow cast. His lips were too pale. His shags of hair whipped out every which way in sharp-ended coils and his eyes weren't his eyes. They were wild, glassy.

There'd been a time she hadn't known Rick's eyes. When all she saw in them was that yearning and need and that mystique that'd course through her. Those eyes hadn't looked like these.

He had a shotgun. The barrel tipped out and up at the sky at an angle. His finger rested across the double trigger. Not on the guard.

"Surprise, Mama," he said, like he was choked up. Like he was a soldier just come home from a war.

They were waiting, he and Anna, for her reaction. For her to speak. She said the only thing she could think of, the only thing that came to her. "Surprise." It was barely loud enough for her to hear.

He took Anna's hand, said, "Come on, now," like none of this was a big deal. He said it like this was any other moment, like they were headed to a drive-in or a visit to Babe and Red's place. He patiently led her down the first step.

Pam wished her own legs to move. To carry her the short distance to the car. But her joints fused in place. She didn't know what this meant. She didn't know what any of this added up to. Rick, Anna, they'd been gone. Pam had been about to be gone. But now they were all here again and he looked as crazy as she felt except he had a gun.

When he stood right in front of her, he spoke. "I know," he said. "What you did."

The van wasn't anywhere. That was right. She hadn't heard it pull up. But he was here. Had he been out here the whole time? When Harley came by? He must've pieced it together. Or Paul told him. Maybe Rick had been the one who was there last night. The one who'd pulled in behind the Jensen place.

"Okay." Her voice scraped against her throat.

"We've just got to make things right." He was measured, like he was holding back. She couldn't tell what.

"Okay." She sucked a breath and searched his eyes. For something familiar enough to make her feel her legs again. To root her feet to the dirt beneath her. Even if it was the misery and need that always wrung her out, that always reminded her of that barn cat at her folks' place who'd lain splayed on the hay and dirt while Pam thumbed the cooling strip of fur between his ears. He'd stared up, body limp, eyes fixed on her with some need he couldn't say. Some need she couldn't do shit about.

She'd take that. She'd take that look right now if it meant she could feel her legs again. But that look wasn't there. She didn't know what was.

For the first time, he glanced down and saw the pillowcase.

"Some clothes," she said. "Soap. Tampons." If he knew, he knew. Maybe he'd see it was no use. Maybe he'd say, *Well, go on, then, I guess. Be on your way. Get.*

Rick nodded. She couldn't tell if what she'd said had registered. She couldn't tell what he'd made of it, if anything at all. He swatted at the air in front of him, at some moth or gnat Pam couldn't see. The gun slipped against his side, double barrel falling dead even with her chest. "We just got to make it right," he said again and propped the stock in the bend of his elbow. He looked down at Anna and back up at Pam. "Come on, now," he said again, voice too gentle. He gestured with the shotgun, nudged its aim in the direction of the far hill, between the trailers.

She didn't try to run. She didn't know if she needed to. She walked ahead of him, bags heavy, shoulders sagging with their weight. Every few steps, the smooth metal barrel brushed the thin hairs of her arm. A hard beat pulsed through her chest and her back. She couldn't tell if the beat was from her feet landing against the dirt or from her heart pumping. As they passed Evelyn Mueller's place, a memory nagged at her till she remembered. It was a time Babe told her about a man forced to dig his own grave before he was murdered. It was in the paper. "Can you imagine?" Babe had asked.

Pam thought she could. She thought she could imagine the weight of the shovel, the grain of the handle in her palms and fingers, the rise and pinch of blisters as the smell of parting soil brought on a flood of small, forgotten things. But if that was what was happening here, if Pam was being led to her own grave, it was nothing like the dread and the weight and the flood of memories she'd imagined. What was happening here was nothing momentous. It was matter-of-fact. Pam supposed that made sense. She supposed it made sense that the brain had a switch. That it turned itself off, let the body be just body when things got to be too much.

When they reached Paul's pickup, parked up on the road closest to the highway, she didn't ask why Rick had it. She glanced in the ridged pickup bed for a spade. There was nothing. The three of them walked around to the passenger side first, where he opened the door for Anna and helped her in. Pam was next. He shut the door, rounded the front end, and got in the driver's side.

The gun was propped between his legs, aimed toward his forehead and the ceiling. She didn't tell him to move it. He did anyway, so it was pinned between his leg and the driver's-side door. He swatted the air again, at the space between his face and the steering wheel. "Yeah, all right," he said, pinched, irritated. She didn't know who he'd said it to.

"What?" she asked.

"Dell Junior. Some hambone-hambone shit."

She checked Anna. Watched for any sign of alarm. The girl looked like an old, dour, shrunken woman. Her head craned upward to try and see above the dash. She swatted, like Rick had, said, Shh, now.

"That's right," Rick said and started the pickup. He whipped it into reverse. The truck heaved backward and stopped. He put it in drive. It jumped forward, and the grille knocked over the Bowmans' trash can with a clatter. "Shit—Bowman." He gunned it.

She gripped the door's armrest. She didn't want to know, she thought, but she asked, "Where we going?"

The blacks of his eyes flared at her. They were too big. "You know better than me. I don't know where the hell you meet him." The pickup hurtled toward the main road. "Heard him headed east on the highway." He made the turn sharp enough that one side of her went weightless. "You both got to know. You both got to know a person can't go and do what you did." He made the turn onto the highway without looking. She held the armrest. She tensed to keep from flying toward him. He gunned it against the pavement. The back end fishtailed. "Heard him headed this way. Need to tell me where to turn."

If Rick didn't know where to go, he hadn't been the one at the Jensen place last night. So Pam knew that much. The tires rolled on the pavement with a steady static. She needed to stall. She needed to think. At the first gravel road past the trailer park, she told him to take a right. He did, muttering. Swatting. When they reached the next road, her head wasn't any clearer. It was vacant. Empty. She picked left this time.

He slowed enough to take the curve without rolling. The

pickup fishtailed again. He hit the gas and out of nowhere, he switched off the headlights. She didn't scream. She didn't know what to scream. He drove, fast. So fast it felt like hurtling through space, like speeding up but also not moving at all. They were floating, disconnected.

"There. You see that?" he said. Pam gripped the vinyl of the armrest. It was cracked. The broken, cracked plastic sliced her skin. Ahead, headlights filled the air past a hill like mist. He shouted above the wind through the cab and the roar of the engine. "You know what they're counting on, Pam? People in that car? You know what makes things work?" He leaned forward into the wheel. His pale, sallow skin was the only thing glowing besides the distant lights. "The unspoken promise I'm not out here hauling ass with no—"

Her arm shot across the dark, elbow grazing Anna's forehead. The last joints of Pam's fingertips caught and curled on the wheel.

He smacked at her grasp and flipped the lights on. "I'm not gonna goddamn do it, Pam. I'm trying to make a point. That's the difference between you and me. I hold up my end."

The haze ahead was gone. The car must've turned.

She felt her legs, her arms, with the ache and tremble that come after swerving to miss an animal in the road.

In the dim light from the speedometer, his nose flared and his lips tightened. His chin puckered. That was familiar. So was the way the sight burned at the top of her stomach. The look was what he did when he pouted. His mouth tightened and his chin screwed up in that pucker. It was a twenty-four-year-old's version of a pout his own toddler was too old to pull.

In the same dashboard light, she saw his jeans. Around his

pocket and lap, what she'd taken for swaths of silver roof coating wasn't silver. It was white. White dust. From the flour he'd dumped in the kitchen.

He'd taken Anna. He'd taken their money.

The whole thing was a goddamn tantrum. Great big babies, her mother had said. Babe was right again. Great big, helpless, fucking babies. Well, Pam was tired. Pam was too tired to be a good mama.

Her words came as low and steady as when she'd asked Babe for the money. This time they came harder, colder. "Guess this is where I step up?" she said. "Where I talk you down?"

He didn't answer. He swatted again.

"You think you can use that gun?"

"Damn hambone-hambones," he said.

"What you ever shot in your life, Rick? Some BBs? At some tin cans on a stump?" For a breath, she pictured him. A kid lying in the grass outside that ramshackle little place of his mother's, a Daisy aimed at an empty Coke bottle. She felt a squeeze in her chest. A squeeze she'd let wring her out too many times, for too long. Pam was not his goddamn mama. He was not her baby boy.

"All right," she said. If that was where he wanted to go, that was where she'd take him. Straight to Harley. "Make a left toward the Bowl. The Jensen place."

31

IT WAS DARK WHEN HARLEY PULLED behind the home place. He'd taken the highway from the west and made a left at the blind intersection on County Road K, where the windbreak shielded the house and barn from view. Where the backyard ended, he stopped on the old Schleswig-Holstein road, the one the county newly named "15," and stood one foot from the cruiser. He shone the spotlight down the low-maintenance ruts that ran along the rear property lines of his folks' place and Ziske's spread, hoping the naked white apparition would turn out to be just that, something the light bled straight through, something no bullet could graze. Some work of imagination from a half-asleep, half-blind old man.

Not even a pair of yellow eyes flashed from the brush. The glow of his side lamp washed across the back of the home place's barn, the grass, the steps to the door they'd always used, the root cellar that, from just the right angle, looked like a portal into something else. From here, the illusion didn't work. From here, the clay sloped into the earth as clear as could be.

He swept the lamp toward the windbreak. The light skimmed where the pile of splintered buckboard wagon wood should've been, where the pile had been stacked as long as he could remember.

The busted-up planks were lower. As if they'd been shifted, some of them scavenged.

Harley shut off the lamp and grabbed the flashlight from the bench seat. He scanned the grass before each step, watching for stray burrows and dens in the dirt. As he neared the windbreak, he saw half the woodpile was no longer stacked. It'd been scattered out, warped and rotted boards laid edge to edge like a shoddy raft.

He rounded them, slow, and saw a gaping darkness. A hole. A grave, he thought first, till he stepped nearer. Its squared-off edges were lined with logs and mortared rocks. Leading down into the earth was a crude, round-rung ladder fashioned from sawed-off tree limbs.

A cellar. Where the splintered wagon boards had been piled as long as Harley could remember, there'd been a cellar.

Harley knelt. He should've called out, he knew, should've announced his presence. But he had no wind in him. He gripped the edge of the hole and shone his light beneath.

He scanned the small room. On the packed dirt floor were trinkets. Part of a child's train set, a locomotive engine forged from metal. A dusty chrome rocket. A deck of playing cards, coated in dust. A small stack of paper. It was comic books. A ball and jacks. A toy top. And toward the edge of the space, where the floor met the wall, ghostly white ropes, roots of tall grass and the windbreak's trees, crooked downward like strands of wiry hair. They pointed to a mess of darkened burlap. Part of it lay flat against the dirt. The rest was pulled back, crumpled against the wall like a discarded shroud. A few sparse coils of black curls lay at one end. Nearby was a snatch of striped fabric, dried and decayed like a dead leaf. Harley saw it was part of a shirt—the rest of it lay neatly folded in the corner, atop a pair of dirty jeans and a child's pair of sneakers.

He pushed himself upward, out of the darkness, to catch a breath. He braced his palms on his thighs. The flashlight dropped to lie at his side, bleeding across the grass and rotted wood.

Ole Braasch knew only the one floor plan, Ziske said. Harley felt the home place at his back. A hundred yards, give or take. A second cellar, just like the one at the Lucas place. Just like the one Rollie Asher had been filling with a spade that day.

Eighteen years ago, a pickup with a dead boy's body in the bed turned west on the highway from the Lucas place, the place Rollie lived in, the place Ole Braasch built identical to this one, right down to the nail for the outhouse paper. And surely Rollie knew that. Ziske would've told him if he hadn't seen it plainly himself. The pickup headed in the direction of the looping Wakonda, but it hadn't stopped at the creek. It'd passed over and driven right here.

When Harley could stand, he did. He left the pit as it was, yawning open at the night. He walked to the cruiser and slid down in the seat.

He backed down the Schleswig-Holstein to where it met County Road K, then drove toward the front of the house, where he hoped the door would be shut like it always was. He pulled to the end of the gravel, to the blind intersection with the highway. He would've liked to stay there, at that blind intersection, not see or know any more about any of it, but he couldn't.

He made the turn and pulled into the overgrown drive. The front door was shut. No red F-250 parked in front of the barn. What was in the yard, perpendicular to the porch, was a black Econoline van that'd seen better days. The side read REDDICK MOBILE HOME REPAIR.

Harley trained the spotlight on the windshield. No one.

The only person Harley knew drove the van was Paul's brother. He and Harley didn't know each other. They'd passed on the highway from time to time, each raising an index finger in acknowledgment. Harley's face heated. It was guilt he felt. Not for sleeping with Pam but for the ruin it'd no doubt brought.

Harley drifted the lamp back and forth, level across the property. He killed the engine and unsnapped his holster break. He stayed put and listened. The only sounds were crickets and a lone cicada's buzz.

"Reddick," he called through the open cruiser window. It felt wrong, using the name to mean anyone but Paul.

"Jensen," came parroted back, cutting through the night and distance from somewhere high up. Harley swore it had the same unshakable calm that always made his teeth grit. But he'd heard something like it in the voice of Dell Senior. Maybe it ran in the family.

He tilted the beam upward. On the porch roof below the second-story window, Paul sat half reclined. He was clothed, at least. He wore the T-shirt with the sexless white angel either plummeting or rising. It reminded Harley of the flames at the Knudsen place, the embers like shooting stars headed the wrong direction. Paul didn't flinch at the light. He was propped back on his elbows, legs stretched out, boots crossed at the ankle. He reached up, waved, sank back on both elbows again.

Harley slipped the .38 from the holster and held it. "Where is he?"

"Need to be more specific."

"Your brother."

"Which?"

Harley didn't answer.

"If you're worried about the live one, rest assured, you diddling his wife is low on my list of current concerns. But to answer your question, I don't know. Somewhere with my pickup."

"Your gun, too?"

"Shitting your britches, ain't you. I didn't tell him, Harley. About the diddling. I also doubt he's a great shot."

Paul told partial truths, but he wasn't prone to lying outright. Harley slid the .38 back in its holster and left the thumb break loose. He unthreaded a smoke. "Come on down."

"Feet first?"

"Don't care." The lighter clanked open, rasped, but only sparked. It was out of fluid. He pulled a book of matches from the glove box.

"Yeah, you do." Paul smiled with his head turned partly away, coy. "Why, though—there's the quandary. I got a theory."

"You got a few."

"Heard of projection? Where what you got inside's all you see outside?"

Less out of courtesy than not wanting to look at Paul's face, Harley dropped the spotlight a hair.

"Don't go feeling persecuted," Paul said. "It's all anybody can see, probably, their own frames of reference." Behind him, one of the windows was open. The split-apart shade was still pulled. The tears in it left sharp, dark gaps. He'd come out through their room. The room with the chifforobe and the mattress that still sagged with his parents' weight. "Ever stop and study the way you live, Harley? No family. No friends. Awake when the rest the world's asleep. Think about it. Your one job? Keep the proverbial peace. Make sure this person over here don't mess with that person over there."

"Seems you've given this some thought. Think that indicates a fixation?"

"You extricate yourself. Keep disentangled," he said. "Come

on—you know where I'm going with this. You seen enough crime scenes to know there's more than one route to self-annihilation. All it takes is not living."

"Deep."

"Then you look at everybody else, see that same thing. Same propensity. But all you're seeing is you. And maybe, Harley, all you really need to do is just lighten the fuck up."

Harley eyed the barn's closed double doors. If there was no old Plymouth in the barn, no F-250, he might've had only the one Reddick to deal with.

"I'm getting out," Harley called up. Paul shrugged. The cruiser door opened with its loud pop, and something behind Paul, something in the room, fluttered white. It could've been the torn shade, though Harley hadn't felt any wind. He left the Fury's door open, nerves too worked to hear the pop a second time as it closed. He watched the darkness of the window. There was no more movement. He left the headlamps and spotlight on and kept the .38 within reach as he stepped from the cruiser. "What brings you here this time? Still looking for something?"

"Nah. Found that a while ago."

Harley took the few strides toward the barn.

"Speaking of finds, you hear they're digging up rhino bones, not twenty miles from where we speak?"

Harley ignored him. He slid open the left door. The Plymouth's taillight and flattened fin gleamed back at him.

"Rhino bones paints an awful big picture, you know it? Dinosaurs got offed, what, two hundred million—some years ago? Give or take? They say these rhinos died not twelve million years back. Mass extinction. Buried just deep enough a hard rain cut the bones loose. A hard rain and ten foot between us and twelve million years, Harley. This shit's transient. Hell, take this house. Here one minute, next it won't be."

"That a confession?"

"Just fact."

Harley didn't need to ask but did. "This your mom's car?"

"Blue Plymouth? Fifty-seven?"

"That'd be it."

Paul took a heavy, dramatic breath. "Mother," he hollered. The word raised the hairs on Harley's neck. "You been found out."

Harley stayed rooted where he was. He listened. No answer came. Even the cicada quit buzzing. The rich tang of dirt and hay in the barn smelled damp despite the dry spell.

Paul said in a loud stage whisper, "She's got what you'd call 'selective hearing.'"

Harley slid the barn door shut. "You make that mess out back?"

"Nah, that was her. I warned her it was trespassing, but she's willful."

Harley didn't know what the best-case scenario was. If Paul was some kind of Norman Bates or if Virginia was really the one. The one who'd torched the clothes in the houses, the one who'd scattered the buckboard planks.

"Granted, I warned her the *letter* of the law. I didn't tell her not to break it," Paul said. "You want to know why, Harley?"

"I got a feeling you'll say either way."

"Paradoxically, the reason law's there to begin with. To protect autonomy." The cicada buzzed again. A few others chimed in. They buzzed like a chorus between verses. "Basic, human, goddamn liberty."

"Get the hell down," Harley said.

"Life, you lose one way or the other. Property? Luck of the draw. Which means all we really got is the right to roam around till we die. Or till somebody like you comes along, locks us up for our own safety or the safety of others. Till we die."

Harley had that urge to grab Paul by the Adam's apple again, shake the voice from him. "That why you dared the Ferguson girl to jump at the quarry? Concerned about her liberty? Her ability to roam around?"

He scoffed. "Sure. Double-dog dared her, and plop." Paul looked out past the spotlight into the dark. Whatever he saw, if anything at all, seemed to sober him. "Nah. Jeannie didn't want to roam around anymore. All I said was she had a right not to. You want to talk about Vern Sawyer next? Vern wanted a chance to prove himself. I gave it to him, and he didn't. But I didn't cut his foot off, did I. The Chevelle did that."

"Guess you can blame the barbwire for the Wagner kid's arm, then."

Paul squinted down, struck. "I get credit for that? Kid's an asshole, but me being there was dumb luck. You want to clear up the water tower deal, long as we're airing grievances?"

Harley took a pair of strides toward the house. "If you're not coming down, stay there. I'm about to let myself in."

"I believe you'll wish you didn't."

"That a warning?"

"Of sorts." Paul grimaced like he'd seen a bad fall on an icy sidewalk. "There's some shit you can't not see, once you've seen it. Don't think I need to tell you that."

Harley stared up, smoke floating from the cigarette pinched

between his lips. He kept his face a practiced blank. It took more practice than usual.

"You were right that night," Paul said. "If I wanted to die, I could've let go. Thought I might've wanted to when I climbed up. Turned out I was just in a mood."

"And making me do it suited your mood."

"That, friend, was a lofty, noble scheme. Don't cheapen it. I thought after you pulled the trigger, found the Winchester unloaded, it'd fuck you up till you finally got it. Got that you never even had a hand in it. Just played the role of fate. Then you might let go of a whole mess of other shit that makes you a pain in the ass." Paul looked out past the spotlight again. "You hear that?"

It was a distraction, Harley knew. Paul was stalling. But if he was honest, Harley wasn't sure he didn't want to stall, too. Who knew what the hell he'd find in there. "Ask you a question, since you're being forthright?"

"Shoot," Paul said. "See, I say that because by now I know you won't."

"Why the clothes? Why break into a dead person's house, steal their clothes, and use them for kindling?"

Paul looked down, face with no more guile than it'd had asleep at the courthouse. "Dead people's?" He smiled a little, in what appeared to be genuine surprise. He looked up and away again, eyes not wide but wider than usual. "Dead people's."

"It's what I said."

"I saw the clothes at the Jipp place. After the fire. But dead people's—that's some attention to detail."

"What's it mean?"

"Inside joke. Long time ago, Dell Senior pulled a prank. Gave her a box of ash and burnt clothes, said it was what was left of him. Dell Junior. Told her to get over it. Needless to say, did not go over well. For one, he burned the wrong kid's clothes. One of the live ones. For another, she'd already found him. Dell Junior. She might've said so if Dell Senior wasn't such a prick."

"That somehow explain her burning trash naked?"

"I know she burned her clothes one time. Symbolic, I suspect. Wrong clothes—living's versus dead's—ashes came from the burn barrel—hell, I don't know, Harley. Good enough dose of scotch-bourbon blend, lot of abstract notions seem concrete." Paul squinted into the dark distance, said, "Shh."

Harley heard it, too. Gravel. He turned back to look as a pair of headlights shone down County Road K.

"Believe it or not," Paul said, "this is an unforeseen turn."

From the shadowy shape, the height of the headlamps' glare, Harley saw it was a pickup. He let himself hope, for a beat, that the driver might be Loren Braasch. But even if Harley couldn't tell the color from this distance in the dark, he knew well enough whose pickup it was, and he knew another Reddick was in the driver's seat. The Ford barely slowed at the stop before hurtling right onto the highway, blowing through the blind intersection. Before it reached the drive, Harley sprinted for the cruiser. He'd take cover there. Radio Carol for whoever she could get for backup.

He pulled the door shut and sank deep in his seat. He drew the .38 from its holster and listened to the roll of the tires. They stopped a fair distance behind the cruiser, close to the road. The pickup idled.

Before Harley could grip the handset, a deep shudder and squeal cut through the night. It'd come from the house. Harley glanced up. Paul was still roosted above, still leaned back on his elbows. Thumb pad on the .38's hammer, Harley nudged himself far enough upward to see past the dash.

In the kitchen, darkness gaped from where a windowpane should've glared in the headlights. Someone inside had lifted the sash. A snatch of pale shone through the screen. Then it was gone.

A faint click. A soft rushing like a faucet. A troop of distant horns faded in and cut away to rushing water again. The sound was a radio between stations. The dial squealed before landing on an announcer. He drifted through the night air. There'd been rain somewhere. The man listed numbers and fractions called in from towns and farms and ranches well outside Pickard County.

The dial hissed again and landed on a muffled croon. Harley knew the croon. It was George Jones. "Least of All."

He sank low in his seat again. He tried to remember if there'd been music in the house after what happened. There had been before. He couldn't say about after.

Behind him, the pickup idled. From the house, pedal steel fuzzed around the edges and another sound filtered through the open window, too clear to come from a transistor's speaker. It was a woman's voice, singing along with the chorus.

For a passing moment, Harley pictured his father reading his paper at the table, humming along.

32

DELL JUNIOR STREAKED AND *hambone-hambon*ed, and Rick and Pam and Anna were all together, all in one place, one-two-three. Here—where they'd had the picnics. The old, dilapidated house with the porch roof coming loose, where Mom said what color she'd paint the rooms, what drapes she'd hang in the windows. The place was here on the highway all along. Passing as many times as he had, Rick had never known it. But now, looking at the house head-on, he did. He'd be damned.

The chrome of the cop car in front of him lit with sparks from the pickup's headlights, and the world was all banners and gleams better than any fireworks show. Rick took a moment. To soak it all in. Revel in it. Because it was the little things. You had to take time once in a while to revel in the little things.

That said, Paul was here, hunkered down high above the earth. Paul was here, and they needed to have a word.

The pickup door opened with a scream that burst in Rick's ears. He left it open so it wouldn't scream again and grabbed the gun so it wouldn't be in the cab with Anna and Pam. They'd be safe from it. He jumped down, clutching it, then thought of the cop. Rick didn't want the cop to misinterpret the gun. Cops did that. He called up to Paul. "Where's the cop?"

"Thanks for bringing my truck, asshole."

"Is he with you? If he's with you, can you tell him—" Rick thought about what all he needed to tell the cop. "Tell him Anna's fine. Anna's right here. Tell him—say I'll pay back Bowman for the gas. And I brought your pickup. The drugs are gone, though." Rick had pitched the last of the pills on the embankment. One less thing to worry about, and he didn't need them anymore anyway. "Tell him the drugs are gone."

"Yeah, I bet."

Rick blinked. "I took your drugs."

"Yeah. Gathered. Put the gun back, you idiot."

"Anna's in there," Rick said. He couldn't put it back with Anna in there. If Paul had kids, he'd know that. Paul needed some kids. Paul needed some perspective. Some ducks in a row. "You and me need to settle this. You can't—it was the same thing with Dell Junior's bike."

"Whatever you're talking about, now's not the best time."

Hambone-hambone-hambone.

"Stop it." Rick swatted with the barrel.

A voice called out behind him. It was Pam. "Harley, he's got a gun," she said.

"You need to go home," Paul said. "Take the pickup. Turn around and go home."

Rick's voice broke. "My own fucking wife?"

"What?" Paul said.

What did he mean, what? "On my sheets. You stank up my own sheets." His voice caught on the last word. Light sparked off the skin around his eyes. The light made it hard to see. "Brut stink on my own goddamn pillow."

"Harley," Pam said, this time like a warning, teeth clenched. Rick wondered if the word should've meant something to him. It didn't.

Someone said Rick's name. The voice was too deep to be Paul

or Pam or Anna, not deep enough to be Dell Junior's *hambone*. Rick couldn't see where it came from. Not with all the sparks and streaks.

Paul was talking again, but he'd sat up bent-kneed and leaned forward. "I took a nap there, you dumbshit. After I got out of jail. I took a fucking nap."

Rick had to think. Why was Paul telling him this? The stink. A nap? A nap didn't explain how nothing was something. "What about the blond number and my leftovers and me not seeing like a gift? You didn't fuck my wife, what about all that?"

"Boy, you need to pass the fuck out."

That was probably right. Rick probably did need to pass the fuck out.

"You need to go home, right now, and pass the fuck out."

A warble. Not a honk. A warble. A trilling warble.

That was why Paul was here. Paul found Mom. She was here. The picnics. Because this was where they'd had the picnics.

"Mom?" Rick called out.

"Rick," Paul said. He sounded tired now. He looked it, too. He was rubbing his eyes. It was late. Rick bet everybody was tired. He sure was.

"*Harley.*" Pam punched the air with her voice.

"What's Harley?" Rick shouted back over his shoulder. "Who you talking to, Pam?"

Nobody said anything. Nobody besides Dell Junior's *hambone*.

"Rick," the deeper voice said again, and Rick saw where it came from. Past all the sparks and streaks. In the cruiser window was the top of a head. The cop. The cop could see him, and Rick was holding the gun. Rick thrust his arms high, held the gun well above his head. Good to let the cop know he wasn't planning to use the gun. He was just keeping it from Anna. From Pam. Keeping them safe. Rick always said: you did whatever you had to, where family was concerned.

Harley.

Rick remembered now. The cop had said his name was Harley. He'd said it when he'd yelled for Pam to open the door.

33

PAM HELD HER BREATH AND WATCHED THE CRUISER.
On the seat beside her Anna knocked the soles
of her shoes together. They were on the wrong feet.
Rick had put Anna's shoes on the wrong feet.

Pam gave a shaking, irritated breath and unbuckled them.
Anna fussed. They're on the wrong feet, Pam snapped. She
switched them. She buckled one and tried to buckle the other.
Anna slapped at Pam's hands. She'd do it herself, she said.

Outside, Rick raved and swatted.

Pam yelled to Harley. He needed to do something. He needed
to get Rick to drop the gun. Tell him to drop his weapon.

Rick asked what Harley was. He asked who she was talking to.

Harley's eyes shot over but didn't find hers through the windshield glass.

Couldn't Harley just wing him? Just wing him so he dropped
the gun? Rick's finger was laced around one of the gun's two trig-
gers. Probably only because he didn't know the difference between a trigger and a guard, but that finger should've been
enough reason to wing him—standing out there, ranting like a
lunatic about hambones.

What's Daddy doing out there? Anna wanted to know. She
knocked the sandals together with a steady pat.

Out there. He was standing out there.

The truck was still running. Pam leaned past Anna to see the
gas gauge. About a quarter-tank. A quarter-tank was enough. It
was enough to get away from here.

She kept her eyes on Rick but pivoted to pluck Anna up by the armpits, to pull Anna over her lap and switch sides. Anna fussed. Of course she did. She was exhausted. And when it came right down to it, she also didn't like Pam much. Which was fair. Pam hadn't given her much reason to. There was no rule a kid had to like her parents or vice versa. Not really. Not in the grand scheme of things.

In the grand scheme of things, you took care of them until they took care of themselves. You kept them alive and taught them to keep themselves alive. Pam had managed that so far. Despite not being cut out for it, despite knowing that and swallowing it whole every day of her life, Pam had managed. That was the best she'd ever do. Manage. That was all she had in her for this.

Babe was right. Pam made her own bed. And she was right Pam didn't deserve better. But deserve didn't seem to factor into a goddamn thing. Not that Pam had seen. What mattered was she could have it for a while. Better. Anna could, too.

"You like Grandma Babe, Grandpa Red," she said to Anna. Anna nodded, not like she understood, more like she was dropping and raising her head to the beat of her shoes. She looked blank and tired. She said their names, repeated them.

In the pickup's headlights, Pam watched Rick's dirt-streaked back and sweat-soaked pits. He held the gun high, like he was giving up, giving in.

She asked Anna if she'd like to stay with them awhile. Grandma Babe, Grandpa Red.

Anna knocked her soles together. When the question registered, she said she supposed. It was a grown-up word, *supposed*. But then Anna was a tiny, jaded old woman these days. She and Babe would get along fine.

The yard was quiet.

Rick called out for his mom. The way he said it sounded like a boy. A sad little boy. The sound of him made Pam's eyes fog.

Harley called Rick's name but didn't move. He peeked from the cruiser. She studied his expression. He didn't look scared. He didn't look angry. He didn't even look intense. That look was reluctant at best. Like he was seeing a wounded animal. One that needed put down but he couldn't steel himself to drop.

Rick had been a wounded animal as long as she'd known him. One whose skin never cooled, one whose eyes never glazed. One who lay there splayed out and looked up at her, needing.

Pam scooched over the hump into the driver's seat. She gripped the wheel. She dropped the gearshift into reverse but kept her foot on the brake.

Rick's arms were sinking. Slowly. "Harley," she called out again, voice thick but breaking.

The gun sank. The butt rested on Rick's hip. The barrel aimed up and out at the sky like it had when he'd surfaced from the darkness of the trailer. Like it had when they'd walked to the truck and the metal brushed the thin hairs of her arms.

Rick turned to face her. He searched for her through the windshield glass. She still gripped the gearshift.

"Who's Harley, Pam?" he said, barely loud enough to hear over the engine.

34

RICK WAS NEARLY BLINDED by the headlights' glare. But in the dashboard light, he made out her face—the pale of it. Around him, streaks and sparks glimmered like his lungs must've. Fiberglass caves, sparkling like quartz. Ruined lungs. Ruined because he'd done what he'd had to. Kept up his end. Ruined because trust was supposed to come from knowing you could depend on someone besides yourself.

She'd had a pillowcase of clothes, tampons, she'd said. She'd meant to disappear. The whole of her. Knowing what disappearing did to him.

He made out her knuckles on the steering wheel. He didn't picture them braced on a mattress edge like he'd done while waiting for her to come home on the far side of the trailer last night. He knew replaying the image of some sickly pale ass rising and falling on top of her wouldn't deaden the sink in his stomach. He knew making himself see it over and over would never make what she'd done the meaningless nonsense of a word said too many times.

His blood felt too thick. Too thick and hot like a sickness. Like his veins could split open with it.

Behind, Mom warbled. Around, Dell Junior streaked and sparked. They were here, they seemed to be reminding him. They were right here.

Rick and Pam and Anna were here, too. One-two-three. Even if it wasn't exactly the way it was supposed to be. Here in the place that wasn't anywhere. Where Mom and Dell Junior were sound and light.

Maybe Pam would be the smell of her hair. That smell like warm soap. Maybe Rick would be the prickled-up skin of a plucked bird. Maybe Anna, his Anna, would be the soft purr of her sleeping breath.

He tried to feel all that itch then radiate through him like the shimmering light. But all he felt was the too-thick blood and the curve of the gun's double trigger.

He raised the barrel. Past it, Pam's face hovered, a pale glow above the steering wheel. He braced the butt against his shoulder.

A pop rang out. It had to be now. If he could salvage anything, it had to be now.

He squeezed.

35

THE POP OF HARLEY'S CRUISER DOOR cut through the silence. Then a crack. A short-lived flame shot skyward as the gun kicked the man back, teetering.

The pickup door screeched shut as the F-250 lurched forward. The back tires spun to kick up a cloud of dirt. Gun trained on Rick, Harley yelled Pam's name. He screamed it. But the Ford plowed ahead. The dusty chrome bumper crushed into Rick's chest. The Winchester flew up to hit the windshield with another crack, then sailed for the trees. The man curved, his boots lifting from the earth. His shoulders and head made a dead thump on the hood. The thump curdled in Harley's stomach. She punched the brakes, and her husband hovered, midair, for a full blink. His body still curled like the front end shaped him. Then he dropped. He unfurled flat with his back to the earth.

Harley stayed put by the open cruiser door. He held the .38 straight from his chest, though it wasn't aimed at anyone. It was aimed toward the windbreak. His eyes darted to the windshield. The glass was intact. The kick had scattered the load's fragments up into the night.

"Jesus Christ," Paul whispered from above, more earnest than Harley had ever heard him.

Then a sound rose. The piercing flute of a child's cry. It broke into stuttering. On the ground, in the tall grass and dirt, a hand skimmed the brush. A knee bent. Rick was moving. He was alive, at least. He was still alive, for the time being.

The child's cry grew louder, stronger, in an unbreaking wail. A hinge creaked. Harley knew the creak. And though he knew it wouldn't come, he listened for the bristles of the straw broom scratching the jamb. Instead came the pat of a step. The porch boards gave a soft groan. He willed his eyes that way, off the idling pickup and the man trying to breathe in the grass.

Virginia Reddick glowed in the glare of the headlights and the cruiser's side lamp, hair a matted mane, wiry and yellow. Her skin, the color of dry dirt, cracked and pleated down from her shoulders and chest. The skin smoothed where her breasts flattened to bob long against the round ball of her belly. Her fists perched on her naked hips.

Below the deep-carved fissure between her brows, Virginia's eyes swept the yard like they aimed to scorch this scene and all past it. If they knew her son in the grass, her daughter-in-law and grandchild in the cab of the pickup, the recognition didn't soften them. The eyes burned like an oak he'd seen when he was a farmhand south of Junco. It'd been struck by a bolt of lightning. The bark split just enough he saw the tree burning from the inside out.

The child in the F-250 had shrieked into breathlessness, sound caught in a patter of rapid breaths.

In the hush, Paul called the girl's name softly. "Stay there, Anna," he said. Harley looked up at him. Paul jerked his head, nudged Harley toward the pickup.

Harley passed where Rick lay and went to the passenger side of the F-250. Before he pulled open the door, he holstered the .38. Inside, the girl sat on the bench seat, features crumpled in a silent shriek. She caught her breath in hitches.

That aside, she looked fine. Not hurt, anyway.

Pam still gripped the wheel. She stared wide-eyed and pale at the woman on the porch.

"You all right?" Harley said quietly. She wasn't. She pretty clearly wasn't. But he couldn't think what else to say.

She looked at him like he was a stranger. Then she blinked like she had from the parted trailer door as night fell. She looked like she was coming to, waking up. Harley wished, for a moment, she wouldn't. It'd be easier if she didn't.

She looked at him, first one eye, then the other. "Get Anna to my folks."

"He got a shot off," Harley told her. "You're not going to jail. I saw what happened."

"I know I'm not."

The cold, dark thought that gripped Harley hours earlier held him again. There was no telling what Pam might do, Babe said, if she was in a tight enough spot. Harley had seen that now. He'd seen it, and the best he could do was stop the hemorrhaging. Stop her from doing anything else. "You're not going to jail," he said again. "Everybody saw what happened."

"I know it." By now her eyes were completely clear. She looked at him like he didn't understand what she was saying. Maybe he didn't. He looked back down at the girl, whose breaths hitched like hiccups. On the floor past her small feet was Pam's handbag. And a pillowcase knotted shut. She was leaving.

"You can't just take off. That's the one thing you can't do."

Though he supposed she could. He'd seen what happened. And if it came down to his word versus Paul's, Harley's account would surely stand.

"You can't leave," he said again. This time it had nothing to do with stopping the hemorrhaging. It had nothing to do with keeping the peace.

She'd looked away, into the rearview. "Get her to my folks."

What had he told her last night? *Not sure what you think can happen here.* Not much, reasonably speaking. Not now. She knew it. He was the one who needed reminding.

Harley nodded, though she didn't see it.

He held out his arms to the girl. She scrutinized him in a familiar way, one that made him feel like a field mouse in a hawk's sights. Then she scooted toward him. He took her up and held her to his side. He nodded again, though Pam didn't see it that time, either. He shut the pickup door. He made himself step away.

The hum of the F-250's engine picked up as it backed out onto the highway, shifted into drive, then roared and died away into silence.

Harley tried to shield the girl's face from the scene around them. He kept her back to Virginia, whose eyes lit well past the yard, as if she saw clear into the darkness. He kept the girl's back to her father, who was trying to catch his breath in the dirt. Rick had maneuvered enough to see the porch and lay transfixed. He looked like death. His skin was yellow-cast and his cheeks sunken, eyes wild but holding their focus. He tried to roll onto his side and winced. Likely broken ribs, no telling what else.

"Dell Junior's here, Mom." His voice was choked and windy.

Harley reached the cruiser's backseat door. He set the girl inside, told her to lie down for a bit. It'd be best, he said, if she'd just lie down for a bit. Harley slid in the front. He grabbed the handset from where it clipped to the radio and told Carol he needed an ambulance. Out at the Jensen place.

"He's right here," Rick wheezed.

"She knows," Paul said from the porch roof. He was sitting up, arms slung to drape over his knees. "She's known a long time."

Virginia walked back into the house.

"You call an ambulance?" Paul asked Harley.

Harley said they were on the way.

Paul scooted toward the porch roof's edge. When Harley looked, Paul stopped and put up his hands to show they were empty. He rolled onto his belly, swung his legs to grip a porch column, and slid to the railing.

He came down from the porch and reached out an empty hand. He didn't look at Harley, just asked for a light. Harley remembered the lighter was out of fluid. He walked to Paul and handed him the matchbook.

Paul climbed the steps and leaned back against the clapboard by the front door. He crossed his arms on his chest, squinted out at the sky, and took a long breath.

Harley watched him. Paul's expression wasn't hardened. The look wasn't soft, but it wasn't hostile or indifferent. He looked tired. The door beside him gaped where Virginia had left it open.

Harley mounted the steps, not bothering to skip the third. When he reached the porch planks, he let them groan as he crossed.

Inside, beneath the unreasonably tall ceiling, Virginia knelt where the cruiser's headlamps cast Harley's shadow. Night's meager light from the front room windows and kitchen entryway glinted off her body. When he caught the sharp metallic scent, Harley understood what he was seeing. From the neck down, she was soaked in gasoline. She knelt where hip bones had risen from the dusty floorboards, not twenty feet from where the cane-seated chair had blown back. A nearly drained bottle of Cutty Sark sat next to her, beside a half-empty tumbler. Her nakedness, the fact she was soaked in gasoline, didn't strike Harley so odd as her bothering with the tumbler.

A cigarette dangled unlit from her lips. Her hand resting on her thigh held a ruined pack of matches. They were soaked, too, either by the gas or the scotch. Harley took a step toward the door. A porch board sighed. She looked at him. She held up the ruined matchbook, one side of her mouth and an eyebrow raised. Like that ruined matchbook was some joke.

In a half circle in front of her she'd spread the clothes. The ones from the chifforobe, from the dresser topped with the brush and comb and dust. Harley recognized a dressing gown with buttons down the front, fabric yellowed with age. Next to it were stockings and slips. They were piled beside a simple dress of cream-colored satin. It was a dress his mother wore once and kept just to keep. Till she'd stopped keeping anything.

The fumes were thick. Harley was light-headed. "Let's get you a blanket. Let's get you covered and out of here," he said. But he had no blanket. He'd used it on the fire in the burn barrel days before.

She dropped the ruined matches and took the cigarette from her lips. She raised the tumbler and sipped. "I don't need covering." She smiled, not happily, more a show of courtesy. Virginia looked tired, too. Her eyes weren't the lit flames they'd been on the porch. "Goddamn, they make you wear it, don't they?"

The fumes ached in Harley's head. They made you wear it. He didn't know what it meant. Maybe grief or the past. Your own skin. Or maybe just clothes. Harley took a step back from the threshold to get his bearings and a clear breath. One not thick with fumes.

When his shadow receded, he saw the far corner of the room. Gas cans were stacked and toppled. His eyes stung so they filled. Like looking through a drinking glass, he saw what lay behind her. A jumble of brown and yellow fragments piled on the scorched army-green blanket. There were hundreds. She must've collected each bone from the cellar. They were clean. Not sun-bleached like a discarded cattle skull. Picked clean by time.

She must've seen him studying the pile. She glanced back, then looked at him again. "Tell him," she said. "Tell him now he can get the hell on with it."

"Dell Senior," Paul said from where he leaned against the clapboard. His voice was still worn out and quiet, but the sound rattled Harley like waking from a dream. "He'll know what it means."

Harley understood. It was what people wanted. To know after a thing like that you'd either overcome or succumbed. You'd moved on or were more broken than they'd ever be. If you didn't persevere, you could be evil or crazy, either or both worked fine, so long as you were something outside what they knew. Like Paul said, outside their frames of reference. Dell Senior wanted her to get the hell on with it. No doubt because Dell Senior wanted, more than anything, to get the hell on with it.

Harley reached absently to his pocket. To finger the foil of his smokes.

Paul looked at Harley's hand, then at Harley. He gripped Harley's shoulder once, brief, like a reassurance. Harley didn't twitch. He didn't tremor.

Paul stepped through the open door. He squatted to his mother's kneeling height. He handed her the matches.

Harley stepped in. "You don't want this," he said. It was instinct, to say it. In truth, he didn't know. In truth, he didn't know if want even applied here.

Paul took his mother's face in both hands. He pressed his lips to her forehead. The wrinkles there flattened and vanished when she shut her eyes. She said something to him. Something soft. When he went to stand, he wobbled a touch and caught the floor with the tips of his fingers for balance. Then he willed himself up. Harley stepped back to let him pass.

Light filtered from the next room, where the walls and ceiling and floor were painted slate-blue, where under the carbide lamp, the whites of eyes once shone like shock from a compound fracture. Shock, Harley knew, was a mind's mercy. Shock was the switching off of pain when a body could take no more. He wished for that shock as the thick knot ached in his throat. He couldn't swallow it away. He couldn't clear it.

He couldn't say the word any more than he could unstop it from where it lodged: Why?

Maybe it wasn't the right question. After all, Paul had already told him. Paul had given all the answers there were to be had. Answers about revenge, compassion, about rage and mourning and making a point. The fact she picked this place, identical to the one where her boy was killed, a place where another person had once opted out of everything—it all linked together well enough. The strands all threaded together like those kinds of answers do. Like loose-knit gauze. Transparent. Easily torn. Enough to make sense for a blink. Enough to leave you asking again and empty, trying to pack the bleeding hole that's left with other, different reasons. All of it so much gauze.

Still. It'd felt natural to ask, even if no one heard it. As natural as the hollow Harley now felt in his chest.

She bent a match down around the edge of its book. Between the strike and the shot of flame, Harley pulled the door shut.

36

SHE'S STOPPED TWICE ALREADY, once to let the ambulance pass, another to leave Paul's pickup at the trailer. The Nova had more gas and her name on the title.

Because the sun rises in the east, she went west, not ready to face daylight. For a long distance, she sped, rising and sinking through the dunes, till she no longer heard or felt the roar of her pulse, till the thick, crackling static in her head ebbed to silence.

Now, pulled off the road on the sand, she breathes. Under the dome of starlight, she feels the air press against her skin. She listens for what there is to hear. Some toads and crickets skittering in the nearby grass. Mainly air.

When she gets back in the Nova, she'll drive to Thedford. There'll be enough in the Butter-Nut can to fill the tank and buy a few things to eat. Passing through Seneca, the clock will turn back an hour. She'll gain time through distance.

When she's out farther, she'll drive down to Chimney Rock, a needle of soft Brule clay cutting jagged and sharp against the lightening sky. It's a place she's seen only in pictures. She once learned it was a signpost, a landmark that told people they were headed the right direction, or at least let them know where they were. She's heard the spire is smaller than it once was, sand and wind having worn at it, year after year.

She'll pull into Alliance when the morning is bright, pale blue. The town, the small city, will be just big enough for her to be a stranger for a while, big enough to stop a bit and still be a passer-through.

There, she'll sleep in the Nova a few nights, maybe more.

She'll use a gas station's bathroom sink as a shower, and she'll find work as a dishwasher or fry cook. Hopefully a dishwasher. Some places, waitstaff tip out dishwashers at the end of the night, and the oily, sweet film of fryers is tough to scrape from the skin. Either will mean a free meal per shift, though, and either will help her stay or leave, maybe drive farther west, to Wyoming, eventually Utah. She doesn't care about getting as far as the ocean but she's always wanted to see the Green River.

She knows, in less time than she thinks, she will miss Anna. The missing will come and go like the rise and sink of the hills, a clenching, burning absence in her sternum when she hears the banter of Ernie and Bert on a lobby or waiting room TV. Then the feeling will pass as quickly as it sets in, gone until it comes again.

She will miss Rick more. She'll miss him whenever a new weariness replaces the old, when the thick callus keeping her from being wrung out turns pliable again. She'll miss his shape and warmth against hers and the tremor when he first falls asleep. She'll miss small, stupid things. The childlike giggle the time he used his toes to slingshot his underwear onto the bedroom lamp. She'll miss the stinging stink of burnt trailer paneling and tar in his T-shirts. She'll miss his dopey, Smokey the Bear insistence that they'll get by when they never had the slimmest chance. She will wish she could've loved him, not more but in the way he needed. She'll wish she could've loved away the need in him.

Pam will miss, and Pam will doubt.

Right now, though, she stands, as small here as she's always known herself to be. Small and unneeded and here for a minute. She breathes deep.

Acknowledgments

Thanks first to my spouse, whose name is either Will or Bill. Whoever you are, closest person to me in the world, thank you. I could have neither written this nor coped with the losses of Rowland S. Howard and George Jones without you.

I am deeply grateful for my family, none of whom are featured in this book because this is fiction, Mom. I love and thank (in no hierarchical order, expressed or implied): Mom, Dad, Greg, Bill, Joy, Brack, Peg. The same goes for my aunts, uncles, cousins, stepsiblings, and in-laws. Thank you to the eleven grandparents I was lucky enough to be born with and know, and especially to those two who helped raise me.

I'm indebted to the family of friends who support me for no good reason: Brittany Dabestani (née Madson), for whom I named a town; Jackie Sterba, who walked across half of Nebraska with me; Jennifer Bryan, my rock, who listened and vented and reread this book twenty times; and Devin Murphy, who championed this novel and showed me I'd written the same sentence for three hundred pages. Thank you to Tracy Johnson and Steve Carmichael, just because. Thank you to every writer and friend who read drafts or spent hours commiserating: Jeff Alessandrelli, Megan Gannon, Kathleen Massara, Heather Akerberg, Jeremy Schnitker, Richard Stock, Jonathan Tvrdik, Nate Sindelar, Rebecca Rotert, Erinn Tighe, Justin O'Connor, Ethan Jones, Gabe Houck, Julie Cymbalista, Rudy Ciavarro, Chris Fischer, Mike Tulis, Jan and Doc Mahoney, Tracy Tucker, Erich Christiansen, and everyone I'm not forgetting—there's just a page limit.

Thank you to my agent, Emily Forland, whose kindness, confidence, and ability to diagnose what I'm doing wrong with a scalpel's accuracy led me to work with my editor at MCD / Farrar, Straus and Giroux: the funny, frank, and charismatic force who is Daphne Durham. Thank you, Lydia Zoells, for your boundless patience and smarts. And to Dave Cole, who copyedited this book: you, friend, are a saint.

Thanks to Richard Duggin, who gave me the swift kick that circuitously led me here, and thanks to everyone else with whom I've studied. I'm awestruck that I even sat in a room *with* Charles Johnson, much less was allowed to call him my thesis adviser. The great Jonis Agee reread this thing more times than either of us want to count and gave feedback I took way too long in implementing. I'm also indebted to Ted Kooser, whose input on my earlier work helped shape the world of this one. Boundless thanks go to my workshop friends, a list including but not limited to: Lowell Brower, Zachary Watterson, Kirsten Rue, Jordan Farmer, DeMisty D. Bellinger, Casey Pycior, Adrian Koesters, Tom Coakley, Kate Kostelnik, and Karen Babine.

I also thank the Sewanee Writers' Conference, where, for the first time, I timidly asked strangers if I could eat with them and wound up chatting late into the night with the likes of Dino

Enrique Piacientini and Richard Bausch. I'm eternally grateful for the opportunity to study with two literary giants, Steve Yarbrough and Bobbie Ann Mason. I'm grateful to have bawled, laughed, and been stunned at readings by Venita Blackburn, Tony Earley, and Randall Kenan. And, of course, I'm thankful for having had the honor of workshopping with incredible writers I'm now honored to call my friends. Among them are Rob Roensch, Emily Chiles, David Bumke, Sheila Lamb, Mickey Hawley, Sharon Bandy, Yang Huang, Jenni Moody, Lynn Schmeidler, and Colin Orr.

I'm thankful for everyone, basically. Thank you.

A NOTE ABOUT THE AUTHOR

Chris Harding Thornton, a seventh-generation Nebraskan, holds an MFA from the University of Washington and a PhD from the University of Nebraska, where she has taught courses in literature and writing. Her other professions have included quality assurance overseer at a condom factory, jar-lid screwer at a plastics plant, closer at Burger King, record store clerk, all-ages club manager, and PR writer. *Pickard County Atlas* is her first novel.